LAYERED LIES

Book One of the Kelsey's Burden Series

KAYLIE HUNTER

This book is a work of fiction. All names, characters, places, businesses, incidents, etc. are the imagination of the author, and any resemblance to actual persons or otherwise is coincidental.

Dedication

To my invaluable friend, James –

How you ever managed to drag yourself through the ever-so-horrid first draft of this book is incomprehensible to me. It must have been hell. And while there wasn't much positive that could be said about that draft, you made me feel proud of myself for writing it and encouraged me to keep writing and continue improving.

At times, you were my grammar coach, my personal cheerleader (without the skirt of course), and often my psychologist. Thank you for being part of this adventure with me. It has been a fabulous journey.

Next round of drinks is on me, my friend. Cheers!

Kelsey's Burden Series:

Prologue

At the top of the third-floor landing, I fumbled with the takeout bags and my dry cleaning as I reached inside my shoulder bag for my keys. That was when I noticed it. My steel-wrapped and encased apartment door, with two top-of-the-line deadbolts, stood partially open. The takeout and dry cleaning slipped through my fingers to the tile floor as I pulled my service weapon from its holster. Setting my shoulder bag down, I retrieved my cellphone and called Charlie.

"What's up, cuz?" Charlie answered on the first ring.

From her end of the line, I could hear music and loud voices in the background, which was a sharp contrast to the absolute silence of my hallway.

"Call for backup to my apartment. Someone broke in. I'm not waiting; Nicholas could be inside."

I disconnected the call before she had time to respond. Charlie would call the cavalry, and soon half of Miami PD would be flooding my block.

I entered the apartment.

I spotted Nicholas' babysitter, Mary, face down on the blood-soaked carpet in the living room. After rolling her to her back, I realized that there was no need to check for a pulse. The long, jagged cut across her throat gaped open.

Not allowing myself to react, I focused on my training and continued to search the rest of the apartment. I crept silently into the kitchen and dining room, inspecting closets and cabinets. The main area was clear. The doors down the hallway appeared closed as I slowly approached.

Keeping my body low and my back against the wall, I reached a trembling hand out to open my bedroom door. The hinges squeaked in protest, announcing my presence. I pivoted my gun into the room first. The closet doors were open, allowing me to confirm quickly that the room was vacant. I backed out into the hall and repeated the same process in the bathroom, finding nothing out of the ordinary.

The last door was Nicholas' bedroom. His door faced directly down the hall. I would be an easy target with nowhere to hide when I opened it. Over the pounding in my ears, I could hear sirens in the streets below. The cop in me wanted to wait. My fear for Nicholas' safety pushed me forward. I silently prayed to find him hiding under his bed or in his closet. I opened the door.

No bullets flashed. No shouts echoed. No quiet sniffles of a scared young boy. The room was silent.

Propped up in the center of the room, facing the door, was Nicholas' favorite stuffed animal — a puppy with a smiling, lopsided grin. I quickly searched the closet and under the bed, knowing as I did that it was futile. My son was gone. My beautiful, sweet, innocent five-year-old son was gone.

Two weeks later, as fast as I could, I packed and left Miami, moving halfway across the country. Burned beyond recognition were the bodies of seven women and a child, along with a note addressed to me: *Leave Miami.* The message was not only a warning for me to leave, but a clue that I was getting closer to finding the answers I was looking for. Unfortunately, the floundering, unfocused investigative trail I had been working could have pointed in multiple directions. Before anyone else died, I ran.

Despite what my enemies think, though, I never conceded. It has been two years since I left Miami. I wait. I watch. I learn. I have my spies searching. I build my fortune. I build my contacts. I train harder for combat. Because I know I will find those responsible for ripping my world apart. And when that long-awaited day arrives, I will send them straight to hell.

Chapter One

I squeezed myself between the shoppers trying to get to the register counter. Women of all sizes and ages shuffled shoulder to shoulder trying to lay claim to the racks of clothes. Only two people between me and the counter, the woman in front of me turned, slamming a tall Styrofoam cup into my chest, dousing me with boiling-hot coffee.

"Bloody hell!" I yelled, as the hot liquid seared my skin. I hurried to pull the steamy shirt off.

Using the driest section of material, I patted my chest to absorb as much excess coffee as I could. My bra was drenched, but I didn't have the luxury of running home to change. I grabbed a clean shirt off a nearby rack and started toward the register again.

"This store is ridiculously crowded," the woman said, stopping my retreat. "The owners should be sued for allowing so many customers inside at once."

"You're right, it is crowded," I said, turning to glare at her. "And since your first instinct was to blame someone else instead of apologizing for bringing a hot coffee into a crowded store, I will start with you. Get out."

I stepped into her space, and she took a step back. "What? What do you mean?"

"I mean, I'm the owner," I said, stepping in her face again. "And, as you can see I have plenty of other customers, so get out."

Her eyes widened at my aggressiveness, and she took another step back. I continued to stalk her all the way to the front door. The other customers parted to create a path. When she was close enough to reach the handle, she bolted through the door and jogged across the parking lot in her high heels through the downpouring rain.

"Stupid bitch," I mumbled to myself. Shaking my head, I rubbed my eyes as I turned to walk back to the register. Three hours of sleep the night before, followed by getting up before sunrise, was putting me in a pissy mood. I sniffed the coffee soaked shirt, appreciating the smell of the strong coffee, wishing I had time to make a fresh pot. But, alas, customers were waiting.

Pulling myself up onto the register counter, I swung my body to the other side and dropped behind it. I proceeded to checkout the long line while fighting to get the clean shirt on. Several customers were grinning, but no one dared to laugh.

After over a dozen customers had been cashed out, I turned to toss a pile of hangers into a nearby bin when I heard a giggle. Glancing around the front of the store, I searched for the source while clipping my hair up in a twist. A little girl with big, smiling brown eyes and long, curly brown tresses was trying to cover her laugh as she ducked her head behind her mom's leg. Her mom smiled, pointed at me, and then tugged on the front of her own shirt.

I looked down at myself and laughed. The blouse was a button-up stretch shirt, but I had failed to notice that only the bottom buttons were secure. The rest of the shirt was wide open, completely exposing my ample breasts behind a lacy black bra. That was one way to dry out the bra.

Turning to the floor-to-ceiling mirror behind me, I quickly fixed the buttons. The rest of me appeared to be in order. With my hair clipped up, away from my face, the fluorescent lights played off the multiple salon-made colors of brown, blonde and red. My lip gloss wore off hours ago, but my thick blue eyeliner remained intact, accenting my bright blue eyes. My hip-hugging jeans were miraculously still dry after the coffee fiasco, and my knee-high boots still had a slick shine to them. Satisfied with my appearance, I turned away from the mirror and winked at the mother and daughter.

The mom gave me an approving nod before returning her attention to the weather outside. It continued to sprinkle but the heavy storm clouds had blown over. The weather channel hadn't predicted any sunshine to grace us today, typical for early April in Michigan.

Looking back at the mom, I noticed her cheaply bleached hair and her worn, ill-fit clothes. Her eyes were alert, but the dark circles under them almost appeared bruised.

"Kelsey," Nicki called my attention away. "What do you want me to do next?"

"What? You mean like work?" I said, rolling my eyes.

The teenager had been pushing my buttons since she clocked in today. She wasn't even smart enough to figure out that I was annoyed with her as she stood there waiting for her next assignment.

"Why don't you try cleaning up some of the hangers and things from the floor and straightening up the shelves, like I asked an hour ago?"

"Fine. Don't forget I have a date tonight, though. I can't stay past 6:00."

Nicki walked to the closest table to half-ass straighten some jeans. I shook my head and checked my text messages. The reply message I was waiting for had arrived and confirmed that Nicki was going to get a couple of surprise visitors soon. I was looking forward to the free entertainment.

Turning my attention back to the register, I checked out another customer. I noticed the woman with the little girl shake her head. She was watching Nicki's poor imitation of being an employee.

"I can pay cash if you can do better," I called over to the woman.

"I could get more done in an hour than she could get done in two weeks," the woman laughed. "I have my daughter with me, though, or I'd take you up on the offer."

"Hey kid," I nodded to the little girl. "Pull up a stool back here with me and let's see your mother school the teeny-bop."

The little girl never hesitated, running behind the counter and pulling up a stool. She grabbed some tote bags and helped bag items as I cashed out customers. Her mother laughed, tossed her purse behind the counter and disappeared into the crowd, grabbing things off the floor and straightening shelves as she went.

"I'm Kelsey," I whispered to the little girl.

"I'm Sara," she whispered back. "My mom needs a job. Can she work here?"

"How about I talk to her about it later, and we'll see how it goes?"

"OK," she grinned, and continued filling the tote bags.

My heart cinched at her happy disposition. I hadn't spent time around kids since Nicholas was pulled from my life. The pain was still as fresh as if it had happened yesterday. I shook my head, forcing the thoughts away, and turned to the next customer in line.

A few minutes later, the woman brought a handful of empty hangers to the registers and was tucking them behind the counter when Nicki's mom and dad entered the store. Before the woman could turn away, I grabbed her elbow for her to wait.

"You're going to want to see this," I grinned.

She looked curious but didn't say anything as she began straightening clothes on the nearest rack so she could watch whatever was going to happen.

"Mom? Dad? What are you doing here?" Nicki asked them.

"Get your purse; we need to go," her mother said.

"But my shift isn't over, and after work Josh is taking me out," Nicki argued.

"Your mother said to get your purse. Now!" her dad snapped back.

Nicki was startled, but stepped behind the counter and pulled her purse out. She turned back to her parents to follow them, but her dad took her oversized, backpack-style purse, opened it, and dumped the contents on the counter. Spilling out were two shirts, a pair of jeans, and a pair of high heels.

"Dad, what are you doing?" Nicki screeched.

Her dad looked mad, but her mother was the one who freaked. Her mom pushed her toward the counter, turning her, and pulled a wad of cash out of Nicki's back pocket, adding it to the pile on the counter.

"Nicole Baxter, I have never been more disgusted by your behavior in my entire life. To find out that my daughter is a common thief!" her mom yelled. "Get your ass in the car!"

"I don't understand. That's my stuff and my money. I didn't steal anything!" Nicki said.

"Don't you lie to us!" her mom screeched. "Your boss texted us a video. It clearly shows you stealing both the money and the clothes. You're not going to weasel your way out of this one. You're lucky she contacted us instead of the police. She can have you arrested! Do you get that?"

"Go. Car. Now!" her dad ordered.

Nicki broke into a wild crying episode that would never fool anyone and ran out of the store. Her mom stomped out after her. Her dad turned back to me as I stuffed the girl's wallet and other personal belongings back into her purse. I grinned, handing it to him. He shook his head, chuckling, and left.

"It might have been good for her to get a set of cuffs slapped on her wrists," the woman next to me grinned.

"Oh no. Her mother's eyes are finally open, which is exactly what her dad was hoping. He's got a very detailed version of boot camp all lined up. After he is done with her, Nicki will wish she had been arrested, though," I chuckled.

"How do you know all that?"

"He's a friend of a friend. I was doing him a favor by hiring her and recording her activity. Not only was it entertaining, but now one of the best attorneys in town owes me a favor."

"Nice," she grinned.

I gathered the cash and clothes from the counter and tossed them all together in a tote bag before stuffing the bag under the counter. I quickly cashed out two more customers before turning my attention back to the woman.

"I have an employment position open now. You interested?"

"Can my daughter stay while I work?"

I looked up and saw hope etched in her eyes. I looked back at the little girl and saw a glimpse of the same. They were in trouble and needed someone to help them get out of it. The question was, how much trouble were they in?

"Sure. You need me to keep it off the books for a while? Pay cash?"

"Is that a problem?" she asked.

"Not at the moment. I'm Kelsey Harrison, the owner of The Changing Room. Welcome to my world," I grinned.

"Anne," she grinned back, shaking my hand. "I better get back to work. I have this mean boss who calls your parents if you aren't up to snuff."

Sara giggled beside us, as Anne kissed the top of her head and went back to the sales floor.

"All right kid, let's get some more customers checked out."

"I like it here," Sara smiled.

"Me too," I grinned back.

An hour later, I saw no end in sight, and I groaned at hearing the bells chime above the entry door. The store couldn't possibly hold anyone else. Looking up, I instantly locked eyes with the man who had entered. Hazel eyes, set on a chiseled face, held my gaze. He had perfectly trimmed dark hair and was wearing an expensive designer jacket. It was obvious he didn't realize this was a resale store before he entered. Even from a distance, he smelled of money. Regardless of the capacity limit, I wasn't about to let him leave empty-handed.

"Menswear is on the south wall, sir. Welcome to The Changing Room," I greeted him from behind the counter.

He still looked hesitant, so I flashed my best flirty smile. He smirked and proceeded in that direction.

Anne leaned toward me and whispered, "Shame on you."

"Hey, a girl's gotta do, what a girl's gotta do."

The bells chimed again, and my sleep-deprived brain snapped back in its direction. My stomach dropped as I realized it was the fire marshal, *again*. It was only Thursday, and this would be his third visit this week. He looked around the store, assessing the situation, and I could see he intended to force the store to close. I had worked too hard to go down without a fight, though.

Climbing on top of the counter, I shouted out to the crowded rooms. "Attention, customers: we have a bit of a situation here. As I am sure you are all aware, the store is a bit crowded, and we are way over capacity."

Several people snickered and tossed out commentary. Most were unable to turn around to face me.

"I need to clear at least half of you out of this store in the next five minutes. Otherwise, that gentleman at the door is the fire marshal, and he's going to write me a ticket that I can't afford."

Okay, so this was a bit of a lie, I could afford to pay the ticket. As far as lies went, though, it was a little one, and I wasn't going to lose sleep over it.

"I am offering a 15 percent off coupon on your next visit if you check out in the next five minutes. You will need to leave one way or another, so I recommend taking the deal while it lasts. Please slowly and carefully move to the front and help us out."

Throughout the store, everyone started shifting forward. I grabbed a fanny pack and moved closer to the door to start a cash-only line, as Anne took over the register for the credit card purchases, and little Sara stuffed the clothes haphazardly into bags.

We worked in a mad frenzy that showed miraculous results as the rooms quickly cleared. Within fifteen minutes only a handful of customers remained. The fire marshal nodded his approval and left with a grin.

Glancing about the rooms, I absorbed the store's complete upheaval. Even with the air conditioner on high, the store temperature felt a muggy ninety degrees at least, and my once-clean shirt cemented firmly to my skin with sweat. Clothes and hangers cluttered the floor. About half of the merchandise was gone and according to the clock we were twenty minutes away from being hit by the after- 5 o'clock shoppers.

Leaning over to Sara, I smiled. "You did great!"

"I did?" she said with excitement.

"You certainly did. I think you are, by far, the best bagger I have ever had," I said. "Do you think you could help straighten up a bit while I talk to your mom?"

"I'm on it," she squealed. "Do I get paid too?"

"Yes, I will pay for your services today and as a bonus, when you are done working, how would you like to pick out some new outfits to wear to school?"

Sara launched at me with a big hug.

"I'll do the best job ever! You'll see!" she exclaimed as she raced over to the first table and started picking the clothes and hangers off the floor.

I released a slow breath, trying to calm the pounding beat of my heart. Burning tears gathered behind my eyes, but I ducked my head and blinked wildly to stop them before they were noticeable. Being around another child was a lot harder than I had ever imagined it would be.

When I was once again in control, I turned to Anne.

"Thanks for jumping in to help," I said, clearing my throat. "It gets a little crazy around here."

"For a little bit there, it reminded me of Alice toppling down the rabbit hole," she laughed.

I could appreciate the similarities.

"You been in town long?" I asked.

"No. I ran out of gas down the road, and we stopped in here to take a break from the rain before we walked to a gas station," Anne sighed. "And, I need to find a motel still. Any suggestions?"

"You're not the type to run out of gas, which tells me you didn't have money to buy any, let alone money for a motel," I said.

Anne looked unsettled as she looked about the store.

"Don't sweat it. I will be sure to pull cash at the end of your shift. Can you stay until closing time?"

She nodded, "Thanks."

"It's all good."

As I turned to my right, dark hazel eyes locked with mine. I had forgotten all about the man with the designer clothes. "Hello, sir. Can I help you find anything today?"

His eyes swept me from head to toe in slow perusal, spending a bit too much attention on my breasts before returning to my face. His expression was one of determination and arrogance. Been here, done this. *Sorry buddy, control freaks are just not my cup of tea.*

I didn't wait for him to reply. "Size 30 x 36? Long-length shirts?" I asked as I started pulling items off the racks and shelves, selecting the precise colors that would complement his fair complexion.

"I'm not sure this is my kind of store, as entertaining as it has been," he admitted.

I could appreciate his honesty, but I wasn't letting him, or more importantly his pocketbook, get away that easily. "Hmm. So, when you got dressed this morning in the clothes you are wearing, were they brand new?"

"I've worn them before," he smirked.

"So, the fact that strangers have worn the clothes is your issue. Not only are all my clothes cleaned first, but some of them, especially in menswear, were brand new with the tags still on them. And, with the $300 you spent on the jacket you are currently wearing, you could buy a new wardrobe here."

"I have plenty of money. I can afford to spend it on expensive clothes. And, I paid $450 for this jacket," he said with a touch of snobbery.

"You overspent on the jacket. It's not worth $450. And, what a shame that you can't find something more entertaining to do with your money than spend it on overpriced clothes."

"Fine. I will buy these," he said, gesturing to the clothes I was holding. "How much?"

"The dressing room is right through that curtain. I will have to insist you try them on." I piled the clothes into his sizable arms.

"I don't try clothes on."

"Well, today you do," I said. "Shoo, off you go."

He shook his head in bewilderment before heading toward the dressing room.

"And, be sure to let us see items you like. I want to be sure they fit well," I said over my shoulder as I walked over toward Anne to help straighten.

"Wow. He is extremely good-looking," she said.

"I suppose," I said as I moved over to the next table.

"Sorry. I didn't mean to offend you."

"You didn't. I'm not so easily offended." I grabbed a pile of jeans and began refolding them. "Personally, I get the feeling he's a class-A spoiled jerk. If you like him, though, go for it."

"Not a chance. I have enough on my plate," Anne said, looking much more relaxed. "So, do you think he will wear anything he buys today?"

"When we get done with him, yes, I do," I grinned. "And if we play our cards right, maybe he will even send some referrals our way."

At that moment, the man in question stepped out of the dressing room wearing a two-tone casual v-neck shirt with pressed navy-striped suit pants. The styles were not a good mix.

"Well, look at you," was the only response I could muster.

"You said I was to show you the wares," he smirked.

"Not quite what I said, but seeing you in *that*, clues me in that you need more assistance than what I can provide today. Let me introduce you to my associate, Anne. She works on a partial commission for direct sales. Anne, can you explain to him why he needs your assistance?"

She looked at me questioningly, and when I grinned, she shrugged a 'whatever you say' response to me before turning to him.

"My name is Anne." She held her hand out to shake his.

"Dwayne Bishop"

"Well, Mr. Bishop, while you are the most handsome customer to enter the shop today, you clearly do not have a sense of how to coordinate clothes. So let's get this straightened out, shall we?" She gestured back to the dressing room.

He threw a smirk back at me before following her lead. Regardless of whether he ever chose to wear the clothes, he would spend enough money to give Anne a good commission.

Confident that menswear was in good hands, I returned to the register.

Chapter Two

The rest of the shift was busy but uneventful. Around 6:00, we had a chance to scarf down sandwiches. Anne and Sara stayed until closing, and we enjoyed laughing and talking with customers. Sara seemed extremely smart for her age, and Anne quickly learned the ropes around the store. When I finally cashed out the last customer, Sara held the door open for her and switched the sign over to "closed."

"That was so much fun! Can I work here all the time?" Sara asked, skipping back to the counter.

"Sorry, kiddo. There's this thing called child labor laws. I definitely can't afford to be messed up with that. But you are welcome to hang out anytime you want."

I laughed at the expression on her face. She was thinking hard about something.

"What are child labor laws?"

"In our country, to have a child work you have to have special permits and then there are limits of how many hours they are allowed to work. And I have never heard of anyone as young as you being allowed to get a permit."

"Well that sucks," she pouted.

"Sara, sweetie, watch your language please," Anne corrected as she carried a load of hangers over and tossed them in a bin behind the counter.

I leaned over close to Sara and whispered, "Yeah, it does suck. You would make an awesome employee," I winked.

Sara giggled.

I pulled two large paper bags out from under the counter and handed them to Sara. "Okay, one bag is for you, and the other bag is for your mom. I want you both to fill them up with clothes for yourselves while I gather your pay for today."

I walked over and locked the door before opening the cash drawer and counting out the sales slips and balancing. I pulled hourly wages and then dug for the commission receipt for Mr. Bishop.

"Holy crap, Anne! You sold $900 worth of clothes to that Bishop guy?"

"*Ya mean Dwayne?*" she laughed. "Yup. I had him so loaded down that he had to make two trips out to his car. He looked quite shell-shocked by the time he left. You have nice, quality clothes. I think he will wear everything he bought. Well, maybe not the cowboy boots, but I couldn't resist," she giggled.

I had to smile imagining the stuffy, but stunning, man prancing around in a business suit wearing cowboy boots. It would appear a bit strange to anyone in Michigan.

"And, you don't have to pay me commission either. I know you just told him that to get him to spend more money."

"I did tell him that to get him to spend more money. And, no, we don't run commission sales here.

Regardless, I keep my word. I don't have enough male customers yet, so until I build that clientele up, I am willing to get a little creative."

Sara was sorting through the girls' dresses and trying to decide which ones to choose.

"Try them all on, girl! You can have a personal dress-up party! Anything you want, just put it in the bag. Be sure to get a couple of pairs of shoes too."

"Really?"

"Of course," I said.

Anne walked over to the counter and smiled, watching Sara gather a load of dresses to take into the dressing room. "She is having a lot of fun. Thank you. I don't mind you taking the cost of her clothes out of my pay."

"Nonsense." I handed her an envelope with her money and the second one with Sara's name on it. "And, you're not leaving tonight without your bag filled either, so you better get to it."

"Umm. You don't have many women's clothes left. The shelves and racks are almost empty," she said, looking around.

"Not for long. My next shift is just starting."

Anne followed me into the back room, watching as I started pulling out racks and bins of more clothes.

"New arrivals that I purchase in the mornings get thrown in the roll-away hampers. The clothes have to be in good quality, no stains, and no third generation hand-me-downs," I explained as I pushed two more racks onto the sales floor. "Later, I sort them out. If it's something I don't want to sell after all, it goes in the donation pile. The rest gets loaded in my truck, and I take it home to laundry. Within a day or two, it comes back to be stored in a tote or on a rack. When the shelves out front need to be restocked, it all gets shuffled forward."

"So how often is it as busy as it was today?" she asked as she helped me load totes on the flatbed carts. We each pulled two carts out to the sales room and started restocking.

"Fortunately, it's been this busy since the third day the store opened. I never even advertised. Unfortunately, when I opened a month ago, I had my entire living room and dining room filled with excess stock, and it's almost gone. I always got my best deals on Saturday afternoons, but the store is too busy for me to leave now to make more buys. Thus, I do need some help," I hinted.

"I can't promise that I can stick around," she quietly said while she continued to stack jeans.

"You can't report your income legally, can you?"

She flinched, but then acknowledged the truth of it with a short nod.

"Are you in legal trouble? Are the police looking for you?"

"It's not the cops we are running from, but they can't help us either," Sara interjected into our conversation in a low whisper.

Neither of us had noticed that she had walked up behind us and was listening. She was wearing a cute dark blue sleeveless dress trimmed with white lace. She nervously chewed on the end of her thumbnail.

"Sara," Anne said.

"No, Mom. She'll help. We don't have anywhere else to go," Sara said, looking down at her dirty socks.

"It's okay, Sara," I reassured her. "I will help. Now, see if there are some white sandals in your size to go with that dress."

Anne was watching out the window, wringing her hands. A voice in my head screamed to throw a pile of money their way and not to involve myself any further. I didn't need any new complications in my life. That voice lost the battle, though, when I admitted that I couldn't turn my back on them.

"Look, I meant it. I will help you. But I need to understand your situation to do so. Are you dealing with parental kidnapping? Did you just try to rob a liquor store?"

"No. Sara's right. The police will never have any interest in us. Sara's father would never file kidnapping charges either. He's not friendly with the police. But if he ever found us…"

"Say no more. The rest is your business unless you ever want to talk it out."

I didn't know anything about hiring someone that couldn't have a record of her income, but I already planned to make some calls to figure it out. She obviously needed some help, and I was in a position to offer it whether I wanted to get involved or not.

"My keys are in my shoulder bag, behind the counter. Run up to the gas station, buy one of those plastic gas cans, and put some gas in your car. When I finish here, I can drive you back to your car, and you can follow me to my house. I have a spare bedroom that the two of you can share. We will figure the rest out as we go. You help me, and I'll help you. Deal?"

"What about the name issue?" she asked.

"I have no idea how all that works," I admitted. "But we will figure it out. Until then, I will pay you in cash. Let's just deal with one thing at a time."

"Mom, can I stay here with Kelsey while you run to get gas? I want to try on more clothes," Sara asked as she paraded out in pink capris and a yellow, ruffled top. Anne looked at Sara, then back at me.

"It's fine with me. I should have most of the shelves stocked by the time you get your car squared away. Then we can load up the laundry and head home."

"Someday, I will find a way to make this up to you," she said as she wrapped me in a hug that took me by surprise. She didn't linger, though. She reached under the checkout counter, grabbed the car keys and went out, re-locking the door from the outside.

Chapter Three

It was after 9:00 by the time we arrived at my house. Sara was asleep within minutes of the bed being dressed with fresh sheets. Anne showered while I started the laundry, unloaded the dirty clothes from my SUV, and reloaded it with the rest of the stocked clothes I had in the living room.

"Aren't you exhausted?" Anne yawned, entering the kitchen wrapped in my terrycloth robe. She started to help me fold the clothes piled on the table.

I shrugged my answer. I switched another load from the washer to the dryer, deciding to quit for the night and refresh them in the morning. It was getting late, and Anne would end up staying up if I didn't call it quits.

"Where do you buy the clothes from?" Anne asked.

"I get some drop-offs in the mornings, but the best deals are garage sales. If you catch people toward the end of their sale, they will sell cheap, so they don't have to store everything for another year. And, if I am hitting up those cute little subdivisions, the quality is fantastic." I rubbed my temples, and for the first time in hours, I sat down to take a break. "I just need to find another way to spike the inventory since the store is too busy to get out."

I grabbed my shoulder bag and dug out some cash. "I have an appointment at 7:00 tomorrow. If you are up in the morning, here's some money for some groceries. I haven't shopped in awhile, so we need *everything*. I'm surprised I still have toilet paper."

"I can pick up groceries in the morning. What time should we be at the store?"

"I will be there by ten at the latest. I might miss a few drop-offs, but I can't miss this appointment, so it is what it is. If you can be in before noon, I will be a happy camper."

"Dang it!" I interrupted myself. "I needed to call the landlord about the parking light being out. I totally forgot." I checked the clock and saw that it was almost midnight. "It's too late now."

"Write down the name and number and I will handle it."

"That would be great." I wrote the name and number on a Post-it.

"It's not a problem. Are you going to be okay with Sara being at the store with me?"

"Sara's awesome," I nodded my approval. "I'll take my laptop and Kindle in for her to use. We can set up an area behind the counter for her, and when it's not too crowded, she can play dress-up."

I got up and stretched. "I pulled out some pajamas if you want them. I left them on the dresser in the spare room. Sara's in one of my long t-shirts," I yawned, heading toward the bedrooms. "Night."

Within the privacy of my bedroom, I pulled open the bottom drawer of my dresser and removed the files and laptop that I kept there. I laid everything on my bed and briefly flipped through the files that I had read to the point of having every word memorized, every lead tracked down. I turned to the laptop and checked the cloud drives to see if any new updates had been left. I searched online news stories for anything flagged as related to those responsible for taking Nicholas. Two hours later, I had nothing. Without bothering to get undressed, I collapsed back on the bed and fell asleep just as frustrated as I had been every night for the last two years.

Being a light sleeper, I woke a few hours later to a strange noise. I sat up and listened but didn't hear anything. I was laying back down when I heard it again. It was Sara.

I climbed out of bed and peeked into the spare bedroom. Anne was sound asleep, but Sara was crying.

"Hey, little bug. Come on. Let's get you a drink of water," I whispered.

She crawled out of bed and wrapped herself around me as I carried her into the kitchen, rubbing her back.

"I'm sorry I woke you," she mumbled into my neck.

"Not a big deal. You can wake me anytime."

I filled a glass of water and carried it, along with her, into the living room. I sat on the couch with Sara on my lap and pulled an afghan around us while she drank. "Did you get scared, being in a strange house?"

"No. I had a bad dream."

"Oh sweetie, I'm sorry. Why don't we see if we can find something on TV to watch to take your mind off things? What do you think?"

She nodded as I grabbed the remote. Keeping the volume low, I found a channel playing old reruns. I moved her glass to the end table, and she snuggled tight to my side to watch TV. I could feel her heartbeat against my skin as her little hands clutched tightly around me. I took a deep breath and kissed the top of her head as I pushed her hair away from her face. It wasn't Sara's fault that I missed my son.

Hours later, Anne shook me awake.

"Your alarm is going off," she whispered as she gathered Sara in her arms and carried her back to bed. I slowly stretched, trying to force my sleepy brain awake. In the bedroom, I turned the alarm off before dragging myself into the shower.

Twenty minutes later, I went to retrieve my shoulder bag from the kitchen and was pleasantly surprised to find a to-go coffee waiting for me. "You didn't have to do this, but I so needed it this morning."

"I've always been an early riser, so no big deal. Honestly, I was surprised to find that you even had coffee in the cupboard since you are out of everything else." She was smiling as she flitted around my kitchen. "Why was Sara in the living room with you?"

"Ah. She had a bad dream. Then we fell asleep on the couch." On the notepad that I always kept on the kitchen table, I wrote my contact information and a few items other than toilet paper that I knew I needed. "If you need anything, just call. I will see you in a couple of hours."

Out in the driveway, I realized that Anne had parked beside my SUV in the narrow drive. For a normal person, this wouldn't be an issue. However, my driving skills in reverse had never worked that well, so I would have to be careful when I backed out. I gently accelerated, staying as far away from her car as possible, smiling when I knew I was safely past it.

KRRRCHHH. My SUV slammed to a stop.

Ugh! I threw the truck in park and opened my door. I had clipped the rear-end of my SUV into the yard light pole. The light lens had shattered, and the bulb was hanging. Crap.

Anne came running out the back door of the house. "What happened?"

"I wasn't paying attention and clipped the light post. I don't have time to deal with it now." I shrugged. "Later."

I pulled the car forward a bit and then tried again to reverse the rest of the way down the long drive. Unfortunately, Anne stayed in the driveway and watched my curvy version of reverse driving, which was always worse when I had an audience. It reminded me of when I was in the police academy. The only reason that I passed the driving courses was because my forward driving abilities rated high enough to outweigh my lack of abilities to parallel park or reverse in a straight line.

I was finally on the road and sighed with relief. I just might make my appointment on time.

"You're late," Katie complained when I settled in the booth across from her.

"I'm exactly on time," I snapped back. I was not a morning person, and Katie knew this. She grinned over her cup of coffee, taking a sip.

I settled my shoulder bag next to me in the booth and made the mistake of putting my hands on the table. Something gooey, which I hoped was syrup, coated the side of my hand. Growling, I grabbed a napkin and dipped it into Katie's water glass to wipe it off. Her grin expanded.

A waitress came over and took my order, and I requested the table be wiped down. A few minutes later, she returned with my coffee and water but forgot about the table as she greeted another customer.

"Don't do anything stupid," Katie said, still smiling, obviously hoping I would do just that. Katie liked a little drama in her life and often used me to fill the void.

"Me?" I asked, while getting out of the booth and walking behind the serving counter.

The waitress started sputtering that I wasn't allowed back there, as I found a clean rag and a spray bottle filled with some mystery-cleaning product. Ignoring her, I returned to the table and cleaned it off myself.

A tall young man covered in tattoos approached me and reached out for the rag and bottle. He carried them back to his table and proceeded to clean it as his fellow tattooed friends held up their drinks and plates. They all wore leather cuts with matching emblems on the back that said Devil's Players. It didn't take a rocket scientist to figure out that the bikes outside the restaurant must belong to them.

"Great. Now the waitress is pissed, and I was going to order breakfast," Katie grumbled.

"You don't want to eat here. There were dead cockroaches on the floor behind the counter," I said, grimacing at the taste of the bitter coffee. "I'm sure all the living ones are in the kitchen."

One of the bikers spit his half-chewed breakfast onto the floor.

He glanced at me before inspecting for himself the bugs behind the counter. "Fuck this shit," he growled before throwing some cash on the table and walking out. His companions ceased eating and followed suit. The remaining couple of the only other occupied table stood and walked out too.

"You do know how to clear a room, don't you," Katie grinned as she checked out the asses of the men leaving.

"It's a special gift. Now, what do you have for me, so I can get out of this dive?"

The waitress stomped over, tossed our bill on the table, and exited through the kitchen. I heard the back door slam shut. I wasn't sure if she was going on a smoke break or had just quit her job, and I didn't care.

"Your cousin, Charlie, just got back from a short vacation in southern Mississippi. She managed to arrest a guy who was abducting a woman. The grapevine is buzzing that her boss doesn't seem too happy about how she spends her time off. That's all I have on Charlie, and there is still no trace of Max." Katie opened her laptop. "I still can't get access to the police files you want. They are keeping them locked up tight. My guy in Florida did manage to get some old financial records on Max, though. I will email them to you, but want you to do a quick glance first and see if anything stands out."

"Any clue on how Charlie ended up being in the right place at the right time?" I asked as I scanned the financial documents from Katie's laptop.

"Best I can tell is she is tracking missing persons reports of young women. She must have believed you about Max's involvement in sex trafficking. My guess is she's hoping she finds him before you do."

"It won't matter which one of us finds him first. I'll have my revenge either way." I took another drink of my coffee, regretting it immediately. "This coffee is putrid. Why the hell did you pick this place?"

"I picked it because those hot bikers have been coming here every morning for breakfast this week. But you screwed that up for me." She picked up her coffee to take a drink but thought better of it, curling up her nose and setting it back down. "Okay, so maybe it's for the best."

I pulled my shoulder bag over my head and threw some cash on the table. "I didn't see anything new in the financials, but I will take a closer look tonight. See if you can pull up the same missing persons reports that Charlie is following and let me know if you find any patterns. She may be onto something. In fact, pull up any unresolved missing persons cases within the last two years. I might see something she missed."

"Sure thing, boss."

It was after 9:00. I was cutting through side roads to avoid most of the traffic when I noticed a service garage and pulled in. I walked into the office, looking around but not seeing anyone.

"What can I do for you today?" a voice boomed from behind me.

"Damn!" I jumped, my heart pounding a mile a minute. "You scared the crap out of me!"

"Sorry about that," the oversized mechanic chuckled, stepping back to give me some space. "Get used to talking loud with all the noise in the shop. Forget myself sometimes when I help fill in for the office."

The mechanic smiled, crossing his arms over his chest as he leaned into the doorway. He was so broad that his other shoulder came nearly to the other side of the doorway frame.

"No. My bad, I didn't sleep much last night, and am running on pure caffeine."

I realized my right hand was tense and gripping my left side, where I used to carry my firearm. I moved my hand to my shoulder bag, hoping that the gesture went unnoticed.

"Okay – well, I am in a rush today, but I was wondering if I could pay you to put on some of that red tape and rig my taillight up to buy me a couple of days before I need to schedule a repair. I cracked the light cover just a bit this morning."

"Let's take a look," he smiled.

I rolled my eyes. I was sure the situation was only supporting his stereotype of female drivers.

"Just a bit? You did a good amount of damage here," he grinned. "You're going to need a new light assembly instead of just the lens. Will your insurance cover it?"

"I'll pay cash. Can you get junkyard parts for it? The truck is old, and not worth the money for the new stuff." Truthfully, the life expectancy of bumpers and taillights with me driving wasn't good, but I didn't need to disclose that to him.

"Sure. We'll get it fixed up enough now so you can keep driving it. Then I will track down the parts, and we can schedule it back in for service." He walked back toward the front of the truck. "Hey, Bones!" he hollered.

"Yeah?" a deep voice answered from the depths of the service garage.

"Grab me some electrical tape and that red lens tape, will ya?"

I dug a business card out of my shoulder bag and wrote my cell number on the back. My phone started ringing. I pulled it out, answering the unknown caller.

"Kelsey."

"Hi Kelsey," Anne said over the phone. "I'm at the store purchasing early drop-offs, but I am almost out of money. Should I tell people to wait or tell them to come back tomorrow?"

The first mechanic was talking to the second mechanic, who was somewhere behind my truck. They appeared to be already adding the tape. I checked my watch.

"I should be there in ten minutes. Try to stall until I get there."

"Got it," Anne said, disconnecting the call.

The mechanic walked back over.

"All set?" I asked.

"Yeah, I will get on the phone and track down the parts you need. It shouldn't be more than a day to find."

"That would be great. I have my number here." I handed him my business card. "Do you know about how long you will need the truck to make the repairs? I will have to figure out how to fit the time into my schedule."

"It will only take about half an hour. It's an easy fix. We are open on Saturdays too if that helps."

"For a normal person, that would be great; for me, not so much. I'll figure it out. How much do I owe you for taping it up for me?"

"No charge. Don't worry about it."

"Thank you. I'm Kelsey, by the way," I held out my hand to shake his.

"Pleasure to meet you, Kelsey. I'm Craig, but my friends call me Chops." He looked down at the card I had handed him. "Is this your business, The Changing Room?"

"All mine, for better or worse."

"My girlfriend, Candi, was yapping about it last week. She came home with three huge bags of clothes. I started getting on her case about spending so much money again when she jammed the receipt in my face. I couldn't believe it. She only spent $80," he grinned.

"Well, we aim to please. We have menswear, too, if you need some duds."

A tow truck pulled into the lot, distracting me. The truck parked perpendicular to my SUV in the row behind me. When I had parked, I had had a full 180-degree wide opening to back out. Now with the tow truck parked there, it was going to be tight.

Chops looked at me and then at the tow truck. "You can't drive in reverse, can you?"

"I can, I just suck at it," I admitted. "And, please, spare me the instructional. I have heard it all. I've even seen the videos and had private driving lessons. Just help me get my SUV out without sideswiping that tow truck."

I was embarrassed, but it was better than having to replace more car parts. Chops didn't say anything else, just got in my truck, reversed it and then pulled it forward for me. A deep chuckle resonated from within the garage. I looked back and glimpsed a rock-hard body, with muscular arms, lean torso, and tight black jeans. Because the light through the bay door angled away from him, his face was in the shadows, but I felt his eyes focus in on me. Shaking off the intense feeling, I quickly thanked Chops again and left.

I pulled behind the store and slammed on the brakes. Along the back wall of my portion of retail space, piles of boxes and bags were stacked, and a dozen vehicles waited, lining the back drive. Turning my SUV out of the way, I parked and grabbed my shoulder bag before jogging to join Anne and Sara near the store's back door. Sara was perched on top of stacked boxes and talking on a cellphone, holding a piece of paper. She gave me a thumbs-up, and I heard her greet someone on the phone and tell him or her that if they wanted to sell their clothes, they needed to bring them in before 10:30. I was completely confused.

"Money – I need cold hard cash!" Anne squealed.

I pulled a bundle of cash from by shoulder bag and handed it over. She had several customers waiting for her as she doled out cash, so I started making offers to the rest of the people waiting impatiently in their vehicles to pull up and sell their clothes.

About forty minutes later, it slowed enough for me to open up the back room and drag out some flatbed carts. Between purchases, we moved the clothes onto the carts and started moving them inside. By 11:00, we made our last buy for the day.

"What the hell was all that?" I was a little shell-shocked as I tried to maneuver around all the new stock. "Fess up. Where did all those people come from?" I grinned.

"It was Sara's idea. I was telling her about how you normally get the clothes on Saturdays when the garage sales are shutting down. Sara said that people are lazy, so the ones that had garage sales last weekend probably still had all their stuff stacked up in their garages. I pulled up the ads from last week's garage sales and the first three I called asked how early we opened. They wanted their garages back. So, I printed the list and drove here. Sara made more calls while I used the money left over from groceries and my pay from last night to buy the clothes. I hope I didn't overspend."

"Not at all. I can't believe you were able to get that much stock built up with what little money you had." We squeezed through the piles and entered the sales floor.

"I also called the laundromat and finagled a deal with them on laundry service. If I can borrow your truck, they will launder some of it at half price for this morning."

"It's all yours." I handed her the keys. "Just be sure to come back, because you no longer have a choice about working here. It's official. You are now the property of The Changing Room."

Anne stiffened. "Property of?"

I laughed while opening the register. "Sorry. I ran into a biker club this morning at my meeting. They must be influencing my vocabulary today."

"Do you know the name of the club?" Anne asked.

Realizing something sounded off, I turned back to look at her. Her pale skin had paled even more, and Sara was listening nervously to our conversation.

"I think they are local, but hang on a minute and I will double-check." I pulled out my cell and called Katie.

"I'm still hungry," Katie complained, answering the phone.

"You're an adult, figure it out," I said. "I need info on the bikers we ran into this morning. Are they local?"

"Yeah. I'm surprised you haven't noticed them around. They aren't what I would call legit, but nothing like the evildoers you have me currently researching. Why? What's up?" Katie asked.

"Nothing. That's all I needed." I disconnected the call before she could ask any more questions. I'm sure Katie would relish the opportunity to dig deeper into the club if I let her.

I turned to Anne and Sara. "They are local. Nothing overly violent known about them, but they aren't exactly law-abiding citizens either. I remember their leather cuts had 'Devil's Players' written across the back of them."

Anne and Sara both seem relieved. I didn't press them with questions, but it was good to know to keep my eye out for any other bikers.

"So, you understand I am not going to let you quit?" I asked, grinning.

"That's good because I have no interest in leaving. I had a lot of fun this morning," Anne said while picking Sara up off the stool and setting her on the floor. "Sara, can you read your book while Kelsey and I get the truck unloaded and reloaded?"

"Sara, how old are you?" I asked.

"Six. I will be seven in a couple of months," Sara answered.

"And you can read by yourself?"

"Mom taught me," Sara nodded. "And, I know how to add, subtract and multiply big numbers too, but mom says I shouldn't tell people that."

"Why?" I asked.

"She says people will think I'm strange because I am too young to know how to do those things."

"Little bug, we are all a little strange. That's what makes life a bit more fun." I tickled her, enjoying her giggles.

Looking around at the overflowing stock, I couldn't help smiling. "And you probably even remembered to buy toilet paper," I said to Anne.

"Yes, I remembered the toilet paper. The landlord also fixed the parking lot light," Anne grinned.

"You are amazing."

"Well, I am glad you are pleased, because I'm not going anywhere. I like it here," she said as she sashayed out the back door with the SUV keys.

The store was busy most of the day, but we were able to keep the crowd moving. Anne made several trips back and forth to the laundromat to ensure we had enough stock for the next day. When we closed, she insisted we leave the re-stock for the morning and that she would come in early with me. I had Max's financials to research still, so that sounded like a good plan to me.

Arriving at home, it felt as if Anne and Sara had always lived with me. Sara ran out to empty the mailbox. Anne started making dinner. I started up the laundry before I found myself at my desk sorting mail and paying some of my personal bills. I even managed to balance my personal checking account.

After dinner, I went to my room and started thoroughly reading the financial records. Nothing out of the ordinary stood out in the documents, but I took notes as I read each page thoroughly until I fell asleep a few hours before dawn.

Chapter Four

Saturday morning was a whirlwind, restocking the store, and after we had cleared enough space in the storage room for more inventory, I reversed my truck up to the back door to unload. Unfortunately, I was on too much of an angle and ran into the stupid cement post. While I was glad the post prevented me from hitting the building, I wasn't happy to see that I annihilated the passenger-side rear light. Ugh! Pulling my phone out of my back pocket, I called the number Chops gave me.

"Chops' Shop," Chops answered.

After the initial shock, I started to laugh. "How in the hell hadn't I noticed the name of the business when I was there yesterday?"

"Kelsey?" Chops asked, laughing.

"Yeah, sorry. How'd you know it was me?"

"The business name is usually the first thing people notice, but you seemed a little rattled when we met yesterday."

"Rattled is my normal mindset these days," I admitted. "I was calling to see if you had already picked up the light for my truck?"

"Not yet. I'm planning on swinging out to the salvage yard later this morning. It didn't sound like you were going to need it done today, so I worked on some other projects this morning."

"I'm not calling because I am suddenly in a hurry. I need to double the order and add the light for the passenger side as well."

"I didn't see any damage to the other light."

"Yesterday there wasn't any. But this morning there was another mishap," I sighed.

I hated admitting such things, but it wasn't as if he wouldn't notice the new damage when he fixed the driver's side.

It took a bit for Chops to stop laughing before he could say anything. When he did, he didn't speak directly to me but yelled to someone else, "Hey Bones, call the salvage yard and see if they can get the same light fixture for the passenger side of that SUV."

Geesh. How embarrassing.

"So Kelsey, should we go ahead and get the front lights too while we are at it?"

"No. It's always just the rear lights," I grumbled.

"You got it. We'll make sure we get both."

He disconnected the call, but I was sure he was still laughing. I rolled my eyes as I squatted to pick up the worst of the taillight lens debris.

We had a line of customers waiting outside when we unlocked the front door at ten and the store filled to max capacity within the next half hour. Anne and I rotated running the register.

The fire marshal stopped in and looked around. "You're pushing your luck, Kelsey," he said before he left. Maybe I should anonymously send him tickets to some vacation destination and give us both a break from each other.

Around noon, my brother Jeff and his wife, Lily, showed up. Lily wanted to shop, so Jeff helped at the register while I hauled more stock from the back. Customers were impatiently waiting as I piled fresh clothes on the shelf, only for them to clear it off again.

"Kel, someone's here asking for you," Jeff yelled as I was dragging out a rack of shirts.

As soon as the rolling rack crossed the threshold between the back room and the sales floor, three women converged, knocking me back into the wall. I didn't want to know what lengths these women would go for a new blouse.

I turned to the counter, where a woman with big curly blond hair and heavy, dark makeup stood grinning at me. "Hi. I'm Kelsey. What can I do for you?"

"It is so great to meet you. I'm Candi. My boyfriend —,"

"Yes, Candi, hello," I interrupted and reached out to shake her hand. "You're Chops' girlfriend. He told me about you yesterday. He admitted giving you a hard time for buying too many clothes," I smiled. I could easily see the jovial woman with Chops.

"He talked about me? That's sweet," she beamed. "And, a girl can't own too many clothes. It's impossible. Your store is my new favorite. I had a ton of fun shopping here."

"Well, be sure to tell all your shopaholic friends," I laughed. "Anything I can help you with today?"

"Oh, look at me going on and on, I almost forgot! Chops and Bones are in the back parking lot. Chops asked me to grab your keys so they can fix your truck. Said it won't take long."

"Wow. That's incredible. I so appreciate this," I said as I dug my keys out of my shoulder bag. "And, if I am busy when they get done, I will leave enough cash up here to pay whatever I owe. Plus, if you have time, do you think you could swing back inside after you give him the keys?"

"Sure, honey, but someone will have to babysit me. Chops says I can't buy any more clothes until I wear the ones I already bought." She laughed at her own joke as I opened the storage room door and let her exit out the back.

Returning to the checkout counter, I pulled some cash from my shoulder bag, handing it to Jeff. "The guy fixing my truck is a nice guy. If his bill looks too low, be sure to throw some on top."

Jeff nodded and tucked the cash in a cup we kept under the counter.

Candi returned a few minutes later. I grabbed two tote bags and handed them to her.

"I need you to pick out some clothes for Chops and his coworker. They'll be free, of course, just a little 'thank you' to them for helping me out. Can you do that for me?"

"Oh, that sounds like fun," Candi squealed. "But I don't know Bones' sizes."

As Anne passed by, I grabbed her by the arm. "Some guys are out back working on my truck. Can you give a head-to-toe look at the guy named Bones and then let Candi know what his sizes are?"

Anne nodded, walking out. The rolling rack I had dragged out had only three shirts left on it, so I exchanged it for a new one. It was like feeding time at the zoo. Crazy ladies swarmed around me, and I jumped out of the way. I decided it was safer to work on totes, so I brought several of them out to restock the almost empty shelves.

Anne returned with a strange smirk on her face. "You haven't seen this Bones guy yet, have you?"

"No. Why?" I said, only half paying attention. Customers were sneaking into the totes I hadn't opened yet.

"No reason," she answered, still smirking, as she squeezed through the crowd to join Candi in menswear.

I didn't have time to figure out why Anne was smirking. The feeding frenzy was multiplying and out of control. One of the women grabbed the tote I was trying to empty and carried the whole thing off while other women were scrambling to grab clothes from it. I was knocked over in the ruckus, landing rump-side-first inside one of the empty totes.

"You are all psychos!" I laughed as I struggled to separate my backside from the tote. The women were either too absorbed in their shopping experience to hear me or simply didn't care. More customers pressed forward, pushing me aside, as they fought over the limited supply. I looked around. The rolling rack by the storage room was empty.

I ducked behind the safety of the register counter and did a 360-degree turn. We were way over capacity. Good thing the fire marshal visited us early today. Glancing at the clock, I noted it was almost 1:00.

"Attention, ladies! Anyone that cashes out in the next 20 minutes *and leaves* will get a 10% off coupon for The Changing Room on their next visit! You only have until 1:20! So you better hurry!"

Jeff and I shrank back as a crowd of people rushed the counter and hit it with enough force that it rocked back toward us. Realizing it might tip over, we jumped forward, throwing our weight on top of it to push it back down flat to the floor. I grabbed the cash-filled fanny packs, handing Jeff one, as Anne returned to take over the register. We all assumed our battle stations to clear out the crowd.

Twenty-five minutes later, most of the customers were gone, but the racks and shelves were barren. We had a short window of time to restock before we would be busy again.

"Hey, big brother, can you call somewhere for food? I need a jumbo fountain drink and something greasy if I am going to make it until 7:00."

He pulled open the food menu drawer. He knew what I liked, so I wasn't concerned.

After placing our order, Jeff joined me hauling all the rolling racks out, and we moved the clothes to wall racks. Next were the totes, taking a little longer.

"Where did Lily go?" I asked.

Jeff snorted. "She checked out so she could get a coupon. She's probably down the strip getting ice cream."

"She's family," I said, thoroughly confused. "She gets clothes for free."

"No, she doesn't," Jeff grinned. "I never told her that she gets free clothes. She pays for them and then I secretly deposit the money in the kids' college fund. She would fill the house to the rafters if she thought the clothes were free."

Knowing Lily and the truckload of clothes my brother donated to my startup, I didn't doubt his logic a bit. If Lily ever found out, though, there would be hell to pay. "Better make sure Anne understands the arrangement before she accidentally spills the beans."

"That was one of the first things I explained when I got here this morning. Anne's on board." Jeff continued smiling as he helped me to stack the now-empty totes. "Dang, you've gone through a lot of clothes today."

"Yeah, and we might end up closing early tonight by the looks of it. That was the last of what we had cleaned and ready to sell. That inventory should have lasted a week. I'm going to need a larger space sooner than I planned if this keeps up."

Lily came back with the food. We were starting to get busy again, so I grabbed my supersize Coke and ran the register while everyone else went to the back room to eat. Just as the checkout line emptied again, Chops came in the front door.

"I figured you guys left hours ago. Was there a problem?"

"No. It was crazy busy in here, and I didn't want to interrupt. We grabbed lunch down the strip. You don't have to pay today, but I wanted to drop off the bill." He handed me the bill, and I reviewed the charges. "And what's with the bags that Candi has? I told her no more shopping, but she said they were a surprise?"

"Then I guess you have to wait for her to surprise you."

As I had predicted, he only had twenty bucks down for labor and the rest was parts. I handed him the cash out of the cup. "Here. And, don't argue. I'm not poor, just really, really busy."

"Yeah, it makes sense now. This place is a nuthouse."

"Yes, but it's my nuthouse," I grinned.

Sara came running out and pulled her stool over next to me, climbing on top of it to sit. She had food all over her face, so I grabbed a Kleenex and wiped her down as she giggled.

"And who's this?" Chops teased her.

"I'm Sara," she giggled, holding her hand out bravely to shake Chops' hand. "My mom works here, and I get to hang out."

"Pleasure to meet you, Miss Sara," Chops grinned back.

"You know what, Sara? I think your mom put some ice cream in the back freezer yesterday. You better get some before Uncle Jeff sees it."

She tore off into the back room again.

"Is her mom the one that came out earlier, asked for Bones, looked him up and down, smirked, and then came back inside?"

I started laughing. "She never said anything else? That was it?"

"That was it," Chops said, scratching the back of his neck. "Is she a little strange?"

"No more than myself or the rest of the people I hang out with," I shook my head.

He grinned, rapped his knuckles on the counter and moved toward the door. "Until next time…"

As the door closed, I had a thought and yelled for someone to cover the register. Rushing out the door after him, I caught him just before he opened his truck door. "Hey, Chops."

"You couldn't have damaged something else already," he grinned.

"Ha, ha." I rolled my eyes. "I have a question. And, I am hoping I don't offend you by asking it."

I was unsure if I was doing the right thing. I didn't know Chops on a personal level, but I couldn't think of anyone else to ask.

"Ask whatever," he said. "Are you looking to buy some weed or something?" he laughed.

"No, I know plenty of dealers."

He raised an eyebrow at that, which made me smirk.

"I find I am entering unfamiliar waters, though. I have a friend that needs to find out how to go about getting some documents, um, created, like the type with a person's picture on them, and maybe a social security number or two. The documents would have to be good enough for filing taxes and getting health insurance."

He slowly dragged his hand over his bristly jaw. "People that are looking for those types of documents are usually running from the law. If you get mixed up with all that, you could get yourself into a pretty tight spot. I recommend that you send the person packing, Kelsey."

"The police aren't the problem. But, I get the feeling this friend would likely end up in the hospital or a shallow grave if someone else found her."

Chops sighed, hands on hips, looking back at the storefront window. I knew he was going to help before he said anything. "Let me make a call and someone will get back to you. But never, ever, tell anyone that I did even that for you, deal?"

"You have my word," I grinned and kissed him on the cheek. "Enjoy your surprise!" I yelled over my shoulder as I jogged back to the store.

By 4:00, I sent Lily and Jeff home. They convinced Anne to let Sara go with them for a sleepover. Sara was excited that she was going to meet my nieces and nephews. I cornered Lily, warning her about Sara's nightmares. "Poor thing," Lily said, but I knew that she would handle it like a pro.

By 5:00, we closed early. We didn't have enough clean and ready-to-sell stock to justify staying open. Anne found a deal on a rental truck and we utilized our time by hauling all the dirty clothes to the laundromat. Being it was early Saturday evening, we had the place pretty much to ourselves, which was good, because we used almost every washer.

My phone rang around 6:00. I answered it even though the display read *unknown number.* "Hello?" I said.

"I was told there are some papers you need. What general information should be on them? How many? How old? First names?" The voice over the line was deep, very masculine and spoke slowly and deliberately.

"Anne, 25; Sara, 6, the rest doesn't matter."

"No concern with anyone calling the cops about the kid missing?"

"None. That's not an issue."

"Good. I will email you an address to send a digital picture of the woman. It will be 5k for the adult and 2k for the kid." The caller disconnected.

You would think brokering such an illegal transaction would make a person sweat, but I was more focused on how incredibly sexy the voice on the phone was. It was probably a good thing this wasn't a face-to-face meeting. Living a life of all work and no play, Kelsey's girly parts were in serious need of attention.

"What are you smirking about?" Anne asked.

I just smiled. I heard the radio playing in the background, Blue Swede's "Hooked on a Feeling," and sang along. I was only a couple words in when Anne started singing too. By the end of the song, the laundry attendant and the only other customer had joined in.

By 8:00, we had all the laundry done and were back in the store. I proudly returned the rental truck without a single new scratch on it. It had turned out to be a great day. It was still early, so we decided to walk to the pub farther down the strip. Our timing was perfect, after the dinner rush and before the heavy drinking rush, so we were able to get a nice tall corner table. I preferred the taller tables, so I didn't have to look up to talk to people.

"So, I may have a lead on the paperwork for you and Sara. It's expensive. I will pay for it and then we can work out a small payment plan down the road so you can pay me back. Total, it will be seven grand. Does that sound okay?"

"Are you sure you can afford to front the money? I will pay you back. I promise. But it will take me awhile. And, I want to pay you interest too."

"No interest. I don't want to worry about Uncle Sam coming after me," I laughed. "I have the money in my personal account. I don't know how much I have in the store account, but I haven't spent any of the profits so that should be sitting pretty good right now too."

The waitress came over and took our orders. We ordered appetizers to split and some cocktails.

"So, are you going to register Sara for school?"

"I don't know," Anne said. "She's so far ahead of other kids her age. I mean, does she sound like your typical six-year-old?"

"No. Not even close," I laughed. "But I like that about her."

"And, she doesn't play well with other kids either. She watched some kids play tag at the park, and she giggled that it was stupid. She would be a nightmare for any first-grade teacher."

"Well, there is always home-schooling. Or, I've heard the online schools are pretty good. Kids can learn at their own pace, which could offer her more challenging classes. We can even set up a desk at the store."

"That might work," Anne said with an excited grin. "I will check that out tomorrow, but we would have to borrow your laptop until I can afford a computer. Is that okay? I can schedule it around you doing the business accounting."

"She can use my laptop. I need to buy another laptop for the store. Mine is outdated and doesn't have enough memory. It will be fine for Sara, but it doesn't like the accounting software."

"Yeah, I heard you calling it a piece of shit yesterday while you were trying to do the books."

We were on our third drink, and I was surprised to realize that I was a little tipsy. I saw a pool table had opened up in the back of the bar, and Anne agreed to play. I settled our stuff while Anne racked the balls. I laughed as I watched. "Well, that tells me we aren't playing for money."

"What?" she grinned. "No one's even broke yet."

"Hey Kelsey!" a voice approaching called.

I turned to see Chops and Candi, and behind them, of all people, was Dwayne Bishop. Chops held his arms out to his sides and did a slow turn. Decked out in his new clothes, he winked at me.

"Hey, Chops – looking good. Hi, Candi. You did great on the clothes. They are perfect for him." I could tell she appreciated the praise. "And Mr. Bishop, how are you?"

"You guys know each other?" Chops inquired with a raised eyebrow.

I could understand his confusion. I was just as confused at Chops' association with Bishop. Bishop seemed too uppity to hang out in a bar with a mechanic.

"We met at the store earlier in the week," I nodded. "Did you guys just get here?"

"No," Bishop answered. "We've been here awhile. We were waiting for a pool table to open, but you beat us to it."

Anne grinned.

We might have only met a couple of days ago, but it seemed we could read each other's minds.

"Doubles? Winner pockets twenty bucks?" she said before I could stop her.

"Deal," Bishop said with a smirk. "But don't blame us if you go home broke."

"Bishop, I am not getting hustled out of my hard-earned money," Chops griped.

"He's right. No money on the table, but we can play doubles still. Just might not be much fun for you boys. Grab a stick and break." I motioned for a waitress and paid for a round of drinks while Bishop completed an amateur break.

"Go for it," Anne said, as she handed me her stick. I already knew she checked to make sure it was straight, but I checked the weight. We took solids, and I left one, plus the eightball, when I finally missed. Chops followed by sinking two and Anne cleared the table.

"Beginner's luck," Bishop grumbled.

"Dwayne," Chops sighed, "for a smart man, you can be damn naïve. These girls are just plain better than us. You can't beat them." Chops shook his head.

"Nah. They just got lucky. Another round will prove I'm right," Bishop insisted.

What a chauvinistic ass.

I turned to Anne and noticed that she was also seriously annoyed.

"Anne's turn to break," I announced.

"Absolutely," Bishop agreed. "Ladies first."

Anne stepped up to the table and turned to Bishop. "Hope this doesn't cause any problems with you shopping again at The Changing Room. We do appreciate your business," she grinned before she broke.

Two stripes split off and sunk. She sank every single stripe one by one before taking out the eight ball. Solids were still full on the table.

"I believe I owe you a shot, partner," I smiled.

Chops and Candi couldn't stop laughing as I ordered a round of tequila shots. In the next game, Chops and Candi played partners against two other people they knew. Bishop excused himself, probably to hide while he licked his wounds.

The waitress returned with a tray of shots, and I was just about to down mine when I heard someone calling my name. Recognizing the person coming toward me, I set the glass down. *Just great.* Now I have to deal with this dipshit.

I looked over to Chops and Anne and warned, "Stay out of this. I will deal with it." Neither would commit by even a head nod. *Ugh. Not good.*

I heard Chops tell his friends to play singles the next game and he led Candi to a chair on the other side of the table, tucked up against the wall. Anne passed our tequila shots off to Chops' friends. I threw the strap of my shoulder bag over my head, tucking the bag to my side.

"Kelsey. What rock did you crawl out from under?" the familiar voice sneered behind me, close enough that I could feel his breath on my neck. I planted a smile on my face before turning to face him.

"Hey, Brett. It's been awhile. Hope everything's good with the family," I said as I moved over toward the pool table. I wanted to increase the distance away from Candi and Anne if things turned physical. And, based on his expression, he was spoiling for a fight.

"Much better. My parents are happy I am no longer with a money-hungry worthless tramp like you. They like the new model much better."

I saw Chops gearing to step forward, but Anne sidestepped in front of him, blocking his path. *Good girl.*

"Well, I am glad they are happy. I was just telling everyone that it's time for me to head home. It's past my bedtime and all. It was good to see you," I lied as I took another step away from him and then started toward the front door.

"What?" he raised his voice, following behind me. "Worried that everyone is going to find out the truth about you?"

I was ignoring most of what he was saying. Been here, done this. Other patrons were watching and listening to the scene as it played out. As I passed our waitress, I placed a twenty on her tray. "Get to my friend. Tell her to wait ten minutes and I will pick her up at the back door."

The waitress nodded before hurrying away. Brett wouldn't mess with her. He already had a target. I stepped out of the bar and onto the sidewalk. I could hear him approaching behind me.

"Don't you walk away from me, whore!" he said grabbing me by the arm.

I twisted my arm out of his grip and pivoted to the side, out of his reach. "Brett, go home. I don't want to fight with you," I said in a controlled voice as I scanned the area.

In the past, I used Brett's volatility as a self-punishment to deal with all the guilt I felt, so I never fought back. I was fully capable of kicking his ass, though. He just didn't know it. But, he was about to find out.

"Oh, this isn't a fight. You want to see a fight?" he snarled.

He grabbed for my arm again, but I managed to slide out of his reach. His movements were slow, dulled by alcohol and probably a bit of weed, adding more points in my favor.

A quick glance confirmed that there were too many witnesses around. I darted for a darker section of the parking lot so we would be less visible. Brett was close on my heels. As I turned to face off with him, I heard motorcycles approaching. They split into two rows and pulled up, surrounding us. Unfortunately, their lights illuminated the area, drawing unwanted attention. One of the riders looped an arm around my waist and pulled me up onto his lap.

"You're okay," a deep voice vibrated in my ear. "I've got you."

"Thanks, but I had it handled." I elbowed the biker just hard enough for him to loosen his grip so I could slide off the bike. I removed my shoulder bag and handed it to him instead.

"Brett, it seems our conversation has been interrupted. I am going to encourage you one last time: *go home.*" I stood facing Brett, only a half-dozen feet away. Witnesses or not, if he still wanted to fight, I was ready.

Brett glared at me before circling his attention to the bikers and the growing witnesses. "Another day then," he sneered.

"You can count on it, asshole," I said as he stalked away into the dark parking lot.

"We would have been happy to kick his ass for you," one of the bikers chuckled.

"I would have kicked his ass myself if you all wouldn't have driven up," I said. I retrieved my shoulder bag, placing the strap back over my head.

A police cruiser pulled up. "Kelsey? Is that you?"

I stepped toward the cruiser and saw Steve was driving. "Steve," I leaned down to peer at the passenger side. "Dave," I nodded in greeting.

"We got a call from the bartender for a disturbance. Was that Brett that just left?" Dave asked, getting out of the cruiser.

"Yeah. You're late for the party. It's already over," I said.

Steve pulled the car into a parking space, and the bikers pulled up to park as well. It was dark, and the parking-lot lights were too far away, so I couldn't get a good visual of any of them.

"So, how bad was it?" Dave asked, pulling out a mini-mag light and shining it on my face and then my hands. Steve and several of the bikers walked up to join us.

"He didn't hurt me. I'm fine."

"He would have, though. We pulled up when he was chasing her," one of the bikers said while rubbing his jaw. He was cute in a rugged-surfer way. He had dirty blonde hair with a touch of wavy curls because it had grown out too long. He wore a leather cut, and I noticed the others did as well. I stepped behind one of the bikers and checked their club name. Devil's Players.

"Did you witness anything that we can use to press charges?" Steve asked.

"No. And, we would tell you if we did. He's bad news," the surfer-biker said.

Dave and I were both trying not to laugh, but Steve had his cop face on, staying firmly in his serious cop role. "We know. We just haven't been able to nail him on anything yet." Steve turned to me. "You want us to put out an alert to pick him up? I'm sure he's been drinking."

"No. You know that would be like pissing on a hornet's nest. I got this. It's just a matter of bad timing," I said.

Dave chuckled but didn't say anything.

"Shit! I told the waitress to have Anne meet me at the back door so I could pick her up." Turning back to the bar, one of the bikers grabbed my arm to stop me.

"It's all good. Chops is escorting her this way."

Perfectly timed, the door opened. Chops and Bishop stepped out, followed by Anne. Anne raced past them when she spotted me. She had tears running down her face as she gripped me in a tight hug.

"Everything is fine. I'm so sorry that you had to see that, but I was safe. He can't hurt me unless I let him." I wasn't sure if she understood anything that I said. She was shaking in my arms. The situation seemed to have stirred up bad nightmares from her past.

She pulled back but couldn't stop crying, and a burly biker with a thick beard turned her into his chest and wrapped his meaty arms around her. I was grateful. I wasn't good with female waterworks.

"Steve, I know it's against the rules, but will you give us a lift home? I have had a few too many drinks to drive, and don't feel like going back in for coffee after that scene that just went down."

"Sure. Should we call in patrol cars to do drive-bys at your house tonight?"

"Not necessary. He'll go home and get shitfaced until he passes out. I will have a couple of days before he surfaces again. I'll handle him then."

One of the bikers growled. "How long has this been going on?" He looked pissed, but it wasn't his problem. It was mine. I said nothing as I walked away, leading Anne to the cruiser.

As we pulled out of the lot, I saw one of the bikers lean against the brick wall outside of the bar. He was listening to his friends as they gathered around him, but his eyes locked with mine, imprisoning my attention until the cruiser drove out of range. I could only make out his rough features: tall, muscular, lean and wearing a cut. The phrase, *bad to the bone*, reverberated in my head. A shiver ran down my spine.

Chapter Five

"Kelsey-," Dave started.

"I know, Dave. We will discuss it some other time. Just please, not tonight." I sighed and rubbed my temples.

I looked over at Anne. She appeared calm now and was using a tissue to wipe her face.

"Do you have a way into work tomorrow or need a ride?" Steve asked.

"I have my car at the house," Anne answered. "I can drive in the morning."

"Are you spending the night?" Steve asked.

Anne nodded before explaining, "Kelsey is letting my daughter, Sara, and I stay with her while I get back on my feet. I recently divorced and relocated. I haven't found a place of my own yet."

"Hey, Dave-" I interrupted. "Did Dallas find a renter yet for the house next to hers?"

"She had a few applications, but I denied them all after I ran the background checks. I think she paid some of them to apply just to freak me out."

"One of them a stripper named Rocket?" I asked, laughing.

"I don't even want to know how you knew that. You and my mother should not be allowed to go out together without supervision," Dave grumbled while Steve and I laughed.

"The house, though," I said, "Can you push Anne through as an applicant? I will vouch for her. I will also pay the deposit and first few months of rent up front. If anything happens, it's on me."

"It's not a problem if you want to rent it for her. But maybe it'd be best if you had company for a while, safety in numbers and all," he answered, turning to look at me.

I shook my head. "Her daughter is the sweetest kid you'll ever meet. I need them a safe distance away from this mess until I figure out what Brett will do next. Hopefully, he won't do anything, but if he does, I don't want Sara anywhere near it. I would have handled it tonight, but the bikers interrupted by thinking I was a mere damsel in distress."

"They had good intentions. You can't hold that against them," Dave said while reaching into his pocket. "I was just at the house today to check on things for Mom. The place is ready; here's a key. You can move in anytime, and I will bring the lease to the store in a day or two."

"You need to run it by Dallas first?"

"Hell, Mom would sign the deed over to you if she thought you would take it. She keeps trying to get me to divorce Tammy so I can date you."

His wife, Tammy, was the domestic type that knitted and baked cakes from scratch. Most mothers would love to have her as a daughter-in-law. Dallas liked life a little more adventurous, though. Her idea of home cooking was once a year on Thanksgiving, and even then frozen dinners were the norm.

"I think Dallas is wrong on that one. You like that Suzy homemaker crap. Someday she'll figure that out. But, thanks for this," I said, holding up the key. "I will see about furniture tomorrow and get them moved in right away."

Anne was staring out the window. I knew she was upset, but I didn't know what to say. Dave saw it too.

"Anne," Dave waited for her to turn toward him, "I'm glad Kelsey has a friend like you to help watch her back. Don't think she's sending you away. She's right. This situation going on is not something you want your daughter witnessing. Kelsey wouldn't be moving you guys if it wasn't the safest move."

"I know she's right. I'll do whatever I need to do to protect my daughter. It just sucks. I like living here," she said as we pulled into the driveway.

"Well, look at it this way. You will be only a few miles away, and I live on the same block, so if you need anything, you just shout out. And, I'm sure my wife will be showing up with a basket of homemade cookies to welcome you to the neighborhood," Dave said.

"Tammy makes awesome cookies too. You need to suck up to her, and she will bring you treats all the time," I said.

Dave jumped out of the car and hurried to open the back door to let us out. The night we met, I had a panic attack from the confinement when he put me in the back of a squad car. I usually can control it, but I have to force myself to stay calm, and that night my stress level had spiked.

"You want us to do a walk-through?" Steve asked.

"No need. He didn't know I would be out tonight, so it wasn't a planned encounter. Thanks, guys. I appreciate the ride and the support."

"We're on until 3:00. Call our cells if you need anything, but we will be doing drive-bys whether you like it or not," Steve said while hugging me and kissing my cheek.

"And get someone to mow the damn lawn," Dave laughed and gave me a quick hug too.

"Yes, sir," I laughed.

I checked all the doors and windows to ensure everything was secure. Anne went to bed, and I pulled out my cell, calling Chops.

"You okay?" he answered the call.

"All good. I won't have any problems tonight. I am sure of that, or I wouldn't have let Anne come home with me. I called to see if I could talk to Candi for a minute."

He didn't ask any questions. Candi was on the line immediately. "Hey, Kelsey, what can I do for you?"

"Is your shopping addiction limited to clothes, or are you into any and all shopping?"

"Any and all, sweetie. Love to shop. Love to find deals," Candi laughed.

"I am moving Anne and her daughter out tomorrow to a rental house. They will need everything — furniture, dishes, towels, wastebaskets, etc. If I supply you with a pile of cash, does that sound like a job you would be interested in taking care of for us?"

"Yes! Yes! Yes! Can I take my friend, Haley, with me?"

"Sure. Don't care how it all goes down as long as it happens quickly. How much do you charge for your shopping expertise?"

"How about Haley and I both get ten an hour in exchangeable value at your store? It will probably take us a full day to get everything. Will that work?"

"I think I am getting one heck of a deal," I laughed.

"I love to shop. Setting up a whole house from scratch is better than a day at Disneyland. And later I get to buy more clothes without Chops being able to complain? I win all the way around."

"Works for me," I said. "I will be at the store in the morning with the money and the key to the house. Just swing through the back door."

We disconnected, and I went to my room. It was still early enough that I could get some work done, so after changing into pajama shorts and an old Detroit Tigers t-shirt, I propped up the pillows at the head of my bed and pulled my files from my shoulder bag.

Every scrap of information I had on Max and Nola laid before me, taunting me. I knew there was nothing more to learn from them, and I tucked them back into the bag. I started up my laptop and checked the cloud sites that I shared with Katie to communicate with the investigators. Nothing new was posted.

Feeling helpless, I reached behind the nightstand and pulled out the picture that I kept hidden away. My cousin Charlie had taken the picture just a few short weeks before Nicholas had disappeared. The warm Atlantic wind blew a light breeze across the almost deserted beachfront. Nicholas had been running in the sand, and I had caught him, tossing him playfully in the air and was rewarded with peals of laughter as Charlie snapped the photo. I could still remember the smell of the salt water and the feel of his warm skin as he wrapped his short arms around my neck to hug me as he giggled. It was a perfect morning.

"I'm not giving up," I told Nicholas, kissing the glass that protected the photo.

I tucked the photo back in its hiding spot and turned my attention back to my laptop. If I couldn't work on the investigation, then at least I could use the time to finish the book I was writing. The books funded my investigations, so even if it wasn't the progress I needed, it was at least progress of some kind.

Decision made, I opened the file and picked up where I left off last. Hopefully, it would distract me from the current mess I found myself in with Brett and the frustration of unanswered questions about Nicholas.

Chapter Six

Over the next few days, I didn't see or hear from Brett and was guessing he either blacked out the whole event or was going to wait until the next time opportunity knocked to strike. Anne and Sara settled into their rental house, and Dave's mom, Dallas, adored them.

She wouldn't let me sign a lease, saying family doesn't do such things. I did make her accept a check for the rent and security deposit. While I missed Sara and Anne staying at the house, they were safe with Dallas living on one side of them, and Dave only a couple houses down the block. And as predicted, Tammy was spoiling them with baskets of homemade goodies.

Candi and her friend Haley ended up filling the house with everything needed while returning a pile of cash at the end of the day. Candi said only a rookie shopper needed that much money.

The store was getting busier every day, and I knew I needed to hire more people. Anne and I scrambled nonstop to keep up. I knew my brother, Jeff, would continue to show up on Saturdays if needed, but he had a family and life of his own.

Friday night rolled around, and Anne, Sara and I were at the grocery store. Sara and I each pushed a cart as Anne ran through her list, filling them for both houses. I rolled my eyes at some of the items that I would never cook that were in my cart and kept sneaking in frozen dinners, condensed soup, and Chef Boyardee. Anne turned up her nose at the Chef Boyardee but didn't say anything. *Food snob.*

We were in the soup aisle when I noticed an older woman. She carried a basket that had bread, peanut butter and Ramen noodles. She looked at several cans before sighing and walking away.

"Anne, I will be back in a minute," I said as I followed the woman. She was probably in her mid-sixties and wore simple navy slacks and a faded sweater. She was looking at frozen dinners and added a potpie to her basket that I knew to be on sale.

"Hi," I said as I walked up to her. "I'm Kelsey Harrison." I held out my hand and was surprised that she smiled and shook it.

"Hi, Kelsey. I'm Hattie. How are you today?" She had laugh lines etched on her face, and she seemed amused by my random introduction.

"I'm great. How are you?"

"Alive and kicking. I couldn't ask for anything else," she grinned.

"Nothing else? How about a job?" I said as I pulled a business card out of my shoulder bag and handed it to her. "I own a resale shop down the road. I'm looking for some new employees. You interested?"

She looked at the card, back at me, and then at the card again. She nodded. "I've been looking for a job for about six months now, but no one wants to hire someone my age. I would love a job." She raised her head, her eyes glassy with the threat of tears.

"Well, that's perfect because I have been looking for the right people to hire, and I don't know, I just realized you were one of them. Can you swing by tomorrow around nine? Tomorrow's Saturday, so we get beyond busy. You will just jump in and help where you can. How's that sound?"

"Amazing, my dear," she smiled. "I will be there. I'm no spring chicken, but I'm a good worker. You won't regret hiring me."

"I already know that, Hattie," I smiled back.

"Hi, I'm Sara," Sara greeted, coming up beside me and latching an arm around my leg.

I brushed her hair away from her cherub face. "Sara, this is Hattie. Hattie, this is Sara. Sara hangs out at the store while her mom works. You will be seeing a lot of her." I turned to Sara. "Does your mother know you ran off to find me?"

"Yup," Anne said, coming up behind me and pulling both carts.

"Hey Anne, I want you to meet Hattie. She is going to start working at the store tomorrow with us."

Anne surprised me next by going up to Hattie and hugging her. "Thank the Lord. We need more hands on deck," Anne laughed. "You'll like it. We work hard but have a lot of fun."

After mooching a free dinner from Anne at her rental house, I arrived at home after dark. The exterior house lights were off, engulfing most of the yard and back porch in dark shadows. Something about the stillness, the absolute quiet, raised the hairs on my arms and had me reaching into my shoulder bag for my Glock.

I turned the interior lights off inside my SUV and opened the door. I stood in the blackness of the driveway for several long minutes, listening for any movement. Nothing. Not even a cricket stirred.

Remaining alert, I went to the back porch and unlocked the door. Reaching inside to the light switch, I turned on the outside lights as I continued to scan the area. No sound. No movements. But my heightened senses told me that someone was out there, watching me.

Still gripping my Glock in my right hand, I pulled my cellphone out with my left and sent a quick text message to Steve. I walked back to the SUV and waited, taking partial cover between the house and the vehicle.

Time stood still as I tried to pinpoint the location of whoever was causing my unease. Somewhere in the outskirts of the outside lighting, someone was waiting to see what I would do next. I continued to scan the area, listening intently.

I heard a car approaching down my road, and as headlights pulled into the driveway, a dark figure bolted into the backyard tree line, giving away his location. I took off running in pursuit as fast as my legs would carry me.

I was a fast runner, but the perp had a good thirty-foot lead on me. My advantage would be that I knew the property well. The rustling of dry brush allowed me to follow his movements as I ran through the dark woods. He was moving northwest, most likely to a parked vehicle waiting in the old commercial district. If I didn't hurry, I would lose him.

Increasing my pace, I took a familiar path that would parallel his movements and keep me from the worst of the briars and thorny wild raspberries. I was barely able to see more than three feet in front of me, but I was gaining on him. The clearing to the commercial district was less than fifty feet away. I pushed myself faster.

And, then I was flying. Tripping over a fallen branch, I flew headfirst, parallel to the ground, before skidding through dirt, stones and tree roots and rolling to a final stop. I fought to suck air into my deflated lungs.

Shit. That hurt.

By the time I was able to stand, I could hear a vehicle tearing off down the road. The distance, the darkness and the density of the woods, all obscured my ability to make out any details. Flashlights bounced around the trees from behind me, and I heard heavy footfall approaching.

"I lost him," I called out.

"Damn it," Steve echoed back, and I heard them slow their pace as they continued forward.

I turned back to the house, joining Steve and Dave on the path. Dave handed me his flashlight, and I led them back along one of my jogging trails.

We were all silent as we gathered my groceries and other belongings from the SUV and carried them into the house. They set the bags on the table before searching the house for any signs of disturbance.

Sensing that the house wasn't breached, I put away the groceries.

The butter pecan ice cream I had bought had partially melted, but instead of throwing it out, I grabbed some spoons and sat to eat it straight from the carton. The cold, smooth, creamy mixture soothed me.

Entering the kitchen, Dave called in their location over the radio as they both sat and picked up spoons to join me.

"Did you get a look at the guy?" Steve asked, throwing a towel under the carton before scooping out some of the ice cream.

"Big frame, dark clothes, that's it. I didn't locate him until your headlights were on him."

"Do you think it was Brett or someone from Florida?" Dave asked.

I shrugged. "It could have been anyone."

"Should we write up a report?" Steve asked.

"Yes, but keep it brief. Trespasser spotted, unable to identify. If anyone is keeping an eye on me, they would expect to see a report written up. So, keep it simple but go ahead and file it."

I looked up at them and snorted. Steve looked perfectly pressed, and his hair styled immaculately. Dave had small leaves and twigs everywhere, thin bloody scratches along his face and a tear in his police shirt.

"You didn't stay on the path, did you?" I grinned.

"I thought I could make a detour and catch up with him, but I ran into those damn wild raspberries," Dave grinned back. "You don't look any better. Did you fall in a gravel pit?" he asked as he raised one of my arms to get a better look at the dirt and blood-coated scrapes.

"I forgot to grab a flashlight and tripped. I'm going to be pretty sore in the morning," I admitted.

Steve retrieved wet washcloths for both of us, but I had so much dirt and gravel on me that I gave up and opted to shower. They left to go file the report.

Chapter Seven

After only a few short days, Hattie fit right in. She preferred working in the back, but dealt well with customers and always sensed when we were busy and came out to jump in when needed. I was pleased to discover she had a special knack for dickering purchases. She also could send the riffraff packing fast with her no-nonsense personality.

I put a $200 cash bonus in an envelope with a note offering my thanks for making the training go so smoothly and that she was already a valued asset to our store. The next morning, she brought in fresh muffins and better coffee. Win-win for both of us!

Thursday morning, I was sorting through inventory in the back room when I realized how much more relaxed I was. I had to grin. The store was running more efficiently, and I had more time for my research and even spare time to work on my writing again. Everything seemed a little brighter.

Hattie entered the back room, setting a package next to me and saying some man delivered it. She returned to cover the register. I turned to look at the package, an oversized sweater box with a wide yellow ribbon tied in a not-so-professional bow. There wasn't a card so I pulled the ribbon loose and opened the box, and screamed.

The scream was a loud, high-pitched — an-axe-murderer-is-chasing-me kind of scream. A huge snake extended itself out of its confined space and started slithering toward me. In my hasty retreat, I knocked over several totes and proceeded to climb on top of them and then on top of the rolling racks alongside the wall. I wasn't thinking. Panic fogged my brain. I was trying to reach out to the next rolling rack when the lack of oxygen caught up with me, and as the world went dark, I plummeted off my perch.

When I came to, I was lying stretched out on the floor between piles of totes and racks. I started instantly panicking again.

"It's fine. Hattie got the snake and got it out of here," Anne said.

Anne was sitting on the floor next to me, holding something up to my head. I went to sit up, but she pushed me back down.

"Stay put. Paramedics will be here any minute. You hit your head on your ungraceful landing."

I could feel my head pounding and reached up to take over holding the towel.

"So," she said. "You're a little afraid of snakes, huh?" She was smiling down at me, but she seemed a bit shaky herself.

"Just a little," I smirked.

Laying on the floor was embarrassing, even for someone like me who should be accustomed to being embarrassed on a regular basis. The paramedics arrived, followed by the police, and it wasn't long before Steve was pushing his way through the cramped space to get to my side.

"What the hell, Kelsey?" He was breathing heavy and wearing plainclothes, so he wasn't on duty. "I heard the call on the scanner. What happened?" He winced when the paramedics removed the towel to check my injury. I could feel the blood drying on the side of my head just behind my ear.

"Someone dropped off a present for me. Wasn't that nice? Inside the box was a thick, shiny snake that looked hungry. I decided I was a monkey and could climb. Then I fainted, so I can't say what happened next."

"Damn it, Kelsey. I knew Brett wasn't going to let this go. I knew it."

"Yeah. But it was a nice dream to think otherwise," I sighed.

The paramedics elbowed Steve out of the way and proceeded to move me to a gurney.

"Is all this necessary?" I asked.

"Yes," was the unanimous reply by Steve, Anne and both paramedics.

They started to strap me down, and I panicked, pushing the paramedics away and trying to get off the gurney. Steve stepped forward and grabbed me by the shoulders, leaning into me. "Calm down. Look at me, calm down."

I looked up at him, not saying anything, but following his lead to breathe in and out, slower and slower. When I felt in control of my anxiety, I nodded to him.

"Okay. Here's the deal. They have to strap you in so you don't fall off, but we will use only one chest strap with your arms on the outside and one more strap around your hips. Can you handle that?"

I inhaled and exhaled a few more times before I nodded again, and Steve held my arms up as they tightened the chest strap.

"Panic attacks?" one of the paramedics asked Steve.

"Claustrophobic. She won't like riding in the ambulance. Remind her to breathe and don't crowd her."

The paramedics wheeled me out. As we passed Sara, I winked and smiled at her to let her know I was okay. She grinned back.

Either my head injury was worse than I thought or the ER was experiencing a very slow day. I was on center stage for attention. They rushed me from one room to another for various scans and tests. After about an hour, a doctor came in with my x-rays.

"Well, luckily your skull is still in one piece. We are going to go ahead and stitch you up now. We have to shave a small section of your hair, but the gash is low enough that the rest of your hair should hide it as it grows back."

I nodded and turned my head away so they could have at it. It was another thirty minutes before they claimed that I was back together again.

"We want to admit you for observation until tomorrow, just to be safe."

"Hell no. I'm not staying. Don't even try it." I slowly sat up and even slower, slid off the bed, bracing a hand on the bed rail for balance. "Where do I sign?"

"It's better if—,"

"I said, where do I sign?" I gave him my best don't-mess-with-me look, which was enough to make him take a step back and nod to the nurse. She pulled out a clipboard and had me sign a liability release.

I started for the door, but the nurse stopped me with a gentle hand on my shoulder.

"You have friends waiting to check on you. Maybe we should see about cleaning you up a bit first." She steered me into a small bathroom, and I glanced in a mirror for the first time. Dried blood painted both the front and side of my shirt. The side of my face also had a good coat of red, and my hair matted together in crusty brownish-red sections. I looked like a cast member in a horror movie, and not the actress who survives at the end.

"Good call." I unbuttoned my shirt, throwing it in the garbage can. Underneath, I had a white tank top on with only a few spots of blood that had seeped through the outer shirt. You could see my hot-pink bra clearly through the light fabric, but I didn't care. I leaned toward the sink and rinsed the worst of the blood out of my hair, before washing my face and neck. I was still white as a ghost but looked less like a flesh-eating zombie. "Thanks."

The nurse escorted me to the waiting room, bracing my arm the entire way in case I decided to body-slam the floor again. I was surprised to see Steve, Dave, Chops and two of the bikers that were out the night of the bar incident. One of the bikers was the guy that I had talked to when Steve and Dave had arrived, the surfer-biker. The other was the badass hottie that held up the brick wall when we left that night. The hottie was even hotter in daylight. His intensely focused, dark brown eyes held my gaze as I approached. He had caramel-colored skin and shoulder-length dark brown hair that shined almost black under the fluorescent lights. Both bikers were giving off vibes of rage, but I instinctively knew it wasn't directed at me.

"I need a ride. Anyone want to volunteer to be my chauffeur?" I asked jokingly, trying to lighten the mood.

"Dang, some girls have all the luck," the nurse winked, releasing my elbow over to Steve.

"We need to talk," Dave said, while walking up next to me and claiming my other elbow. Chops and the bikers followed us out.

"I need to get out of here. It smells like bleach, vomit and urine. Can you drive me back to the store?"

"We already decided that Chops will drive you. Doctor's orders were no driving for two days, and someone has to monitor you for the next 24 hours. Steve and I are heading to the station to talk to the officer in charge and gather info. Close up the store early tonight. We will meet at your house at 6:00. Bring Anne and Hattie along so we can figure out a schedule of who is babysitting you overnight."

"I'm fine. I don't need a babysitter," I said, rolling my eyes.

"Shut the hell up!" Chops scolded. "You look ready to pass out any minute."

Ugh. I knew better than to pick a fight I wouldn't win so I just let them do their thing.

Chops drove me in his truck back to the store with the other two bikers trailing behind us. We parked next to my SUV in the back lot. When I got out, I was instantly woozy, so I held onto the door as surfer-biker came over and held firmly to my arm until the dizziness passed.

Feeling stable again, I stepped over to my truck, pulling out my keys from my shoulder bag, and just stood there, staring at my SUV.

"Umm, by chance, are any of you fans of snakes?"

I was shuffled back to lean against Chops' truck as he took my keys and all three of them thoroughly searched my SUV and the gym bag I kept in it.

"Snake free," said surfer-biker.

I approached cautiously, and carefully looked in my bag before I deemed it safe to pull out some fresh clothes. The vehicles blocked the view to most of the stores so without caring beyond that, I removed my tank top and changed into a clean shirt. Hottie-biker stepped up next to me, lifting the side of my shirt, exposing the tattoo on the side of my ribs. I pulled the shirt away from him and lowered it to cover the tat before pulling my hair up in a messy bun to cover up the shaved portion of my scalp. He reached past me and pulled out the Handi Wipes lying on the floorboard. He used one to wash the back of my neck. A warm shiver ran down my spine from him being so close and touching me. I closed my eyes and took a slow breath so I wouldn't pass out again. *Kelsey, get it together.*

"You have blood on your pants too," Chops pointed.

Sure enough, down my hip, more blood trails had dried and stained my jeans. *Stupid head injuries.*

Kicking off my shoes, I asked them to turn around as I slid out of my jeans and into a clean pair. When I slid my feet back into my shoes, I started to sway. Hottie-biker reached out and grabbed me above my hip, warm fingers extended to graze my stomach.

When I looked at him, he had a smirk on his face. I looked back at surfer-biker and Chops, and they grinned as well, leaning comfortably against Chops' truck. They hadn't turned around as requested. "Not very gentlemen-like, boys."

"Where's the fun in that? We just got to see a fine ass in a hot pink thong," Chops laughed.

"I'm going to tell Candi," I said.

"No, you won't. You're not the type to tattle for no reason other than to start shit," he laughed.

I had to smirk at that. I wasn't into all that girly drama.

"So, now that you have all seen my ass," I turned to Chops, "are you going to introduce me to your friends or am I going to keep referring to them in my head as surfer-biker and, ummm, the *othe*r biker?"

"You talked to James that night in the parking lot at the bar. He's the president of the Devil's Players," nodding his head toward surfer-biker. "Bones helped me fix your truck and was also there that night. He's the one that pulled you up on his bike," Chops said, nudging an elbow into a grinning Bones. "They're club brothers of mine."

"Why don't you wear a cut?" I asked Chops.

"I usually do when I'm not at work. The night at the bar was a rare exception for Candi's benefit so I could show off the clothes the silly woman was so damn proud of." Chops rolled his eyes.

I smiled. I didn't think there was much that Chops wouldn't do to make Candi happy.

"Well, gentlemen, nice to meet you officially. I appreciate the back-up at the bar that night." I shook James' hand first. "And, Bones, thanks for also helping on the truck."

I noticed his Devil's Players cut had a patch on it naming him sergeant for the club. I wasn't sure what a sergeant for a motorcycle club did, but by the looks of him, I assumed it was some type of physical position.

"I'm surprised you haven't needed any more repairs in the last couple weeks," Bones grinned, leaning back against my SUV and lighting up a cigarette.

"Ah, well, you know," I shrugged.

"What did you hit?" Chops laughed.

"I didn't hit anything. I sort of, maybe, just a little, ran over something. Now, stuff is noisier than it was before. But it seems okay to drive, so I haven't worried about it." I repacked my gym bag and closed the door.

Bones moved to the rear of my vehicle and slid underneath to have a look. I heard him say "Holy shit!" and laugh.

Chops went back to join Bones under the truck, and I rolled my eyes. When they came back out, they both pretended to be mad, glaring at me with hands on their hips.

James leaned in, whispering, "Somebody's in trouble…"

"I'm not scared. I battled a snake today. I can handle them."

"Darlin', the snake won. You ended up with sixteen stitches in your head."

I couldn't think of anything snappy to respond, so I stuck my tongue out at him. "Okay, guys. Drop the act. I know it's not that bad."

"You ripped half your exhaust loose, cracked a fuel connection, and we're pretty sure you damaged the left rim and strut. How big was the rock?" Bones smirked.

I shrugged. "I've done worse. The important thing to remember is that no one was hurt," I grinned.

I was not about to tell them the truth, which was that I backed up over a fallen tree. It was hard enough to admit to myself that I somehow managed to do it. It would remain another one of my little secrets.

"I'll call a wrecker. We'll keep your keys and get it put back together as cheap as we can," Chops said.

"Thanks. But I will need my house and store keys off the ring first."

"Yeah, think I will keep your house key for a bit too. We are going to have some of the guys search your house and make sure nothing is slithering about."

I visibly shivered at the thought of a snake in my house. Chops reached out and patted my shoulder.

"Hang in there, girl. You're dealing with all this amazingly well. I keep waiting for you to crack."

"This ain't my first rodeo," I mumbled, writing down my address on one of my business cards. "Can you vouch for the men that will be searching my house? Can I trust them?" I asked Chops.

"You have my word. You can trust them," Chops nodded, squeezing my shoulder gently.

Other than a few files and my other laptop, there wasn't anything that they could find that could be used against me. It was worth the risk, to live in a snake-free environment. I nodded and handed the address over.

Chapter Eight

I entered through the back door and spotted Hattie sorting clothes. She stopped what she was doing and looked at me from head to toe with a look of concern.

"Hi, Hattie. How's the day going?" I stuffed my shoulder bag into the cabinet and relocked it with the key we hid off to the side.

"Don't you 'Hi Hattie' me, girl. You got blood on your shoes still, you're pale as a ghost, and you look shaky." She walked over to me and turned my head. "Your hair up helps, but we need to change your shoes. I'll find some. Anne keeps some makeup in a basket on top of the cabinet. You need a layer of foundation. Your brother Jeff is here, and if he sees you like that, you'll have a new roommate."

Yikes. I followed orders, adding a fine layer of foundation and slipped my feet into a pair of strappy sandals that Hattie dropped in front of me. She looked me up and down one last time before nodding her approval and returning to the task of sorting clothes.

I laughed at how easily I was dismissed and walked through the doorway to the sales room. "Honey, I'm home!" I hollered.

Sara ran to me. I didn't pick her up because I still wasn't too steady on my feet, but I leaned over, pulling her closer to my leg. "Hey Sara. How's my favorite little bug doing?"

"Good. Can we get lunch now?" Sara seemed unfazed by the events of the morning, and I was glad for it.

"Sure," I smiled.

"Everything okay?" Jeff asked from behind the register.

"Great! What brings you in on a Thursday?"

"I had the day off work, and it sounded like more fun to be here than work on Lily's never ending to-do list," Jeff grinned.

"Are you up to running out for some food then?"

Jeff quickly agreed, and I passed off a wad of cash to him. After taking everyone's orders, he left to walk to the bar down the strip. I'm sure he would manage to enjoy a beer or two while waiting for the food.

As soon as Jeff was out of sight, Sara, Hattie and Anne converged. Sara climbed onto a stool and started inspecting the side of my head. I pulled out the stool next to her and sat, giving into exhaustion. The thump to my head took more out of me than I realized, and it was going to be a long afternoon.

"We barely got all the blood cleaned up before Jeff got here," Anne said.

"Thanks. I appreciate it," I said.

"Who's Brett?" Sara asked.

"He's my ex-boyfriend."

She looked from me to Anne and waited.

Anne shook her head. "No, he's not like your dad, more like Uncle Digger," Anne answered the silent question. Sara just nodded.

"Sara, I don't want you to worry about this. I will deal with Brett. I have my friends that are police officers coming over tonight, and we will figure it out."

"It won't work. You can lock him up, but if he's like Digger, it will just make him meaner," she said.

Oh, how I wish she were clueless. "I know. I'll figure it out. I can handle Brett, though. He isn't anything for you to worry about." I pulled her over to my side, stool and all. "If he messes with any of us, I will put a cap in his ass," I said. Sara giggled. "Now, get back to your school work! You're slacking, short stuff!"

She jumped from her stool and skipped back to her 'school cubby'. We were amazed at how well the online school was going. She shocked us by placing in sixth-grade reading, and she was ahead of her age in all the other categories as well. The online program was a good fit for her. Anne had been right. Sara would have been bored silly sitting in school, trying to pretend that she didn't know how to color between the lines.

"You sure you can handle him?" Hattie asked.

"I'm sure. I might be scared of snakes, but I'm not scared of Brett."

That seemed to satisfy both her and Anne, and they went back to work. I decided to stick close to the stool and run the register for the rest of the day.

Chapter Nine

At 5:30, we closed down early as ordered, despite the customer complaints, and went to my house. I was happy to see two bikers wearing Devil's Players' cuts sitting on the front porch.

"Howdy," I smiled.

"You must be Kelsey. Bones asked us to hang out and make sure no one came here after we searched the place. Name's Whiskey; this is Goat." He thumbed over his shoulder to the other biker.

Whiskey himself was stocky and wore a thick, scraggly beard with a hint of red tone in his hair. I was sure he was the one who held Anne while she cried that night at the bar. While he looked a little dangerous with his bulging, tattooed muscles and a wardrobe consisting of a lot of leather and chains, his eyes were jovial. Goat was taller, about ten years older and slender. He had a distinguished polite manner and smiled warmly.

"Nice to meet both of you. These are my friends Anne and Hattie. And this here cutie-pie is Sara," I said while tickling her. "Thanks for helping out today. I will sleep better knowing that you searched the house."

"I can appreciate that. Heard you took a hell of a knock on the head earlier. Bones and James were both clear on our orders. We searched every gap. We even sent a prospect into the crawl space on the back side of the basement," Whiskey said.

"Oooh, poor guy," I shuddered at the thought of going into such a confined area. "That was above and beyond the call of duty. But I will feel better next time I have to go down to change the furnace filter."

"No need," Goat said. "I got bored this afternoon and cleaned out the furnace, just some preventative maintenance. I changed the filter too. You should be good for a while. And Whiskey mowed the lawn."

My visual blinders were usually firmly in place so that I wouldn't see how bad the yard looked, but now I turned to look around, and sure enough, everything was in top-notch status. The few neighbors I had should take pictures to remember the occasion.

"Wow! Maybe my luck is turning," I said.

"You look familiar," Goat said.

"She's the one that ruined our breakfast a few weeks back by announcing the dead cockroaches," Whiskey chuckled. "I haven't been able to eat breakfast since then without gagging."

"What were you thinking, eating food in a dive like that?" I asked, realizing that Whiskey was the one that had spit up his food.

"It was because of that blond woman you know," Goat answered, rolling his eyes. "Tech, one of our members, spotted what he referred to as a blond goddess at the diner earlier in the week. After that, he insisted we have breakfast there. I have no idea why. It's not like he ever made a move to talk to her. The closest he got to her was walking up to you for the cleaning rag."

"It was probably for the best that they didn't meet," I smirked. I doubted that even a biker could handle Katie and her penchant for seeking out trouble.

"Kelsey, where are your manners?" Hattie scolded, passing me on the porch. "Let's get inside so I can prepare refreshments and such for your company."

"Yes, ma'am."

We all obediently followed her through the door.

Hattie brewed a pot of coffee and mixed up a pitcher of lemonade before she began rifling through the cupboards for snacks. She had only been to my house a few times, but I was glad to see she was at ease in my kitchen to do her thing. Hostess with the mostess, I was not. Everyone chatted about meaningless things while I stared out the window, distracted by random thoughts. A baby-blue truck crept along the road in front of the house. I knew that truck.

I pulled my Glock from my shoulder bag and walked out the front door. Anne and Whiskey followed behind me. I live on a dead-end road with a cul-de-sac and no other turnoffs past my house, so the driver would have to drive by again. I waited by the big maple tree near the road.

As the truck re-approached, I raised my gun and fired. The driver stomped on the gas, squealing tires as he fled. I walked out into the road and watched as the truck traveled to the end before turning toward the business district. I started back to the house.

"You missed," Whiskey grinned.

"Hard to justify killing someone for just driving by my house," I grinned back.

Whiskey and Anne followed me back into the kitchen as if nothing happened. My cellphone rang, and I answered it, "Kelsey."

"This crazy call just came in over the radio," Steve said without a greeting. "Something about a lady on your road firing a gun at a blue truck."

"Neighbor must have been drinking," I said.

"Hide the Glock, Kelsey," he said, before hanging up on me.

I unloaded the gun and stuffed it in the back of the silverware drawer. I planned on target shooting out back with it later, so there was no sense cleaning it and putting it away.

"Police coming?" Goat asked.

"Only the friendly ones that were already scheduled to meet with us," I replied. "Steve will shut down the alert. Hell, most of the cops probably already guessed it was me, and would only show up to make sure I was okay."

"Nice," Whiskey said.

"Yeah. I got lucky when I met Steve and Dave. Dave's mom, Dallas, even forced me to move in with her, while I got my head on straight." Thinking of Dallas always made me smile. I laughed when I realized that Goat was Dallas' type. "You single, Goat?"

He grinned. "Why?"

"Just a random thought," I smiled. "Probably best if I left it at that."

He let it go, looking amused.

It wasn't long before both Steve and Dave arrived in Steve's truck, followed by several motorcycles. Dave was the first one through the door, grinning while asking, "Did you hit him?"

"Nah. I wasn't trying to hit him. I just wanted him to take off for a while."

Steve came in through the back door followed by James, Bones and Chops. James pulled a few beers from the fridge that they must have stocked themselves earlier in the day. Hattie set out bowls and platters of chips, crackers and cheese. She also had something cooking in a pot on the stove that smelled like vegetable beef soup.

"Where did you find all this?" I asked her.

"Anne had me stock your kitchen yesterday. It's a good thing too. Otherwise, I would probably be serving a stack of stale saltines and tap water."

She was right about that. I wasn't home enough most days to worry about groceries.

Everyone settled down and Steve, being ever so serious, started up with business. "Maybe Sara should go into the other room and play while the adults talk."

Sara looked up at me, from her perch on my lap, and I shook my head no. "She's fine. Speak freely. I am not going to hide this from her." She grinned at me and went back to drawing with the paper and pen that I always had on the table.

"Hattie confirmed in a photo line-up that the person who dropped the package off was Brett. The detective assigned also found a video showing Brett walking across the parking lot with the package and a few minutes later walking back without one. It would have been nice if we had video from inside the store, too," Steve grumbled, giving me his best cop stare.

I just rolled my eyes and took another drink of my coffee. I wanted a strong cocktail, but my head was still throbbing, so I didn't think it was a smart idea. I heard another car and leaned back to look out the window. "I'm not expecting anyone else."

"We are," Dave said, greeting a man and woman at the front door. The man wore a badge clipped to his belt, and the woman was wearing a suit, carrying an attaché. "This is Detective Garrison and Assistant DA Pamela Tanner. I thought it would be more efficient if we figured this out together. They picked up the case from this morning's incident."

"We think that with a little more information, we may be able to push this as a stalking case. But we need your help to do that," Ms. Tanner said. "One incident doesn't qualify, but I was told that this wasn't the first time you have had encounters with Mr. Thompson." She looked at me expectantly.

"No, it wasn't. But before today, he was always careful about witnesses, and I wasn't in the best mental state myself during most of the prior situations. Trying to pin anything on him other than today's incident would be a waste of time." I looked down at Sara, still doodling on the notepad. "Could you arrest him for the stunt today, make him sweat it a bit, and use this to get me a restraining order?"

"Yes, but with just the snake incident alone, it will probably result in a plea deal for a misdemeanor crime. He won't serve any time. A judge probably wouldn't even make him post bail. He doesn't have a criminal record that amounts to anything," the detective answered.

"I know. I just want the restraining order on record." I didn't say anything else as they all watched me.

After a long pause, the detective nodded. "If that's what you want, that's what we will do. We just have to find him. We have an APB out on him, and county boys are sitting at his house. His truck is there, but he isn't home."

"He's in town, driving his cousin's truck. If you agree not to impound the truck, his cousin Derek would probably help set up a meet so you can pick Brett up," I grinned. "Derek loves his truck. Just don't let on that he was in on it, or Brett will beat the crap out of him."

"Derek is more likely to go along with it if the call comes from you," Steve advised.

I picked up my phone and called. Derek was agreeable and said he would call me back. Within minutes, he confirmed the meet at the Turnaround bar out on Gull Road. The dive bar was one they frequented often. I relayed the information, and Detective Garrison and Ms. Tanner left.

"I can't believe you're just going to let him walk away from this, Kelsey," Steve said. "He's been harassing you for too long. It needs to stop."

"Yes, it does. And, it will," I answered. I was just as determined as Steve to end this, I just preferred to do so on my own terms.

"What are you up to, Kel?" he questioned.

"She's establishing a documented pattern of behavior," Sara answered for me, still doodling on her notepad. "With the misdemeanor and the restraining order, when he comes at her again, then she won't be looking at prison time when she *caps his ass*."

Everyone stared at Sara like she was from another planet, except for Anne, Hattie and I who just grinned and shook our heads.

"You are my favorite little bug in the whole world," I laughed, kissing the top of her head, "but you shouldn't swear."

"How old are you?" Goat asked.

"I turn seven in a couple of months," she answered with a grin.

Changing the subject, I asked, "How long before they will have to release him? Will he be out tonight?"

"He'll be held for arraignment until tomorrow, probably be out by mid-morning, noon at the latest. Pam will get the restraining order signed at the same time and make it a condition of his release."

"Sounds good," I grinned. "Are you up for some target practice?"

Steve returned the smile and answered "hell yes," as he pulled a beer from the fridge. I reloaded my Glock and followed him outside.

A few hours later, my head was pounding, but I felt better releasing some pent-up frustration on the targets in the back yard. In the garage, I disassembled and cleaned my gun.

"Nice shooting," Bones said, coming up beside me.

I still held my undefeated status in Steve's version of the game Horse, which we play with bullets instead of basketballs. Bones took second, which riled up Steve. I grinned because I knew Steve would be at the firing range every day for the next few weeks hoping for a rematch for his second-place status.

"Thanks. I was actually off target tonight. Probably has something to do with the pain pill I took, but the doctor's orders didn't say I couldn't shoot, only that I couldn't drive."

Bones grinned while looking down at me. "Who taught you how to shoot?"

"I grew up in a hunting family, so I was familiar with guns, but never had any interest in them until a few years back. I've had a few training sessions since then. What about you? Military?"

"Yeah. I never even saw anyone shoot a gun before I signed up, but ended up having a knack for it. I must be out of practice if I can get beat by a girl," he teased.

"Wait until I'm feeling better and we will compare our skills with rifles," I grinned back.

"Should be interesting," he smiled. "I hear that Anne is mad that you won't let her stay to keep an eye on you tonight."

"I moved her and Sara out to keep them safe; that hasn't changed. I will be fine on my own."

"Yeah, except for the doctor's orders are to wake you every hour through the night. Hattie, Goat and I are staying and taking shifts. That going to be a problem?" he asked with a raised eyebrow.

"I'm honestly too tired to argue about it." I put my gun back together and checked the safety. Re-entering the house, I told everyone I needed to lie down. Hattie was serving soup to those who wanted it. Whiskey and James were going to follow Anne and Sara home to make sure they were safe.

My first wake-up call was Hattie, bringing me a warm bowl of soup. "I know you're tired, sunshine.

But you didn't eat earlier, so make an old lady happy by putting some of this in your stomach."

I was hungry, so I ate most of the soup before setting the bowl aside. I curled back up in bed and fell back asleep. The other wake-up calls were much briefer, and I had to answer some silly question with each one. 'What's one plus six?' 'What color is your truck?' 'Who was the third president of the U.S.?' I was left alone after the last question generated an '*I don't give a shit who it was*' reply.

Closer to morning, a familiar nightmare interrupted my rest. I was searching for Nicholas but couldn't find him. I started to panic, yelling and searching throughout the dark apartment. Warm arms wrapped around me and words whispered in my ear calmed me, and the dream faded away as I drifted into a deeper sleep.

Chapter Ten

When I woke in the morning, I found myself half-lying on top of Bones in my bed. I disentangled myself and rolled away. *Whew, not good.*

I had noticed that all the bikers seemed to be relatively attractive, but after growing up with five older brothers, I paid little attention. I wasn't looking for a man and had turned off that part of my life while I focused on the rest. But for some reason, it was harder to flip that switch to the off setting with Bones. Waking up wrapped around him, half on top of him, hadn't helped. I mentally forced the switch back to the off position, grabbed my robe and went to the kitchen. My headache was better this morning, but the side of my head was tender.

I found Hattie already up with coffee made.

"Good morning, Hattie. Thank you for making coffee." I kissed her on the cheek and took the cup of coffee she offered.

"Good morning, sunshine," she greeted me with a smile.

I curled up in my favorite kitchen chair, the one offering the most morning sun, and enjoyed my first sip of the dark brew.

"Good morning, Hattie," I heard Bones' deep voice and looked up to him giving Hattie a kiss on the cheek, too, and retrieving his cup. He winked as he pulled out the chair next to me and sat.

Hattie was all smiles as she went over to the oven, pulling out a tray of fresh, hot cinnamon rolls that smelled divine. Soon after, Goat strolled in to join us, and Anne and Sara entered the kitchen through the back door.

"Sara, who was the fricken third president of the U.S.?" I asked in frustration because I couldn't get the question out of my head.

Bones laughed, and Hattie and Goat looked puzzled.

"Thomas Jefferson, elected in 1801 and served two terms," Sara answered.

Bones laughed harder.

"Did you even know the answer?" I asked him.

"No, but it was fun to hear you swearing at me, half asleep," he said with another wink. Hattie laughed at this as well.

"Is my daughter behind in school?" Goat asked with a look of concern.

"No. Sara is just ahead of the curve," I assured him. He just nodded but still seemed unsure. "How old is your daughter?" I asked.

"Amanda is nine. I'll bring her by sometime. I know she would have fun shopping at your store and her mother never takes her anywhere."

"She's a good kid," Bones added.

"I don't have any friends. I would like to meet her," Sara said surprisingly.

"You have lots of friends. We are just older than you, little bug. But, yes, it would be nice if Goat brought Amanda by to hang out with us. Either this afternoon, when she gets out of school, or Sunday, would be great."

I looked at Goat, and he nodded. "After school today would work. I usually pick her up on Fridays and do something with her for a couple of hours."

We were all enjoying the warm cinnamon rolls when Bones leaned closer to me and whispered, "Who's Nicholas?"

Startled by the question, I knocked my coffee cup over. Everyone scrambled to clean up the mess before it spread too far. During the chaos, I turned to Bones and hissed back, "None of your damn business."

He seemed surprised but slowly nodded, accepting my answer.

It may have been rude, but my past was mine, and I wasn't about to share it with him or anyone else. I turned away from the table and filled a cup with fresh coffee from the pot. My hands shook, and I spilled more coffee as I poured. Hattie reached over, taking the pot away from me and placing a comforting hand over mine. I looked up, and she offered a gentle smile before replacing the pot and wiping up the spill on the counter. I took a deep breath to calm myself before taking my seat again.

It was pushing 9:00 when Anne and Sara left for the store. I excused myself to get ready for the day, and forty minutes later, Hattie and I left as well. Bones and Goat were going to nap since they were up most of the night checking on me. I wasn't surprised to hear that they set up prospects to guard the house for the next few days. The real question was whether they were preventing more snake deliveries or if they just enjoyed ordering the prospects around.

Dave and Steve kept me informed, and as expected, Brett was set loose by 10:00. I didn't expect him to try anything for a while, but just in case, I was wearing my shoulder harness and gun under a blazer.

"Hey Anne?" I hollered.

"Yeah?" she answered, coming around the corner from the menswear section.

"What day would you say is our slowest?" I asked.

"Sundays. We get a good crowd, but they don't buy as much. Why?"

"We need a day off. Working seven days a week is too much on all of us. And, it's not good for Sara to be here so much either."

"Can you afford to close for a day?"

"I think so," I sighed. I had caught up on most of my to-do list items the last few days but had been avoiding the accounting books. Beyond paying the bills that came in, I hadn't paid much attention to where the account balances landed. "I will try to get through the books today and figure that out."

"Start with a bank deposit. We have too much money in the filing cabinet. I had to open another drawer to use."

I followed her to the back room, and sure enough, we had a drawer and a half filled with cash deposits ready to go. I pulled them all out and was surprised that there was about $8,000 in bills.

"Cripes. The people at the bank are going to think I'm a stripper, carrying all this cash."

"Nah, too many 10s and 20s. They're more likely to think you're a drug dealer," she laughed as she helped me fill a large paper tote bag with the cash.

The bank was within walking distance, but I borrowed Anne's car and drove, despite doctor's orders. When I entered, I noticed that there were enough people around that I didn't want to advertise the amount of cash I was carrying. I walked over to the security guard and showed him the contents of the tote bag. "How do I make a deposit a little more discreetly?" I asked.

He laughed, waving to a woman sitting at a nearby desk and indicated that I needed private banking assistance. I followed her to a side office. After making sure no one had a clear view, I dumped the bag on the desk.

"Sorry," I cringed. "I am behind on my banking."

"I can see that," she said. "We will get you squared away." She called a teller to assist, and they efficiently recounted the deposit before the teller took it with her in several large leather bags. "We can set you up with night drop bags, so you can drop off deposits through our drop chute and not have so much accumulating next time. The chute goes directly into a safe in the basement."

"That would be great. It's not always easy for me to get away during banking hours."

She stocked me with a month's supply of large leather bags, and the teller returned with my deposit slip. I verified the amount of the deposit matched and then looked at the bank balance. I was shocked and found myself suddenly sitting in a guest chair.

"Wow. I knew the business was doing well, but didn't know it was doing this well."

The woman turned to her computer and reviewed my accounts. "Yes, I would say it's a success." She looked a little shocked as well while she reviewed the computer screen. "You also have another business account that is accumulating pretty fast too. Do you want to move some of the funds into a money market or cd account?"

"Ahh, no. Thanks for asking. Can you print the balance in the other account for me?"

She printed out a summary page of all my business and personal accounts, and I thanked her for the assistance before gathering my stuff and driving back to the store. I was smiling from ear to ear. I had enough funds to secure a bigger store location, a year ahead of my scheduled plan.

I spent most of the remainder of the day going through the books between cashing out customers. It was steady, but not overwhelming, and Anne and Hattie had the sales floor and back room under control. By the time I had the bookkeeping caught up, it was almost closing time. I started rummaging through a drawer in the back room when Goat entered through the back door.

Goat had dropped Amanda off a few hours ago. She and Sara were getting along well. They had little in common except they both liked to try on clothes. It reminded me that Sara needed to interact more with other kids, and I had a plan that I thought would help.

"Hey Kelsey. Do you know if Amanda is ready to leave?" Goat asked.

"She's up front, still playing dress-up."

"She likes it here. Sorry if we are intruding."

"Not at all. You're welcome anytime. Ah-hah. I found it," I said, pulling out a razor blade.

"Whatcha doin'?" Goat asked.

"About to kill off our Sunday shift," I answered, heading to the front door.

Anne and Hattie came around to watch as I scraped off the bottom line of stickers, removing Sunday hours. Anne and Hattie cheered as several customers in the store booed in good humor. I must have made Goat nervous because he grinned and took the blade away from me to finish the job.

"What on earth are you going to do with a whole day off from work every week?" Hattie asked.

"Well first, Saturday nights we should invite people over. Amanda and maybe some other kids could hang out with Sara while the adults enjoy a few age-appropriate beverages. Then Sundays I can work on all the things I never get done. I will most likely end up here most Sundays, but at least it will be a break from the customers."

Hattie and Anne liked the idea of Saturday night get-togethers more than they cared about having a day off. They huddled together and started planning food. Sara and Amanda were excited about playing together and proceeded to hound Goat until he agreed they would attend.

Chapter Eleven

The first weekly gathering went well Saturday night, and several of the Devil's Players, especially those with kids, joined us along with Dave, Steve and their families. The adults played cards and sat around eating and drinking in the kitchen and dining room while the kids tore up the living room and played in the back yard. Goat said that Bones was out of town, making it sound like this was a common thing and that James had some business to handle. Chops and Whiskey both looked concerned about something, but I didn't ask any questions.

By 9:00, I decided it was time for the kids to settle down, so I pulled a movie out of my DVD collection for them to watch. Unfortunately, I couldn't figure out how to work the DVD player, so Sara had to start it for me. The kids asked what movie it was, and when I told them it was "Star Wars," they all gave me blank looks.

"None of you have ever watched 'Star Wars'?" I said in disbelief.

It wasn't long before I was on the floor with all the kids watching the movie, and half of the adults drifted in to join us. By the time the movie ended, all the kids were asleep, and the adults agreed they would pick them up in the morning. Hattie and Anne decided to stay as well. Hattie took my room, and Anne took the guest room. I agreed to sleep on the couch in case one of the kids woke up and needed anything.

By 10:00 Sunday morning, the house was once again empty. Not having any specific schedule allowed me to relax and putter about getting projects done at home. Chops had dropped off a truck for me to use while my SUV was being repaired, so I grabbed the keys and drove to the store to clear a few more to-do items there. I wasn't surprised to see Anne and Sara show up an hour later.

"We thought we would find you here," Anne laughed.

"Not for long. I just want to finish this paperwork and then I plan on going to the gym, followed by dropping off the clothes for the homeless shelter."

"We'll load the truck while you finish your paperwork. What gym do you go to?"

"One downtown. It's more of a fighting gym than the commercialized cardio clubs," I said.

"Can we go?" Sara asked.

I looked up and saw Anne and Sara's hopeful expressions, and laughed.

"It's not a very nice place, but yes, if you guys want to follow me down there, it's not a problem. You can watch some of the practice fights."

They both bounced around the store gathering clothes appropriate for the gym. I was already dressed in sweats and had a sports bra on under my sweatshirt. I finished the papers I was working on and then shut down the lights and locked everything on my way out the back door. I had to smile when I realized that not only had Anne loaded the truck, but she had also turned it around so I could pull straight out.

Anne followed me in her car downtown, to the older city section. I carefully maneuvered around broken glass in the back parking lot before pulling into an open space. Anne pulled up and parked beside me, looking cautiously around. I grinned, getting out of my SUV and grabbing my duffle bag.

"Is it safe here?" Anne asked.

"If you're with me, you're safe," I said, walking up to the side entrance of the gym with Anne and Sara hurrying alongside me. "If you come alone, call Calvin for an escort to and from the parking lot."

"Who's Calvin?" Sara asked as we entered the gym.

"That would be me," a gruff older voice called out. Calvin was in his late sixties but still looked mean enough to make people think long and hard before they messed with him or his gym. "About time you came in, Kelsey. You're probably all flabby and slow from all the time off."

"Find me a sparring partner, and we'll see about that," I grinned, leaning in to give Calvin a quick kiss on the cheek. "These are my friends, Anne, and Sara, a.k.a. little bug."

"Your friends don't look like fighters," Calvin grinned.

"Not yet, but everyone has to start somewhere. Think we should start them on jump ropes?"

Calvin nodded and walked to the center of the gym, pulling some ropes out. He set up an area for them to work out that was near the practice ring I used. Anne pouted, taking one of the ropes, but her expression quickly altered when she realized that she wasn't very good at it.

"Start slow, and build up speed and control. The first step in learning to fight is quick footwork," Calvin instructed.

I set my bag near the ring, stripped off my sweatshirt, and pulled my hair up on top of my head. Calvin yelled at a few of the other men to focus on their workouts and called one of the guys over to spar with me. I couldn't remember his name, but I had sparred with him before. He used a mix of boxing and street fighting that worked well against my own training.

"Let's see what you got, girl," Calvin called as I climbed into the ring.

Two hours later, and on my third sparring partner, I called it quits. I had held my own through all the matches, but my muscles were burning, and I was having trouble controlling my breathing.

"You're back on the weights on your next visit. Your strikes were weak. By the sound of your breathing, you better up your game on your cardio too," Calvin complained as I climbed out of the ring and he handed me a towel.

"Wow, thanks for all the praise, Calvin," I laughed.

"If you're looking for flattery, you're in the wrong gym," a deep voice chuckled.

I turned to see Bones approaching, sporting a lopsided grin. He was in workout clothes, and a light sheen of sweat accented his honey-tinted skin.

"Nice fighting," he said.

"Thanks. Do you fight?" I asked.

"Best I've ever seen," Calvin answered for him.

"You going to teach me some new moves?" I asked.

"No," Bones stated, reaching out to pull my hip closer and to the side as he grazed his hand over the tattoo on the side of my rib cage. He stroked his thumb down the blade of the knife to the tip, where it pierced the image of a human heart.

I stepped away, visibly shivering from the contact.

"I don't think that would be a good idea for either of us," he grinned.

"Okay then," I said, taking another step back, trying to calm my hormones.

"Aunt Kelsey," Sara interrupted, "Can you teach me to fight like that?"

"Maybe someday, little bug. For right now, I think we should stick to the jump rope and maybe some simple kicks."

She seemed pleased by the thought of learning how to kick, and Anne said she wanted to learn too. We laughed at their excitement.

"We are going to head back to your house and start dinner," Anne said.

"You don't be walking in this parking lot without an escort," Calvin ordered. "I'll give you my cell number, and you call from the parking lot so I can personally walk you to and from the building when Kelsey's not with you."

"Yes, sir," Sara and Anne grinned.

Calvin followed them out as I pulled my sweatshirt from my bag.

"What's the deal with the tat?" Bones asked, his eyes piercing into mine, demanding a response.

"Everyone has a past," I answered as I grabbed my bag and walked away.

Chapter Twelve

After the gym, I drove to the mission to drop off the donation clothes. Father Eric stopped me during my visit, and after being properly guilted into parting with a few large bills for the food pantry, I exited out the back door.

Driving out of the parking lot, I took the side street to avoid traffic and cut through the downtown district. I heard loud yelling and stopped when I saw four men beating another man just inside of an alley. I pulled over to the curb and hit the alarm on the truck to scare them off. They paused to look up, but continued kicking their victim who was now on the ground in a fetal position. It wasn't dark yet, but with the sun dropping behind the horizon, the area was filled with shadows. There wasn't anyone else around. I opened my door and stood up on the running board as I pulled my Glock out of my shoulder bag. I fired into the grass about twenty feet away from me.

The gunshot got their attention. They took off running. The man on the ground groaned, and I climbed down and slowly approached him, keeping an eye out for his friends. "You look like you're having a bad day."

He tried to smile but winced in pain.

"Should I call an ambulance?"

"No. I'll be fine. Nothing's broke." Using the cement wall, he pulled himself as upright as he could stand.

"I can't just leave you here. They might come back. Is there someplace I can take you?"

He shook his head no. "I was on my way to the shelter, to see if they had an open bed tonight. They require ID, though, and those guys just made off with my wallet." He turned and started limping down the sidewalk. "I'll just go to the park. Thanks for your help."

"Hey – what's your name?" I asked.

"Alex," he turned and answered.

"Alex, do you do drugs?"

"No. Not my style."

"Are you dangerous to kids?"

"Hell no. Lady, you got the wrong guy," he said, shaking his head while he started to walk away again.

"I think you misunderstood the question."

He stopped and looked back at me.

"Get in the truck. You're coming home with me to get some ice on those bruises." I got behind the wheel and watched as he stood there, looking at me for a minute or two before he started to limp my way. I pulled up closer to shorten the distance.

"You must be crazy, picking up a black man that just got jumped in an alley," he said as he gingerly climbed inside.

I just laughed and drove home.

When we arrived, I helped him inside the house and into a kitchen chair. Sara retrieved a wet washcloth from the bathroom while Anne pulled ice packs from the freezer. We helped him clean up a bit while he held the ice pack on the side of his face where the swelling was the worse.

"You're welcome to stay here a couple of days while you heal up. I have two rules. You don't hurt anyone I care about, and you don't steal from me. It's that simple. I feel I should warn you, though. I have a mean ex that knows where I live. It's not always safe to be around me."

He laughed. "Lady, I think my chances are better with you than out on the streets tonight."

"The name's Kelsey. This is Sara and her mom, Anne. I'm sure Hattie will be around soon and you can meet her. Let's get you settled in the spare room. You can rest a bit before dinner." I helped him to the spare room before returning to the kitchen.

"He a new stray you're adopting?" Anne asked as she stirred something in a pan on the stove. Whatever she was cooking, it smelled fantastic.

"Looks like it. Of course, we will have to see if he is interested."

"How do you do it? Sara can do the same thing — meet someone and know if they are good or bad, just like that."

"Always watch the eyes," I laughed, though it probably wasn't funny. "And, it doesn't always work.

Brett, for example, he could be the nicest guy ever and then turn on you in a second."

"You worried at all about this Alex guy?"

"No, not at all. The sneaky ones like Brett can't hide when they are cornered or stressed. Alex was at his worst when I found him and was still calm and polite. He's safe. I wouldn't have brought him around Sara if he wasn't."

I winked at Sara and she giggled while she continued drawing on the kitchen notepad.

"Hey, Aunt Kelsey?" Sara said.

"Hmmm?"

"You do know that homeless shelters aren't like animal shelters, don't you?"

"What do you mean?" I asked, confused.

"Well, if you go to an animal shelter, they hope you adopt a pet. You went to a homeless shelter and adopted a full-grown man. Normal people don't do that," she giggled.

"Smartass," I laughed.

Chapter Thirteen

Tuesday morning, I met the realtor at an empty car dealership out on Highway 43. I knew immediately that the building would be perfect for the relocation of The Changing Room. I heard the front door open, and Katie sashayed my direction. I asked the realtor to excuse us so we could talk privately.

"New store location?" Katie asked.

"Looks to be," I answered. "I wanted to talk to you about moving you in-house. I would still want you to be in contact with the investigators and run any leads that come up, but if you work at the store, you could also help me protect everyone."

"That new guy that you rescued, Alex, checked out. He's had a shitty life so far, but has a clean rap sheet," she said, continuing to look around. "What would I do if I worked at the store? It's not like I am very customer-friendly."

"No. You wouldn't be the best at customer service. Eventually, you can help me run the books and maybe assist in menswear. For now, though, you would handle the remodeling of this building and make it more boutique than warehouse in appearance."

"What will my cover story be?"

"We can say I picked you up hitchhiking and hired you. Nobody would question it."

"It's not far from the truth, either."

I had spotted Katie about six months ago sitting in an airport in Chicago. Her army unit had just returned home, but she sat alone, surrounded by her duffle bags. Unlike her fellow soldiers only a few feet away, no one was there to greet her. I sat and asked her which direction she was heading. She admitted that it didn't matter where she went, and she had no plans, no family. We continued talking, and a half an hour later she was booking a flight to Michigan. She agreed to work for me, managing the investigation I was running. Unfortunately, as of yet, there were not enough leads to keep her busy.

"Okay," Katie simply said. She pulled out some files and handed them to me. "These are the missing-person cases that are still open. To me, it appears that your cousin Charlie is chasing random clusters along the southern coastline. I wasn't able to see any other patterns, but maybe you will spot something I didn't notice."

"Doubtful," I grumbled, while jamming the folders into my shoulder bag.

"What's wrong?"

"I'm just frustrated. This investigation isn't going anywhere. It's been two years, and I haven't been able to find anything useful on Max's whereabouts. I think it's time I consider sneaking back into Miami." I rubbed the palm of my hand across my forehead before thrusting it through my hair. "I need this case to be my priority."

"It is your priority. But so is building your wealth and training so that when you do find them, you are ready. If you deviate now and go to Miami, you'll just get people killed. You know this. You'll get your revenge, just keep putting one foot in front of the other until the timing is right."

While I understood what Katie was saying, there was one big piece of the puzzle that I never told her. And it was the piece that haunted me, night after night. But that secret didn't change anything. She was right. If I jumped the gun and showed up in Miami, I would lose my advantage. I had to stick to the plan.

I signaled the realtor to join us and then shocked her by telling her I wanted to close on the purchase of the building by Friday. She spat and sputtered that four days was not enough days to close on a commercial property. Katie interrupted her tirade and explained that if she wanted the commission, she would make it happen.

They both proceeded to make phone calls and fill out paperwork. By noon, we had an approved purchase agreement, and the title company was already running the deed check. Katie had several contractors meet up with her and signed for one of the companies to start work on Saturday. We would relocate by month's end.

Chapter Fourteen

We all worked hard to keep The Changing Room a success and to launch a seamless relocation into the new building. I was able to purchase the new building and property with cash. The first three weeks in the new location had been a success, and I was already rebuilding a nest egg.

Since the new space was originally a large car dealership, it accommodated ample parking and provided three sides of glass windows in the front for natural lighting on the sales floors. The back of the building offered a service area that Katie redeveloped for purchasing, laundry and excess inventory.

To address the need for larger bathrooms and dressing rooms, we knocked down and moved many of the prior office walls. After softening the walls with warm colors, changing some light fixtures, and adding the faceless white manikins to the windows, the inside was elegant and inviting. An expansive emerald green awning with white script lettering of 'The Changing Room' softened the exterior design, along with well-placed oversized potted bushes and trees.

The new store offered the space to expand both menswear and bridal and gowns. Both departments were on the west side of the building and the office that Katie and I now shared, was nestled between them.

Anne runs bridal and gowns and is learning the fine art of dealing with nervous brides and their overbearing mamas. Sara still attends an online school, and based on her whim of the day, sets up in the break room or the office. Katie runs menswear. Her strong will and independent streak allow her to handle the clientele with efficiency and a slight touch of bitchy that seems to entertain the male customers. No one so much as blinked when I fed them the story of picking her up hitchhiking on the side of the road.

Hattie works inventory intake, laundry and some boutique gown alterations. She has shared more of her past, and I discovered she had retired just before the stock market crash. With most of her retirement fund depleted, she found herself, like many others, needing to re-enter the workforce.

Alex's wounds all healed from the beating he took, and he is now part of our strange, makeshift family. He recently moved out of my house and into the other half of the duplex where Hattie lives. I put him in charge of restocking and purchasing, and he was able to maintain the inventory for the small store while fully stocking the new location. He is handsome with dark mocha skin, deep brown eyes and usually sports a single diamond earring that is glaringly fake. Alex has also proved to be our own class clown. His continuous pranks, unconventional outfits, and constant jokes keep us laughing through the long days.

The front checkout is mostly part-time employees. I end up spending most of my shifts behind a register. I am hopeful that I will eventually find someone to run the front. Until then, we all dig in and do what we can.

My personal life, what little there is of it, is the same. I continue to re-read the same reports and files, searching for any scrap of information on Max or Nola, but nothing new has developed. The lack of information left me with excess hours at night to spend on my writing, and I released another book last week as a result.

I have only seen Brett once since the snake incident, and he parked far enough away not to be in violation of his restraining order. I'm sure he will turn up again, but he's the least of my worries.

Our Saturday night get-togethers have continued. Many of our friends with kids enjoy the event, and it has turned into a potluck setup. Occasionally, all the kids spend the night for a giant sleepover. Having the kids around reminds me of Nicholas, but they are good memories.

James has finally come to a few gatherings, and declared them fun, even if they were a little PG-13 for his taste. He probably wishes the women would wear skimpier clothes. Bones has attended only one gathering, but most weekends I hear he is out of town. I still see him on brief occasions, but usually, it's in the store or at the gym. The club seems worried about him for some reason, but I have been careful not to ask any questions. It's none of my business.

"Your boy-toy is back," Alex sing-sang, startling me out of my thoughts.

Ugh. He could only mean Bishop. Dwayne Bishop has become an unwelcome regular in the new store. His presence alone drives my blood pressure higher, and that's before he opens his mouth and his arrogance vomits all over me.

"He's not mine," I griped. "I claim no ownership, nor does he have any claim on me."

"If only he agreed," Alex smiled over his shoulder as he went up to assist some women looking at coats.

Today Alex was wearing white patent leather shoes with a black suit that appeared to be from the Roaring Twenties. On top of his head, of all things, he wore a white fedora. I wasn't sure where he came up with the multiple costumes he wore in the store, both men's and women's, but admired his sense of style and creativity.

"Kelsey to menswear. Kelsey to menswear," Katie squealed over the PA system.

Her voice was an octave or two higher than normal, which was an indication that I should hurry. Crap. And, the day was going so well, too, I thought as I jogged that way.

Chapter Fifteen

It was immediately apparent what the problem was when I entered menswear. Katie was alone in a sea of about thirty Devil's Players. I wasn't even aware that their club had so many members. I spotted Bishop grinning, sitting comfortably in the corner and knew he was the culprit. It was common practice for him to bring in referrals during his weekly visit to harass me into a date. However, encouraging the whole club to visit at once was over the top, even for him.

"All right, boys, what's on the agenda today?" I asked.

"We have a club wedding and need nice shirts and decent jeans. One of the member's daughters is getting married," Whiskey said.

"Very well then, if you can all line up over here," indicating the center of the room, "We will see if we can take the pain out of this process and get you moving in the right direction."

The men didn't have any issues following orders, and Katie and I started doling out shirts and jeans for each of them. The first half-dozen men went off to the dressing rooms while we continued sorting and gathering clothes for the rest.

I was avoiding Bones, while fully aware of his every move. He was even sexier today somehow, and I kept thinking of what colors would look the best with his caramel skin. I felt him watching me as I worked. I finally couldn't stall anymore, and pulled clothes that I thought would complement him well.

"Here you go," I said, handing him the clothes.

As I was turning away, I realized that he was undoing the button on his jeans.

"Umm... Bones, you have to wait until a dressing room opens," I sputtered while simultaneously wondering if he was a boxer or briefs kind of guy, knowing I was about to find out.

"I'm not waiting half an hour just to hide behind a piece of fabric to try on a pair of jeans."

His slow, deep, confident voice sent a shiver down my spine. I swear my boobs even stood a little higher. He read my facial reaction and grinned as he tugged his jeans slowly over his hips, one hip at a time – *fricken teasing me!*

The other men laughed, following his lead and stripping off their clothes. I looked up into the main room, and several women shoppers had already stopped, openly gawking.

"Ah, shit!" I said as I rushed over and hit the button to bring down the big overhead steel door. The door separates the two areas, with the only remaining exit being the employee-only hallway that connects to the back storage rooms. Of course, it wasn't long before Alex made a surprise visit through that hallway.

"And here I was worried you were being assaulted or something," he said in mock disdain, pointing between Katie and me. "Sluts, the both of you."

The bikers less familiar with Alex's antics stiffened, and those who knew him well chuckled.

"You're trespassing. This is a private party," I said as I threw a pair of jeans at him.

"Fine. I will go slave away while you two get to have all the fun." He stuck his tongue out at me and then left the way he came. It wasn't until he was walking away that I noticed he was carrying one of the baseball bats that I had discreetly placed around the store.

"Hey, Alex," I called out to him.

"Yah?"

"Thanks for checking up on us."

"Anytime, love, anytime," he called over his shoulder before the door swung shut.

"Strange friend you have there," Whiskey said, standing beside me shaking his head.

"That's what makes him so perfect," I smiled. "And, look at you in your new duds." I checked the length and general fit. "Very nice, Whiskey. About time you came into The Changing Room for a new outfit. I've only been bugging you for weeks now. Did the rest of the clothes fit well?"

"Yup. I'm buying them all. I just wish someone had told me that we don't have to use those girly dressing rooms. I would have changed out here too."

"Ha. No. It seems Bones doesn't like to follow the rules, is all."

"Hey, Bones. Are you giving Kelsey and Katie a hard time?" Whiskey asked in good humor.

Bones looked up as he was buttoning a white shirt over his sculpted abs. His muscular chest was exposed, offering a display of intricately inked images and a sprinkle of dark, fine chest hair. *Damn.*

He locked eyes with me and grinned as if reading my thoughts again. "Somehow I think she can handle it."

After checking on the other men to make sure their clothes fit well, I was confident that the red hues on my cheeks had subsided enough to have a word with Bishop. James was now sitting next to him, grinning.

"Well, Bishop, how unsurprising of you to visit us once again. I do hope you find something a little more worthwhile to do than to shop with us *every* Saturday morning."

James raised his eyebrow and smirked, turning to look at Bishop.

"Just making sure that I do my part toward helping local businesses," Bishop said. "And it's always a pleasure to see you in the process, Miss Kelsey," he tried to charm.

"I assure you that we are doing just fine. Feel free to share your charitable self with someone else's business."

Saved by the bell, the PA system called me to the registers. Checking first to make sure that everyone was wearing at least pants again, I re-opened the overhead door.

On the other side of the door stood Alex, two police officers and several customers. One of the customers was a middle-aged woman who was having a bad hair day, and currently bellowing a lecture on morality.

"What's the problem?" I inserted myself into the mix. Whatever was going on, I was glad to see that the officers in question were Dave and Steve.

"This woman called in stating that naked men were running around in the store," Steve said, leaning back to peer into the menswear area.

"That's a bit of an exaggeration. The dressing rooms were full, and they didn't want to wait so they started changing. I closed the overhead door to prevent customers from getting upset. The end."

"But that doesn't give you the right to expose good Christian people like myself to this sinful behavior," insisted the woman while swaying a finger in my face.

"Lady, if you don't like what happens in my store, then get the hell out." I stepped directly in front of her. "I don't need your business or your judgmental, condescending opinion thrown in my face." I took the clothes out of her hands and handed them Alex. "And, unfortunately, not a single one of them was naked! Believe me- I looked!" I said loudly as I walked away.

I could hear a round of laughter from menswear but kept my head high on my way toward the registers.

Chapter Sixteen

As I was opening a register, I snorted at the uppity woman as she stomped out of the store.

"Bye, Kelsey," Dave and Steve both said as they passed.

"Bye, Dave. Bye, Steve. Thanks for coming." It wouldn't have helped them any if the woman knew that we were all friends.

"It was our pleasure, truly," laughed Dave, before gallantly bowing and turning out the door.

Finding my rhythm of checking out customers, I forgot about everything else around me. It didn't take me long to catch up the lines, and I decided to take one more customer before I closed the lane back down again. A short, skinny man with oily skin stepped up next. He wasn't one of the men that I saw earlier in menswear. He shifted his hands up to the counter, and I started to pull the women's shirts from him when I realized his other hand was holding a revolver, pointed directly at me.

Without moving my upper body, I slowly reached my foot under the counter and set off the silent alarm. The alarm wouldn't call the police, but it would set off strobe lights in several rooms to warn the employees of a problem. One of the employees would call the police.

"Quickly fill a shopping bag with cash," he instructed.

Of all the lanes this dumbass could have chosen, he had the unfortunate luck of choosing mine. I have been in much scarier situations, so it only managed to piss me off that this slime-sucking scum bag walked into my store with a gun, twitchy hands that I can only imagine being drug related, intending to rob me. I was even more pissed that my gun was in the back-room lockers today.

My hostile thoughts continued to build as I grabbed a plastic bag to use for the money. When I opened the drawer, my hand went first toward the bills, but I stopped myself and started adding the rolls of change. We kept several rolls of each coin in the drawers, so it didn't take long for the bag to become heavy. I filled the rest of the bag with the bills from the drawer. *Stupid mother-fucker.*

I turned as if to hand him the bag but looked behind him to the main entrance door and made a gasping-surprised sort of noise. Honestly, I can't say what kind of noise it sounded like to others; acting was not my thing, but it did the trick.

He turned swiftly in that direction, turning the gun away from me, pointing it toward the floor. I swung the bag at him, hitting him on the side of the head, *hard*.

He staggered.

Taking another swing, I hit his shoulder, causing him to spin away and drop the gun. The bag tore open, and the money erupted into the air and scattered everywhere.

With the bag no longer useful, and the gun no longer in his possession, I pulled myself up onto the counter and jumped, tackling him to the ground. All the anger, frustration and crippling fear hidden behind an emotional wall broke free as I hit him, over and over again. I pummeled him with my fists as he tried to cover his head.

"Somebody, help! Get this crazy bitch off me!" he screeched.

Strong arms reached around me and pulled me off the would-be robber.

"I think you got him, sugar," James whispered in my ear with a chuckle.

I forced myself to not fight the restraints of James' arms and concentrated on slowing down my rapid breathing. *Shit*. I needed to focus. Just breathe, Kelsey, I thought to myself.

I looked down and couldn't help the snort that escaped.

The man was a mess. I had broken his nose, split his lip, and one of his eyes was already swelling shut. He wailed loudly, as he curled into a ball on the floor.

Bones leaned over, grabbed up the junkie, and manhandled him out of the store as Whiskey casually trailed behind them, looking bored. I snorted again.

After a moment of reflection, the reality of the situation penetrated my brain. "What was I thinking?" I realized too late. I turned, to see Anne and Katie glaring at me.

"Yeah, I think they are about to give you a bit of hell. I will wait for the cops outside with my men."

"Thanks for the help, James," I said over my shoulder.

"Thanks for the entertainment, sugar. Most fun I have ever had shopping."

"Yeah, we aim to please here at The Changing Room," I said. "Be sure to fill out the customer survey card."

James was barely out the door when Bishop was in my face. "How stupid can you be? You could have gotten yourself killed," he snarled, grabbing my arm roughly and pulling me into his body.

"*LET - HER - GO!*" Anne ordered from behind him.

We all turned in surprise at her forcefulness. She was glaring with such rage at Bishop that I was expecting laser beams to blast his ass any minute. The look was enough for Bishop to release my arm and step back.

"This isn't over," he hissed as he went to the door.

I noticed Bones and Whiskey had stepped back inside the doorway. They must have heard Anne yelling. Bones raised his eyebrow at me, and I just shrugged in response. What could I say? Anne was a bit overprotective, and Bishop was being, well, Bishop.

Turning back to my friends, I said, "We have a lot to do, and unfortunately, I am going to be busy with the cops so you both will have to wait to chew my ass out later."

They seemed to accept my statement as an order and Anne went back to work while Katie helped sweep all the money into a big pile and tossed it into a bag to take to the office. Dave and Steve directed other officers to question witnesses before cornering me yet again about getting a surveillance system. I agreed to look into it but wasn't thrilled with the idea. Money wasn't an issue, but the time to research equipment seemed daunting. Electronics was not my thing.

Overall, I was busy for about two hours with the whole mess. And by then the store was beyond busy, and I was stuck running cash-only sales for the rest of the day. Thoroughly exhausted by 6:30, I announced final call over the PA for all customers to make their way to the checkout and turned the sign to closed. As the final customer checked out, I locked the door and rang the bell to let everyone know it was quitting time.

"You would think that an armed robbery would have slowed down business a bit, but I could barely keep the racks stocked," Alex said as he collapsed onto a nearby stool.

"And, new drop-offs were rolling in all day too. We got some great new items in for next week," Hattie added.

"Bridal and gowns sold a third of our inventory today. We will need to find some more merchandise," came from Anne.

"Menswear was freaking awesome today!" Katie squealed and gave me a high-five as I grinned back at her. "And, when Bones started stripping – *holy shit* – I about had an orgasm right there! *Best job ever!*"

We all had to laugh with her on that one. And, I was trying hard not to think about how great he looked in nothing but his low-rider black boxer-briefs.

"I am so damn jealous," Anne pouted. "The first time I saw Bones, Kelsey had sent me out to the parking lot to figure out his sizes. One brief gaze at him, and I was speechless. I couldn't say anything; I just turned around and went back inside."

"Yeah, then came in smiling but never gave me a warning as to why. Thanks a lot, by the way!"

"Girl, you needed to experience it for yourself," Anne laughed.

I had to admit, if only to myself, the day at the hospital, head injury or not, I was sure my panties were damp when I got my first full view.

"Okay, let's switch conversations," I said, trying to physically and mentally shake the image of a strip-teasing Bones from my mind. "I agree. Today was definitely a unique day. I'm glad sales were good. And the entertaining customers today were a nice touch."

"Yeah, like the druggie with the gun you pounded the shit out of?" Alex added questioningly.

"Not my brightest moment. I can appreciate all of you being mad at me on that one. I promise to think it out a little more in the future before I decide to beat someone with a roll of quarters."

"We were just worried about you," Anne said. "That's why we got mad. We don't want to see anything bad happen to you, and sometimes you tend to do things that scare the crap out of us."

"You're all a bit scary, if you ask me," laughed Hattie. "Now, let's lock up, close down and go to Kelsey's house. We will make some of those fruity cocktails for the Saturday-night potluck and figure out who had the weirdest customers today. I love the weird customer stories," she said as she waddled off to the back room to shut down.

Chapter Seventeen

It was barely daylight when I heard the back door opening. I buried my head under the blankets, knowing it was Hattie. I had given her a key for mornings such as this. She would wait for me to get up, and while doing so, she would start a pot of coffee and probably clean my kitchen.

We weren't a 'get up and go to church' group, so we usually met up at my house to chat about meaningless topics and drink loads of coffee before I went to the store to catch up on projects. Often the rest of the crew would follow me in to do the same.

I waited until the aroma of the coffee was too much to bear before crawling out of bed and stumbling in that direction. I stayed up too late last night after everyone else had left. Once again digging through the missing-person files, looking for patterns. I couldn't shake the nagging feeling that I was missing something.

I knew that whatever it was, though, it didn't have anything to do with Charlie, Max or Nola. Charlie was following a scattered pattern along the southern U.S. coastline. I could easily predict her next location. And, there was little chance that her game would lead her back to Max anyway. He was a creature of habit, and I would put my money on him still residing within the underworld of Miami's jurisdiction. And,

Nola was a ghost with no roots, no emotional ties to anyone.

No, the nagging feeling I had was that I saw something else, but my brain hadn't completely put it together because it was completely separate from what I was looking for.

"Good morning, sunshine," giggled Hattie.

I was sure her laughter was in response to my sleep-deprived appearance.

"Good morning, Hattie," I said, kissing her on the cheek as she passed me a cup of black coffee. I think I purred at the first taste of it.

I attempted to drag a hand through my hair, but it became snared in all the tangles. I set my cup down and proceeded to comb it out with my fingers until I was sure it didn't look like a bird's nest sitting on top of my head. Beyond that, I didn't care.

Within a half an hour, Alex, Anne, Sara and Katie arrived. Sara and I were having an intellectual conversation about which donut was better: the standard glazed or the apple twist with cinnamon and sugar. Alex was trying to convince Katie on a new haircut, and Anne and Hattie were puzzling over new sources for bridal gowns.

The front doorbell rang, startling all of us. We all turned toward the front room. I wasn't expecting anyone. Pulling Sara from my lap and placing her on the chair beside me, I went to see who was interrupting our morning, though my guess was that it was just a salesman. No one who knew me used the front door. I pulled the curtain aside to look on the front porch, and Bishop smiled at me. James stood next to him, grinning ear to ear and another man, looking quite miserable, stood on the other side. I released the curtain, returned to the kitchen and settled back in my favorite chair. Everyone was staring at me as I drank my coffee.

"Well, who was it?" asked Katie.

"Nobody important," I said.

They all shrugged and resumed their conversations.

The doorbell rang again, but I didn't get up. Katie turned to go to it, when I pleaded, "Please don't," and she stopped.

"Who is it, dear?" asked Hattie.

"Bishop."

Everyone, including Sara, snarled at that bit of information as the back door opened, and in waltzed James.

"I smell coffee. Oh, and you have donuts too," he said as he poured himself a cup and joined us at the table.

"You know that the vermin will just follow your path," Katie snapped.

"I know. But I came along for the entertainment, and it's not as funny if you don't let him inside," James continued to grin, thoroughly amused.

Whatever was going on, I didn't want to know. Unfortunately, my time had run out. Bishop entered the back door, followed by the stranger who still looked miserable. The stranger moved past Bishop over to the table and selected a donut as Hattie handed him a cup of coffee. He didn't join James at the table but leaned up against the wall. I had to smirk when Hattie moved to block the coffee from Bishop, and Anne pulled the box of donuts out of his reach.

"Bishop," I sighed. "What the hell are you doing in my house?"

"Well, if I would have known there would be donuts, I would have come earlier," he said in his over-bearing way as he took the other half of my apple twist.

As he was about to take a bite, Katie grabbed the donut out of his hand and pitched it across the room into the trash.

"You need to leave," I glared, gritting my teeth. "You're not welcome here."

He was a good-looking man, confident, financially secure, but between his controlling personality and unwavering snobbery, I had had enough of him. Luckily, my friends didn't care for him much either.

Hattie slapped his hand as he tried again to get a cup of coffee. He sighed, giving up and turning his attention back to me.

"Yesterday that junkie could have killed you. And yet, you jumped him, putting yourself in further danger. So I have decided that if you are not able to make rational decisions to protect yourself, then it's my responsibility to protect you some other way," Bishop said.

"I am not your responsibility, Bishop," I said. "And, I am more than capable of taking care of myself."

"Whether you have accepted me as your champion or not is irrelevant," Bishop shrugged. "It's my duty to ensure your safety if we are to have any future."

There was a punch line coming. I could tell by how James' grin rolled into a full-out smile that was wide enough for me to see his back molars sparkle.

"Ensure my safety? Future? Bishop, what are you talking about?"

"Meet Donovan Carter," he gestured to the man leaning against my kitchen wall. The man in question saluted us with his cup of coffee but didn't say anything. Then the other shoe dropped. "He's your new bodyguard."

Sara must have sensed my instant anger because she bailed from the table and moved next to Donovan near the wall. My brain went into overdrive processing what he had just said.

The arrogant SOB hired a bodyguard for me?

With that knowledge, I launched.

"Get out of my house, you arrogant, ..." I went flying at him, arms swinging, "self-involved, pigheaded," my right fist made contact with his face as he staggered backward, knocking a chair over, "Asshat!"

I stalked toward him as he backed up to the front door.

In the dining room, I grabbed my baseball bat and reared it back in a full swing.

Bishop ducked a moment before the bat smashed hard into the wall, throwing chunks of drywall between us. He dove out the front door, and I kicked the door shut after his exit, locking the deadbolt.

Sara approached me and put her hand on my arm. "Good job, Aunt Kelsey," she said, grinning.

Donovan had followed close behind Sara and had his hand extended toward her as if he was ready to pull her back if I continued my rant. I handed him the bat and followed Sara back into the kitchen. I took up my prior chair and slowly sipped my coffee to soothe my nerves.

Anne, Alex and Katie all seemed unconcerned by the entire situation. They had been trying to convince me to ban Bishop from the store for weeks, but I never felt he had done anything to justify it. I might have to rethink that.

Sara went to the box of donuts and dug me out another apple twist, climbing back onto my lap to share it. Hattie refilled everyone's coffee and started a new pot. We were back to normal except for having two extra guests staring at us.

"So, that went well," Donovan said, pulling out a chair and joining us at the table.

"I tried to warn him," James chuckled. "I think he's going to have a black eye."

"Well, he almost had a cracked skull, so he should consider himself lucky," Donovan said.

I rolled my eyes, and Hattie snickered.

"No, Donovan," Hattie grinned. "If Kelsey wanted him to have a cracked skull, he would have one. She pulled back long enough to give him time to duck. She wanted him out, not dead. She's got a lot of skill with her Louisville Slugger."

They looked to me for confirmation, and I just shrugged. I think the real answer was that I just didn't want to clean blood out of my carpet. It was nice carpet. But I still hoped Hattie was right, and I was a better person than that.

"So," I said, turning to Donovan, "You realize, you are fired, right?"

"I wish. Bishop paid me in advance. When I found out the real story, he wouldn't let me back out of the deal. I'm all yours for three months," he grimaced.

"No can do. I don't want a bodyguard."

"I gave him my word," Donovan said.

Ugh. I couldn't fault him for wanting to keep his word. I lived by the same code. And my friends knew it too as they stood there smirking. Katie had the balls to laugh out loud.

"There has to be a way out of this," I said.

"I have an idea," James declared as he took another drink of his coffee and peered into the box of donuts to see what remained. "What if you do less bodyguard work and more security and training work?" James asked Donovan.

"What do you mean?" I asked.

"Well, you do seem to find yourself in threatening situations more than most people. You're good at handling yourself, but Donovan and Bones are the best fighters I know. Donovan used to train in Krav Maga and Ju-Jitsu. I also heard your friends on the force getting on you about not having surveillance systems set up in the store. I agree with them that the new store is too busy and too big not to have some systems installed. Donovan runs a security company. He can train you in self-defense and help upgrade the store."

Donovan shrugged that he was fine with it. I looked at my friends, and they all mimicked the same shrug. I looked down at little Sara and knew that I had no choice.

"I have a few conditions. Katie and Anne have to join in the training. I already have some basic training, but some specialized training could prove beneficial. I also will not blindly agree to whatever security recommendations you have, but Katie will review your recommendations. Lastly, I want Anne and Sara to learn gun safety. I have a concealed permit, and want to make sure they understand guns enough to respect them, and it would be good for Anne to learn how to shoot properly."

"She's too young," Donovan said, nodding to Sara.

"She will surprise you; don't worry about her age. Do we have a deal?"

Donovan looked to James, who was smiling like a Cheshire cat and then back at me. "Deal."

Anne and Katie squealed in delight. We asked Alex if he wanted to train too, but he announced that he was a lover, not a fighter. Hattie had no interest either, but surprised us all when she said she carries a 38 Smith and Wesson in her purse. We all looked at her floral purse setting on the counter. *Huh*. I would have never guessed that one.

"So what hours are we talking here? Is this a 9-5 gig?" I asked Donovan.

"Depends on when you need me around. I only know about the tweaker at the store. Anything else I should know about?"

"She has an ex-boyfriend, an oversized blockhead that shows up randomly. She has a restraining order out on him and a bullet with his name on it, but Bishop doesn't seem to know about him. We intentionally haven't volunteered the information to him either. He would only get in the way if we had to step in and help her out. She's an excellent shot with her Glock though, and probably won't need any help when the time comes unless she needs to bury the body," James said nonchalantly.

"Brett's not an issue at the moment," I said. "His sister Barb was in the store last week. Apparently, Brett's distracted by a tall blond bimbo with jumbo-sized fake boobs from the Battle Creek area – Barb's description, not mine. She said someone will try to give me a heads-up if things change."

"Sounds like it would still be a good idea for me to stay close until I get the lay of the land. I'll just sleep in my car in the driveway if that works for you. Then I can keep a better eye on things. When I feel more confident that all is as it should be, I will switch over to a hotel for nights and stay at the store with you during the day."

"You're not sleeping in my driveway. What would the neighbors think? And more to the point, Hattie would beat me with a broom!"

Hattie smiled her confirmation. I shook my head, trying to remember that none of this was Donovan's fault. It will only be for three months; I reminded myself. I can be the bigger person.

"I have two rooms upstairs that are empty of everything," I said. "You'll need to run a vacuum and wash the windows and shelves yourself because I am not your cleaning lady. But you can rent some furniture and set yourself up however you please." I was certain I would regret opening my big mouth, but I could always pay him to move back out later.

Donovan seemed intrigued and set his coffee down before going upstairs. James got up and followed. It had never been a priority to furnish the upstairs rooms since I lived alone, and the downstairs offered plenty of space and a guest bedroom. They both came back down a few minutes later, talking about furniture.

I heard motorcycles pulling in my driveway and raised my eyebrow at James. He smiled and answered my wordless question. "Whiskey, Bones and Goat."

"Where do you guys get these names from?" Alex asked.

"You don't want to know," Donovan laughed, grabbing the last plain glazed donut out of the box.

The additional bikers walked in the back door as if they lived here, and Hattie had cups of coffee ready for them. Each one of them smiled and gave her a kiss on the cheek as they claimed a cup. I couldn't help but roll my eyes. I couldn't decide if they had her snowed, or if she had them wrapped around her little finger.

"So, how did it go?" Whiskey asked.

Bones was getting ready to sit when he looked past me into the dining room and then at the bat that was sitting in the corner. He smiled.

"Hey, Goat – think you can fix the drywall in there?" Bones chuckled, motioning with his coffee cup that direction.

Goat looked into the dining room and nodded. "Yup, I can start it later today. Be done by tomorrow."

"Well, guess that answers my question now, doesn't it," Whiskey grinned. "At least, there's no blood to clean up. It would be a bitch to clean it out of that tan carpet."

I had to smile at his thought process and did a coffee cup 'cheers' with him in agreement.

"It was epic," James laughed. "You should have seen the look on Kelsey's face." I stuck my tongue out at him before giving Sara a kiss on the cheek, getting up, and going to shower.

Chapter Eighteen

Between the store and our new training adventures, the following two weeks evaporated from the calendar. I had surprised Donovan with my shooting and fighting capabilities. He taught me offensive fighting moves, and I gave him a few pointers on shooting. He was also pushing me to my limit on weights and cardio workouts. Katie and Anne were learning the basics, and being already in overall good shape, they were doing well with the workouts.

Donovan and Katie had made a lot of security upgrades. New garage overhead doors now separated the back rooms with the push of a button, in addition to the ones that bridal and menswear already had. They installed new steel doors with security bolts to the break room and office, along with electronic passcode access points to unlock the back entrance doors from the outside. Security cameras fed streaming video into a hard drive that someone more talented than myself could retrieve remotely.

Katie assured me that she was monitoring the expenses and researching the purchases for the best deals. When I heard Donovan telling her she was a tight wad one morning, I became less nervous about all the extra expenses, but I still wanted to catch myself up on the books. Katie had taken them over, and I had been reluctant to pay too much attention to them recently. I preferred working the register over doing the accounting work, and that was like saying I would rather eat worms than tarantulas.

Therefore, this morning, I dragged myself into the store, well before daylight hours, to go through the books. I was glad I had. Katie was not only doing an exceptional job managing the budget and accounting, but the store profits were off the charts. Katie was right. We could afford all the security changes easily, and they hadn't been as expensive as I anticipated. There was also plenty of money in the account to make some payroll and benefits improvements, and start the next expansion phase.

"I was wondering when you would get around to looking at the financials," Katie greeted from the door. She passed me a fresh cup of coffee and sat in a guest chair. "I have wanted to meet with you and review the files, but it seems like the days take us in separate directions."

"Katie, this is impressive. You have been doing an amazing job running the books. I'm sorry it took me so long to give you my praise!" I got up and high-fived her. She was beaming, which was out of character for our snarky Katie.

"And, that's not all I have been working on." She reached over, pulled open the lower cabinet drawer and handed me a blue folder. "These are some other recommendations that I have. Some are security, but the rest are changes to insurance benefits, better retirement plans, maintenance projects, some service vehicles for the store, etc. If you have the time, I would like you to go through them."

Determined to make the time, I started reading through each item. I went from one proposal to the next, stacking them up on the desk. When I got to the end of the pile, I realized I had been at it for two hours. I signed off on all the proposals except one and called Katie over the PA system into the office.

"Well, what did you think?" she asked excitedly, as she closed the door.

"You have my approval on most of them, and I made notes on the rest. I have some additional payroll changes that I want handled too. I would like to promote you to store manager and bump you, Anne, Alex and Hattie to an executive salary level. Can you meet with them and make that happen?"

"Oh, let me see… you mean, give not only myself a raise, but my friends as well? Yeah, I think I can manage it. What about you? There is plenty of room in the budget to give you a raise, too," she asked.

"No, if I need to pull some funds, I can always draw from the business account. And, I haven't had a need to touch the book sales business account in a while either, so I am sure that is accumulating."

"You haven't even looked, have you?" Katie snorted.

I had confessed to Katie about my writing when she started taking over the accounts. She found it amusing that I wrote erotic romance novels to supplement my income and loved knowing the secret while everyone else was left in the dark about it. She was also one of my biggest fans and would drive me crazy at times questioning me on release dates and progress reports.

I mostly used the writing account to fund the investigation, but with no new leads to follow, expenses were low, and I hadn't touched the account in weeks.

Katie handed me two red folders that she retrieved from the bottom drawer of the filing cabinet.

"Why red?"

"If someone is carrying a red folder, they are in serious trouble. Red folders mean confidential documents such as bank accounts, employee files, etc. Blue is for projects and budgets. Black is for Uncle Sam."

"That sounds easy enough to remember. I will be sure to keep my eye out for red folders in the future."

"Fair warning, the plumbing contractor we use also uses red folders. I found that out the hard way," she frowned.

"Are we going to be sued?" I laughed.

"Nah. I took him and his ice pack to lunch and got him drunk. He says I can tackle him any time I want now."

I didn't doubt that she tackled him, nor did I doubt that she got him drunk to avoid charges. I finished writing the payroll changes that I wanted and handed them to Katie before opening up the red folders. We had two desks in the office, so she went to her desk and began updating the payroll files.

"If it's all right with you, I would like to wait to tell the others of the pay changes until tomorrow. I want to give them job titles to go with their raises. I can go to a printing shop and get name tags made to give them at the same time."

"Sounds perfect," I agreed. "As long as they know by the end of the week, I am fine with however you want to handle it. Can you see about getting us on a group phone plan too? Alex and Hattie don't have cellphones, and I'm on a crappy plan. We can just run a new plan under the business."

"Sure. But that means you'll have to learn how to use a new phone," she laughed.

"It will be fine. Sara will help me. Just don't let mine have too many bells and whistles."

I focused on the bank statements, trying to understand the numbers. My personal accounts didn't surprise me. I didn't have time to spend the paycheck I drew from the store except for a few automated bills, and my house was mortgage-free, so the account had accumulated. The business account from my writing was unreal. It had too many digits in the balance column.

I logged into my Amazon account and started reviewing purchases. I couldn't believe the number of book sales, nor the reviews, that I had received. The sales were ten times what my previous books had been, and the other books had done well enough to support me for years.

"You knew there was this much money and didn't say anything?" I asked.

"I figured it would be a nice surprise if you ever popped your head up to look. You had to have known your books were selling well, didn't you?"

"Yes, no. They had always sold at a steady pace," I shook my head in disbelief. "You know what this means, don't you?"

"That you're rich?"

"No. It means that I can buy the adjacent lot and the one behind it. Can you call my realtor and get her over here today? I want a cash offer to go out immediately."

"I'm on it," she started dialing.

"Wait. There's something else I've wanted to talk to you about." I pulled a folder out of my shoulder bag and handed it to her. "I've been working on the missing-person files and ran across something. It's not related to our search but wanted to see if you could help me piece it together."

Katie opened the file and flipped through the summary sheets inside as I explained. "There seems to be a pattern of every four months a pre-teen boy goes missing along a certain highway route. The boys are about the same age and similar in appearance. There is one gap in the pattern, though, that keeps throwing my theory off. What were the parameters when you pulled the sheets?"

"If the victims turned up eventually, dead or alive, then they were out-sorted. I also removed any solved cases that resulted in an arrest. I kept them, though. I can go back through and see if one of them fits the missing date. It could be the perp was in jail or had a medical issue during that time, though, and your theory would still hold."

"I don't think so. I think there is another victim that was either not reported or is in your out-sort pile. If whoever is doing this had an interruption in his schedule, then he would have been desperate to grab the next kid as soon as he could. It would have shown as a hiccup in his timeline."

"I'll call the realtor and then go through my files," Katie assured me, once again dialing the phone.

Chapter Nineteen

On Tuesday, Donovan was training me on the new surveillance equipment when a young woman entered. I welcomed her to the store and let her know to ask anyone if she needed assistance. She acknowledged with a respectful reply and went on her way down the main aisle.

"Earth to Kelsey," Donovan said.

"Sorry." Focusing on the monitors, I asked, "Can you show me again how to backtrack the video, say the parking lot video, about five minutes ago?"

He looked puzzled. Whether it was because I wanted to see the parking lot video or because he couldn't believe I still didn't remember how to do it myself, I wasn't sure.

I watched the video footage come up and hit pause when I saw the woman pull in and park her car. I looked up from the screen and scanned the store. The woman was over by women's shirts, sifting through the racks. She was tall, with dark olive skin and straight, long black hair. I stood to head her way, forgetting about Donovan until he gently grabbed my arm.

"What's wrong?" He scanned the store before turning to scan the parking lot. My reactions must have triggered his alpha protective instincts.

"That woman is in trouble. I want to see if there is anything I can do to help her."

"What do you mean? She looks fine to me," he said as he inspected the woman more thoroughly. "What did I miss?"

"She drove here in a rust bucket, looks like she hasn't slept or showered in days, and is wearing a scarf on a humid summer day."

He looked at the woman again but still couldn't figure it out.

"Look at her outfit. That is a high-end tailored suit, worth at least a couple thousand dollars. Her jewelry is custom work and even if they are fake, which I doubt, would be worth good money. The scarf is also high quality, but most likely covering up bruises."

"Okay. You talk to her. I will have Tech from Devil's Players run the plate on her car."

As I approached the woman, she seemed to tense but didn't run. "I want to help you if I can. I won't hurt you, and I won't let anyone else hurt you. I just want to offer you my spare bedroom, some clothes, food and a hot shower while you figure things out."

"Why?" She stepped back and looked ready to bolt this time.

"Because that's what cuckoo-crazy Kelsey does," Katie answered for me as she approached. "She picked me and my suitcase up alongside the interstate a couple of months ago. Best damn day of my life. Hi,

I'm Katie and this," motioning to me with a head nod, "is the owner, Kelsey."

The woman took another step back.

"Relax. Kelsey's right. You're safe here. You're not the first, second or even third person she has helped. You can trust her." Katie hollered toward the back room, "Hey, Alex!"

"Yo!" Alex said as he popped his head around the corner.

"Size six, woman's wear, long lengths, a full week's wardrobe."

Alex walked out, quickly assessed the woman's features, nodded and went back to inventory.

"Come on into the office while Alex gathers you a new wardrobe. If you decide not to stay, you will still need the clothes. I'm afraid we don't carry the line of labels you are currently wearing. Our clothes are clean, though, and you will blend in a bit better." Katie walked toward the office, and the woman followed without thinking about it twice. I could relate. When Katie was on a roll, it was natural to follow.

"We don't need to know any details, but did you put enough distance between you and whoever bruised your neck to believe you're safe?" I asked.

I gestured to a guest chair that she collapsed in as she thought about the question. I pulled myself up to sit on top of my desk, giving her some space.

"I don't know. I think so. I was careful. But I'm exhausted," she admitted with defeat.

"Did you use any credit or debit cards? Cellphone?" I asked.

"No. I don't have a phone, and I have only used cash since I left town," she said.

"That's good," I said.

Donovan knocked on the frame of the door, startling the woman again. He put his hands up in an open palm display. He looked at me, and I knew he had intel. I nodded. She had a right to know, whatever it was. It's her life.

"I don't want you to get upset, but I ran the info on your car," he said to the woman.

She instantly bolted to the other side of the room and braced herself against the wall.

"Donovan, I adore you, but you're an idiot sometimes," Katie said, rolling her eyes.

"What? What did I do now?" he asked.

"Never, ever, start a conversation with a woman with 'I don't want you to get upset.' It's like a built-in trigger. No matter what you say after that, we are going to be upset," Katie explained.

"Well, now I know," he snapped back.

I just shook my head at him. "What did you find out?"

"You purchased the car with cash in Detroit, which is good, but I have a feeling the name that you used for the title transfer is a real name, and the New Jersey driver's license, I am guessing, is real as well. That car puts you in Michigan. I want to send it somewhere else to throw off the trail."

We turned to the woman for confirmation, and she nodded. "I'm sorry. I don't know what I was thinking. I'm just too tired to think straight anymore," she cried.

Donovan moved over to her and took her hand. "It's going to be fine. Give me the car keys and let me get it out of here as quickly as I can." She nodded again and dug the keys out of her purse, handing them to him.

I pulled out an envelope of money from my desk drawer, handing it to Donovan. He looked at me, then the envelope, and then the desk.

"How many times do I have to tell you to lock up the cash around here?" he scolded.

Katie giggled. She had been on me lately about the same thing. I just ignored them both.

"Ditch the car, but make sure to dump it a few states away in a populated area, where someone will easily find it. I'm thinking Atlanta or Pittsburgh; either city would be good. Let's have the rat-bastard searching through a half-million people to try and find her," I said.

"I can pay for that. I have money," the woman said as she pulled out a huge pile of hundreds from her purse. It must have been at least twenty grand.

"Damnit. What is wrong with you women?" Donovan grumbled as he stared at the woman, the cash and the purse, before turning and stomping out of the office. Katie and I both broke out laughing.

"I'm on the run. Where the hell did he expect me to put the money?" the woman asked.

Katie and I laughed harder.

"Yo, big B's," Alex said as a way of announcing himself. "I got the cream of the crop right here." He stacked a couple of bags on Katie's desk and moved over to the filing cabinet by the door. "We don't sell undergarments for women, but for reasons that I don't want to know, Anne stocks some for the queen B's and herself. You are about the same size as Katie so we will steal from her stash." Alex pulled an assortment of new bras, panties, stockings and such from the drawer and added them to the bags. "Other than possibly a few more shoe options, which those Louboutin sling-backs you are wearing are far better than anything we've stocked, you are all set."

"Thank you. How much do I owe?" she asked.

"Please. If the owner and the manager are telling me to set you up, I already know they aren't running a tab. I'm Alex, by the way," he held out his hand.

"Glad to meet you, Alex. I'm Annalyssia," she said, shaking his hand in return.

Katie and I both jumped from our desk perches. "No, no, no. Alex, love, forget you ever heard that name," I said.

"Yeah, that just isn't going to fly," Katie added.

"How about Lisa?" I asked Annalyssia.

She shrugged, appearing too exhausted to care.

"Yeah," Katie agreed. "Lisa will work. Simple names are harder to trace. Lisa Matthews. I'll get started on the new paperwork right away."

Katie went over to her computer and started doing her thing. It was a little scary how adept she had become with ordering fake IDs.

"Well, Lisa Matthews, welcome to our madness," Alex smiled. "And girl, ditch that scarf. You aren't fooling anybody with that thing. I will pick up some cosmetics that will work to cover the bruises, without giving you a rash."

Lisa untied the scarf and threw it in the trashcan at the end of Katie's desk. By the look of the bruises, she was lucky she still could breathe, let alone talk.

Alex leaped for the trash, retrieving the scarf. "Now girlfriend, I did not say throw away the hand-sewn silk scarf. I just meant that you should not be wearing it today because it's too hot."

He shook the scarf gently and held it up for inspection.

"It's yours if you want it," she shrugged.

"You are my new BFF," he smiled before skipping out of the office, the scarf waving around in the air while he danced beneath it.

The door opened again. Hattie walked in carrying a tray of food and drinks. "Alex gave me a heads-up that Kelsey picked up another stray," she winked at me. "I brought you something to eat, dear. It's nothing fancy, just the usual sandwiches and such I keep here to make sure these two eat at least once a day. I'm Hattie. If you need anything, don't hesitate to find me." Hattie turned and walked out just as efficiently.

"You do know, don't you, that none of you are normal?" asked Lisa while drooling over the plate of sandwiches.

"What fun would that be?" said Katie as she continued typing away on the computer.

I let Lisa know to make herself at home, and told her she could nap on the office couch. I had a couple more hours of work to do before I could leave.

Katie caught up with me before I made it too far. "Hey, we need to talk," she said, leading me into menswear and then around the corner and into the employees-only hallway.

"What's up?" I asked, checking to make sure the hallway was clear.

"It's about those missing-person files you had me send to my friend at the FBI. He called this morning and said they caught the creep. Apparently, the guy was a truck driver who they now suspect was responsible for over a dozen murders. He also has a remote cabin in the area you marked off as his possible residence. They have already found the remains of three of the boys and figure they will find the rest in the next few days."

I sighed. "And the FBI is keeping our names out of the case, right?"

"Yes. He said it wasn't an issue since we had no firsthand knowledge of the case."

"And the father that was on trial for kidnapping his son?" I asked. His son had been the missing piece of the puzzle in the timeline.

"The FBI is working with the local authorities to get him released."

"The families will at least have some closure. That's the best we can do for them."

"I just wish we could find you some closure too," Katie admitted.

"My day will come," I patted her on the shoulder and walked away. Hot tears burned just behind my lids and my hands trembled. I shook my hands out and blinked several times, burying it all deep, as I had for over two years. *Soon.* My day needs to get here *soon.* I knew that I couldn't wait much longer for something to break in the case. I was barely keeping my emotions under the surface these days.

Chapter Twenty

I went back to the security system, surprised to see the monitor still paused on the image of Lisa getting out of her car. I hit a few buttons to move the screen to real time, and everything went black. I stood gaping, mouth open, at the very expensive piece of equipment. If Donovan found out I'd trashed his new toy, he would never let me touch it again.

Panicking, I called James.

"Hey, beautiful," he answered on the second ring.

"Stop flirting with me!" I exclaimed over the phone. "I have a problem."

"What's wrong?" he said, his voice instantly going serious.

"Donovan is out doing an errand, and I touched the security system!" I knew my voice was a little shrill, but I didn't care.

There was a long silence before he finally said, "I don't understand. What exactly is the problem?"

"I killed his brand-new toy! He's going to be furious. He will probably make me run on the treadmill as punishment!"

I could hear James laughing, and then the line was disconnected.

"He hung up on me! What does that mean? He's not going to help?" I said to my phone.

"*Please*. If you were talking to James, then the NSA will most likely be dropping from the sky any moment to fix the thing for you," Anne laughed as she picked up the box she was after and went back to bridalwear.

Still staring at the monitors ten minutes later, I didn't hear the bikes pull up or the door chimes. I didn't notice anything, until large arms wrapped around me and pulled me back into a muscular chest.

"Hello, Sugar," James whispered in my ear before kissing me on the temple.

"Please tell me you can fix this," I said, leaning back against him.

"Nope. But Tech probably can." He turned me to see the man standing next to him. Tech was tall, well over six feet, young with a narrow build, and sporting a goatee.

"Hi, Tech. Welcome to The Changing Room. I've seen you at the Saturday night potlucks, but I don't think we ever met."

He nodded, but he was already focused on the blackened-out system and pulled a stool out to start working. "Yeah, I was all-in as soon as I heard you were playing all the Star Wars movies. I'm a Star Wars junky," he said while moving electrical cords around and flipping some switches. "Damn, you did kill it."

"As in, *permanently*? Or as in you just need to put the electrical paddles to it and bring it back to life?" I whined.

Tech looked at me as if I was an idiot before turning back to the monitors.

"I'm hoping we can keep this on the DL and get it up and running before Donovan gets back," I said.

"How long do we have?" Tech asked.

"That depends on whether he runs the errand himself or decides to sub it out. So I would guess anywhere from 36 hours to, I don't know, say, five minutes?" I said.

James laughed and sat on a nearby stool. Tech connected his laptop to the hard drive on the security system, and strange letter and number codes started scrolling across his screen. I pulled another stool out next to James and sat, feeling useless.

"So, James, why don't you have a nickname?" I asked.

"I did. It was Tagger," he shrugged.

"So, why doesn't anyone call you Tagger anymore?"

"Bones decided that it wasn't for me anymore, and told everyone to call me James. Nobody argues with Bones, so they did."

"It's scary that I don't know anything about you guys. I mean, you are all regulars at the store, at my house, but I don't know anything about any of you. I tried to Google you all once but didn't come up with anything," I fully admitted with a grin.

He smiled at me with a wicked grin of his own. "Baby, you don't have to do online searches. You're welcome in my world any day, and most definitely any night."

"Stop flirting! Now, tell me about the nickname," I shoulder-bumped him.

"Afraid it was from the service and not that pretty. Part of my job was to pick up the pieces and tag the parts to identify the fallen soldiers, thus the nickname Tagger."

"Ugh. That sucks. What a horrible job."

"It was. And, it screwed me up for a long time. But there were others like Donovan and Bones that had it worse than I did."

I didn't ask why Donovan and Bones had it worse. It wasn't my business, and it wasn't James' right to tell.

"So you knew them before the club? When you were in the service?" I asked.

"I knew Donovan. Donovan knew Bones. I met Bones after we were all back in the States. Donovan started his security firm, and Bones and I pledged to the MC life."

"So where does Bishop fit into all this? I can never figure out why he's always around."

"I knew Bishop from the military too, met in basic. I was back a year before I ran into him again. He prospected for about two months with the club, but it wasn't his thing. He was too cocky to take orders and refused to do some of the grittier jobs. How he survived the military without getting court-martialed is beyond my comprehension," James laughed.

I had a mental image of Bishop cleaning toilets as part of his prospect duties, complaining about how beneath him it was. I would love a picture of something like that.

"So what's the deal between you and Bishop?" James asked.

"Ugh. I am not having that conversation," I said.

My blood pressure increased a few notches, remembering Bishop in the store the day prior, attempting yet again to harass me into going out on a date with him. It seemed that swinging a bat at his head hadn't dissuaded him at all.

James looked at me curiously, but changed the subject. "Did Donovan get moved in upstairs?"

"Sure did. Candi helped him find some furniture. I barely know he's around most of the time until I smell his fantastic cooking, and then the aroma draws me out of my room. I've probably gained ten pounds since he moved in."

He snorted at that. "And the training?"

It was my turn to snort. "He has his hands full. We're making progress, but he yells at us a lot," I said.

James' chuckle vibrated along my side as he pulled me with one arm and kissed my temple again.

I pulled away and stood, distancing myself from him to prevent any further advances.

"Actually," Tech said, while not taking his eyes off his laptop, "Donovan told me that the three of you were doing great. Said Katie has a mean right hook and Anne's improved at blocking and evading. You surprised him with already knowing extensive fighting techniques. And, you continue to surprise him with how fast you are learning the new techniques he has shown you. I also hear that you are quite the little sharpshooter with a Glock or a rifle." He looked over his shoulder at me with an inquiring raised eyebrow, before turning back to the monitors.

"He did?" I grinned. "He just bellows things like 'Do it again' and 'That was too slow' and then makes us get on the treadmill as punishment. I thought I was in pretty good shape until he proved me wrong."

"Well, it must be working if he told Tech you were doing well," James grumbled, looking displeased by my obvious physical retreat.

"Maybe. The only thing I know for sure is that I'm going to have to buy a hot tub. We are so sore most of the time it's difficult to crawl out of bed in the mornings."

They seemed to find our pain humorous, which earned them both fake glares, but I was glad to see James switching back to being jovial.

I looked up at the security system right as Tech did something that flicked everything back to life again. The color monitors displayed their respective feeds, and green lights were flashing on the black box, which I assumed was a good thing.

I gave Tech a big hug from behind. "You're my hero!" I squealed.

"What about me? I brought him over here," James complained.

"And, I thank you as well, James," I smiled but turned back to Tech.

"So what were you trying to do before you crashed the system?" Tech asked.

"The screen froze on a still shot, so I tried to change it back. But I really need the entire morning footage deleted."

"Anything to do with the license plate I ran for Donovan this morning?"

"Maybe," I vaguely answered as Tech nodded and started typing again on the keyboard.

"Well, consider it all deleted," he said with a few more clicks of the keyboard.

"That's it?" I said, completely amazed.

"Yup. Next time just call me. It will be easier to delete it myself than restore the whole system."

I pulled my phone out and handed it to him. He took the phone and raised an eyebrow at me.

"She doesn't know how to program someone's name and number in her new phone. You either have to do it yourself or call her so she can hit the save button," Katie explained as she passed by on her way into menswear.

"How do you run a business?" Tech laughed as he entered his contact information into the phone.

"I can handle the basics of computer programs, Excel, Word, accounting programs, online shopping. Just don't ask me to program the time on your coffee pot or your favorite stations on a car stereo. Bad things happen," I answered. "So, what do I owe you for fixing the security system?"

"Not a thing, ma'am. You're a friend of Donovan's and the Club's, just happy to help."

"No, there has to be something. And quit the ma'am crap, it's just Kelsey."

"Clothes," James answered for him. "He doesn't like to go clothes shopping, but he is down to one pair of jeans and two shirts. Several of the guys have offered to bring him over here, but he's avoided it."

"Done," I smiled. I stepped back and took in Tech's measurements by sight before heading to menswear. If he hated shopping so much, I knew not to push him into trying on the clothes. I gathered up several pairs of jeans, a pair of black dress pants, a variety of shirts and a warm coat. Katie had come up and added a few pairs of shoes to the pile. We also had started to carry packages of new socks and underwear to fulfill the one-stop shopping needs of our male customers, so I threw in a couple of packages of plain white socks and some boxer-briefs as well. Katie pulled out the boxer-briefs from the pile and exchanged them for plain boxers. I didn't question her or the grin she was sporting.

We carried everything up front and piled it into two tote bags. I opened up the cabinet under the register and retrieved a red bow, sticking it on the side of one of the bags. I handed both bags over to Tech.

"This is all for me?" Tech asked, peering into the bags.

"Yup. If you think of something else you need, just let one of the guys know, and we will send it back with them. As long as you bail me out once in a while with the electronic shit, I will keep you stocked on all the clothes you could ever want."

"Deal," he agreed, walking out the door, still looking in the bags.

"Later, sugar," James whispered, as he slapped my ass on the way out.

I sighed. I was eventually going to have to set James straight.

Smothered giggles erupted behind me, and I didn't have to turn to know it was Katie and Anne, probably Hattie as well.

"Back to work!" I hollered.

Chapter Twenty-One

Lisa was sleeping like the dead, so I stayed at the store, not wanting to wake her. I was busy restocking shirts when out of the corner of my eye, I saw Alex skipping through the salesroom. I instantly knew two things—neither of which was good. One, Bishop was here. Two, Alex was going to push things to a completely new level today.

Bishop and Alex had hated each other since the first day they met. As Bishop became more arrogant and controlling, Alex acted out more in my defense. It escalated further when Alex found out Bishop was a homophobe. Alex would flirt and tease Bishop until — knowing better than to act out against Alex or he would suffer the consequences with me — Bishop would storm out.

Alex must have had time to see him coming today, though. Outfitted in a burgundy silk blouse, short black mini skirt, net nylons and stripper boots, Alex was on the prowl.

I saw Bishop walking toward me in the second aisle, but Alex intercepted him first.

"Hey there, sexy," Alex purred not so quietly, as he dragged a scarlet red press-on nail down Bishops arm. "How about you and I find some cozy dark spot to share a drink or two and get to know each other better?"

Bishop knocked Alex's hand away with enough force that Alex lost his balance on his hooker heels. Luckily, I was right behind him to level him out before I stepped between them, facing Alex.

"Alex, dear, how's inventory coming in the back?" I asked.

"Everything is splendid, love. We are ready for the weekend. I just saw this sexy little thing," he said, gesturing his press-on nail toward Bishop, "and thought it was a good time to take my break." He smiled at Bishop and *blew him a fricken kiss.*

"Alex..."

"Bishop, sweet, what do you say about that drink?" Alex winked at Bishop.

A cluster of customers openly gawked at the exchange. I glanced back at Bishop. His face was almost purple, and his neck veins looked ready to pop.

"Alex, I think it's time you go to the back room," I insisted.

"But I'm on my break, love. It's the law and all. Everyone gets one." Several of the customers nodded their heads in agreement. "And, I thought maybe Bishop here would like to give me a *ride.*" Alex thrust his hips forward and rotated them toward Bishop.

Hearing someone approach, I turned to the left. Bones, Whiskey and Tech doubled over laughing at the exchange. That was all it took to push Bishop over the edge. He dove at Alex, knocking me off to the side in the process.

Alex, not thinking out the hooker heels thoroughly, lost his balance as he tried to jump back, giving Bishop the opportunity to grab him by the throat. Bishop pulled back his other arm, ready to throw his meaty fist into Alex's face.

I threw a solid side punch to Bishop's lower abs, knocking him away from Alex. Then I executed a leg sweep in conjunction with a forearm thrust to his upper chest that threw him flat on his back with enough force to knock the wind out of him. I was positioned to defend myself, but he just laid there, looking up at me in disbelief.

My coworkers emerged from the far corners of the store and took fighting stances on both my sides. Even Hattie stood next to me with an umbrella, ready to swing it like a baseball bat.

The only one not in a fighting stance was Katie. She turned to Alex with her hands on her hips. "Alex! Seriously? Pissing off a guy that is twice your size? *You idiot!* Get your skinny ass in the back room and stop screwing around," she ordered.

"But he deserved it! How many times does Kelsey have to tell him to get lost before he is going to figure it out? The arrogant dickhead needs to leave her alone."

Katie stepped in Alex's face and her expression currently was not one of affection. "No. You need to get this straight. Kelsey is a grown- ass, self-sufficient, independent and educated woman. Who, as you can see, is more than capable of dealing with Bishop. So, back off!"

Alex didn't argue, but turned and stomped his hooker heels down the aisle toward the stockroom.

"And find me a pair of those boots in my size!" I yelled to Alex, to which Katie just shook her head at me.

Bishop was still on the floor when Bones approached. He scanned me, still in my defensive stance, and nodded at me as if I passed some secret test.

He then stepped in front of Hattie. He held out his hand, and she handed him the umbrella-bat. He turned the umbrella around, placed one of her hands in the middle of the length and the other on the handle end. Then he showed her to use it more as a jabbing weapon than a bat.

Passing me again, Anne stiffened when Bones held his hand out to take hers. She glanced at me, but I could only shrug. Slowly, Anne moved one of her hands forward, and he grasped her fingers, uncurling them from the fist she had made.

"Anne," scowled Katie, "How many times has Donovan told you not to tuck your thumb? You'll break your thumb."

"But it makes my fists feel bigger, like I can hit harder," Anne defended her actions.

Bones snorted, retrieved something from his back pocket, and dropped it into Anne's hand. Then he turned and forced Bishop up, giving him a hard shove toward the door. Bishop didn't argue. He went willingly.

We all turned to Anne.

"This is awesome!" In her hand, she had a giant set of brass knuckles. She put them on and started shadow boxing.

"Okay, everybody. The show is over. If you're on the payroll, get back to work. If you are a customer, get to shopping before I decide to close early today." As expected, everyone quickly scattered.

Chapter Twenty-Two

The rest of the day was uneventful. When Lisa woke up from her nap, we packed up for home. My house wasn't anything special, just a one and a half-story old farmhouse with two bedrooms downstairs and two bedrooms upstairs. Entering through the back door, I explained the living arrangements to Lisa.

"You can make yourself at home here, food, laundry, TV, whatever. I will set you up in the guest bedroom. I have the other downstairs bedroom, and Donovan occupies the upstairs. Currently, the living room is serving as our home gym. My furniture is in storage while Donovan trains us on self-defense. I'll warn you, though, he is meaner than a boot camp drill sergeant when it comes to cardio workouts."

"I heard that," Donovan complained from the kitchen.

"Sounds like fun. I used to run every day but haven't been able to for a while," Lisa said.

"Well then, you and Donovan will hit it off splendidly."

"Finally, someone who appreciates physical fitness," Donovan smiled when we entered the kitchen.

"Whatever," I rolled my eyes. "What's for dinner?" I asked, snooping in one of the pans. I wasn't kidding when I told James that Donovan was a good cook. The extra bonus was that he liked to cook Italian, which was my favorite.

"Get out of there," Donovan scolded as he reset the lid on the sauce. "The sauce has to simmer. It will be about an hour before dinner." He pushed me farther away from the stove. "I moved a TV into the spare bedroom. Let me know if you need anything else moved."

"Thanks. And, this is officially Lisa Matthews, just so there is no confusion."

"Got it. Did Katie get the paperwork straightened out?" he eluded to the fake ID.

"Yeah. She said it would be ready to go by tomorrow."

"Good. Now both of you, off to do whatever women do, and let me finish with dinner."

I carried Lisa's bags into the spare bedroom, and she pulled out a change of clothes. I had some work to do in my room, so she decided to soak in the tub before dinner.

Forty-five minutes later, I surrendered to the smell of the marinara sauce, saved my work, and followed the aroma.

"You're killing me, Donovan. I can't focus, smelling all this yummy food."

Lisa was grating cheese at the counter while Donovan crushed fresh garlic.

"And, why is she allowed in the kitchen and I'm not?" I poked.

"Because she has kitchen skills and you don't," he poked back. "Are you ever going to tell me what you do in your room for hours and hours?"

"I have orgasm, after orgasm, while thinking of you," I grinned, and Donovan rolled his eyes.

Lisa seemed puzzled, so Donovan explained. "She goes in there before dinner, comes out to eat and work out, before going back in again, door shut. Some nights she stays up until almost dawn then takes a nap before heading into the store. By Friday nights, she is so exhausted that she goes straight to bed and sleeps about twelve hours to catch up."

I ignored him and turned the subject back to the real priority, which was my stomach. "I'm really hungry. Can we eat yet?" I whined.

"We were just getting ready to serve, so perfect timing," Lisa said.

She grabbed the potholders to move the pasta bowl to the table. Lifting the bowl, she winced, and I reached out quickly with a towel and grabbed the bowl as it was free-falling.

"Sorry, I am such a klutz. Thanks for making sure dinner didn't land on the floor," she said nervously, not making eye contact. She started moving smaller items to the table, favoring one of her arms.

Donovan and I locked gazes.

"Sorry, I just have to send a quick text," I said, fiddling with my phone. I sent a message, and a few seconds later, I read the reply. "All set, let's eat."

We dug in, and as usual, I overate. I was desperately hoping Donovan didn't make me run on the treadmill tonight. If I didn't have personal motives for being as fit as possible, I would have told Donovan to kiss my ass weeks ago and started a couch-based strike with a jumbo bowl of mashed potatoes and fatty gravy.

While clearing plates, I heard my phone chirp and checked the messages.

"Lisa, I promised to stay out of your business, but I am worried about your arm and possibly your ribs. I asked a friend to send a doctor. There will be no paperwork trail, and I will pay in cash. I just got a text that Doc will be here in a few minutes. I am not trying to control or manipulate you. We just need to know if you have any broken bones or other injuries that need medical attention."

I held my breath, waiting for her reaction. Donovan was trying to look busy, but I knew he was nervously awaiting her response too.

"I want to pay the bill myself. I have money. My ribs are most likely just bruised, but I may have broken my arm again. So it would be a good idea to get it checked out."

"And, will you agree to a full check-up? You have your bedroom, so there is plenty of privacy."

"I don't want to be alone with someone," she whispered. Her eyes pooled with tears, and I reached for her uninjured hand.

"You don't have to be alone. I can stay with you the entire time. But it's important that we get you checked out," I assured her.

She nodded her approval.

"How much money should I get out?"

"I always drop him a thousand. I overpay him because he runs a medical clinic, and I know he helps a lot of others for free that can't afford his services."

She nodded and blinked back the tears that were threatening to fall.

We all turned when the back door opened. James and Doc entered, and I gave Doc a hug. James winked at me on his way to get a plate and started filling it up.

"Hey," complained Donovan. "That was going to be my lunch tomorrow."

"Yeah, right. The pasta queen would have cleared it out on a midnight refrigerator raid, and you know it," James laughed.

Donovan agreed and grabbed another plate. "Doc, I will fix you a plate before James eats everything. It will be waiting for you when you are ready."

"Sounds great," Doc said as he went off toward the bedrooms and Lisa and I followed.

Doc picked my room, most likely because it was larger. I moved the laptop off the bed while making introductions and explaining to Doc that Lisa wanted me to stay with her. He did a thorough exam, and while Lisa was getting dressed, I could tell he was having a hard time shutting out his emotions. She had many injuries, and they were all in different stages of healing.

"Is she safe here?" he asked.

"We think so. We got rid of the trail."

"And if he finds her?"

"He won't live long enough to regret it."

I would kill the man without hesitation after I saw the damage he had inflicted on Lisa's body.

Doc nodded and pulled an arm brace and sling out of his bag, which he started fitting to Lisa's arm. "Lisa, your ribs are bruised, and your arm is at least fractured. I want to get an X-ray tomorrow morning, and I predict that I will need to put a hard cast on it. I also want you to take these antibiotics for the next ten days. Take them until they are gone. I will run the blood work under Kelsey's name, so we keep your name out of the records."

"Ummm," I interrupted. "No offense, Doc, but my name has been used too many times through labs and pharmacies around here lately. People are starting to think I sell more than just clothes. Can we use Katie's name this time?"

"Sure" he laughed, "as long as Katie doesn't care, I am fine with it." Turning to Lisa, he explained, "If you looked at all the test results in Kelsey's medical file, you would understand. I get a good number of patients that can't have their names documented. I run a lot of them under Kelsey's name. According to her file, she has had just about every STD except AIDS. It's so crazy that I started keeping her real test results under Anne's name," he chuckled.

"Oh!" she said, trying to cover up her laugh.

"If Bishop doesn't decide to leave me alone soon, I might have to have Doc leave my file out for him to snoop in. That should send him packing."

"Who's Bishop?" she asked.

"A pain in the ass," Doc answered for me while he made the last adjustments to Lisa's arm sling.

I had met Doc a few months back when I took a teenage runaway to his clinic after I found her living on the streets. He helped fix her up and get her in a good foster home. Shortly after that, I found out he was also friends with the club. He's a hell of a humanitarian, and the only person I've known him not to like is Bishop. He has never said why.

"This will have to do until tomorrow. Now I need to claim my dinner plate before James steals it." Doc went back to the kitchen, and I sat a moment longer with Lisa.

"I just want you to know that I meant what I said. If the man that did this to you ever shows up, I will kill him," I whispered.

"You won't have to. Just give me a gun and I will happily take care of him," she whispered back.

I got up, opened my nightstand drawer and loaded a spare gun that I kept there. I made sure the safety was on and passed it to her.

"Do you know how to shoot?"

"Yes. My father taught me," she answered while expertly checking the clip, before sliding the gun into her purse.

"Well, it's almost time for the girls to show for our workout. I guess you have the excuse of bruised ribs and a broken arm, but what excuse do I use to get out of running on that medieval torture machine called the treadmill? I had to unbutton my pants at dinner just to make room for dessert."

Lisa laughed while we made our way back to the kitchen.

Chapter Twenty-Three

Anne, Sara and Katie arrived for the workout on schedule. Doc and James decided to stay and enjoy a few beers while they made jokes at our expense. I wasn't surprised when Whiskey, Tech and Bones arrived with a case of beer shortly thereafter.

I was whining like a baby running on the treadmill, covered in sweat and queasy from my dinner rolling around in my stomach. Sara ran on the treadmill next to me while egging me on with "Come on, Aunt Kelsey!" and "Why are you breathing like that?"

By the time the treadmill dinged, indicating our time was complete, I wasn't sure if I could stand. I looked over at Sara, standing next to me grinning, looking as perfect as when she had started. I just rolled my eyes at her, while she continued to giggle.

Wiping down with a towel that Lisa handed to me, I asked Donovan, "Can we fight now?" The hand-to-hand was my favorite part of the workouts.

"No!" Katie whined. "I want to do a longer cardio tonight."

"Chicken?" I teased, knowing that her plea was more to stay off the mat while I was on it.

"Come on, Kel. You are too good. I don't think Anne and I should spar with you anymore," she admitted.

"She's right," Donovan said.

"Run that by me again and a little slower, please. You're saying I'm getting too good at this?" I bounced my weight from one foot to the other, getting excited to get on the mat.

"You're not THAT good," Donovan grinned as the rest of the guys laughed.

When he turned his back to me, I stuck my tongue out at him. With the threat of the treadmill so close, I wasn't brave enough to disrespect him to his face.

"But you are beyond Katie and Anne in skill level, so it's not helping you or them to pair you together. And, when you spar with me, I can't coach you as well. James? Will you spar with Kelsey tonight?"

James was taking a drink of his beer and almost choked when he heard Donovan. "You want me to fight a girl that is half my weight and a foot shorter than me?" he asked.

"Are you chicken too?" I prodded.

That was all that needed to be said. It didn't take much to convince a biker to brawl. James had a huge smile on his face as he stripped down to just his jeans. With bare feet and a muscular, bare chest, wearing a pair of low-rider jeans that I remember picking out for him, he stepped onto the mat in front of me. Wowzer!

"Damn," Anne and Katie said in unison.

I shook my head, trying to clear it as Donovan commanded me to focus.

Sara told me to *kick his butt.*

James just snorted.

"Okay," Donovan instructed, "James, your job is to pin or trap Kelsey by whatever means. Kelsey, you need to defend yourself, prevent being pinned and drop him to the floor. Refrain from full punches, and avoid any groin or throat attacks, Kelsey. Remember this is just practice, so keep your focus."

I nodded that I understood, and James looked at Donovan questionably. Donovan turned to him and smiled. "Good luck, man."

At first, neither of us moved. Katie and Donovan usually charged me immediately so I wasn't sure what to do when James held his unmoving position.

"She can't defend herself if you don't attack her, James," Donovan scolded.

"What the hell am I supposed to do?" asked James.

"Try to slap her. As hard as you can," Donovan instructed.

James still seemed unsure.

"*Do or do not,*" Tech quoted Yoda, "*There is no try.*"

"*Judge me by my size, do you?*" I quoted back.

James finally reached within my space to slap me. I quickly knocked his arm away and pushed him off balance. He seemed a little surprised by this, but more focused and determined when he faced me again. It wasn't long before he was trying to punch, kick or bodyslam me, but I kept evading him and striking back. The fourth time I threw him flat on his back, he finally called uncle.

"Hey, prez," Tech called over to James. "I forgot to tell you that in the store this afternoon Kelsey dropped Bishop on his ass in two moves. It was beautiful."

Whiskey and Bones chuckled. Anne and Katie went silent. I cringed and moved over to the wall, trying to hide in the open-floor-plan room.

"And you just thought to tell me this now?" asked James, still on his back and trying to refill his lungs.

"I wish I could have seen that," laughed Doc.

"I downloaded it from the security feed before I left. I will send you the video," Tech told Doc.

I stared at the floor, still cringing, as I felt the anger rolling off Donovan as he stepped up behind me.

"We made a deal. You promised you wouldn't use the techniques I am teaching you unless you had to protect yourself. You need to learn to manage that wicked temper of yours. You could have killed him or caused permanent injury."

"She didn't act in anger," Bones defended me, stepping in front of me while facing off Donovan, who still stood behind me.

If I weren't so nervous that I was about to lose my fight training, I probably would have enjoyed being the center of a testosterone sandwich. Bones reached out, grasping my hand and gently squeezing it. I doubted that anyone could see the gesture since it was on the side that faced the wall.

"She stepped in to defend Alex. Bishop was about to knock him unconscious, and I was too far away to stop it. In two moves, she had them separated and Bishop on the ground and held her position until I removed him from the store," Bones said.

"*A Jedi uses the Force for knowledge and defense, never for attack,*" Tech whispered in a perfect Yoda impersonation.

I wanted to laugh, but I didn't dare.

I felt cool air drift across my back as Donovan stepped away. Bones gave my hand another squeeze before he released it and stepped back as well.

"What did Alex do to provoke him this time?" Donovan roared.

"Don, brother, you wouldn't believe us if we told you. Luckily, I have the flash drive right here so you can see it for yourself. All of the customers were silently gawking at the scene, so we even picked up the audio," Tech smiled.

Since the living room no longer had a TV, everyone filed into my bedroom. I quickly moved my notepads and laptop inside my desk drawer while Tech set up the TV. When I turned around, both Donovan and Bones were watching me with raised eyebrows. I just ignored them.

We watched the video four times before I finally had enough and kicked them all out of my room. It was funny watching Alex ruffle Bishop's feathers, and

I decided the security system finally had proved to have value.

I showered as everyone else sat around enjoying a drink. When I came back out, my jaw dropped. Donovan and Bones were both on the mat, bare feet, bare chests and bare fists. It was the hottest thing I had ever seen. I looked at the other girls and confirmed they were staring in open lust as well.

Lisa even went over and opened a window, exclaiming it was getting a bit warm. I had worked out enough with Donovan that I knew he rocked the abs, but, Bones? *It should be a crime for that man to wear clothes.*

Bones and Donovan both busted up laughing and turned to face me. My face heated with embarrassment as I realized I said that last thought aloud.

"Night all," I said as I scurried off to my room and shut my door. *Whew.* I need to write while my hormones are on the rise. That scene alone should elicit enough naughty thoughts to fill a few chapters.

Chapter Twenty-Four

A month later, Lisa's arm was finally out of the cast, and her ribs no longer bothered her. She still lived with us, and we made it more permanent by repainting the walls in her room and buying some items to make the room more personable. She and Donovan were two peas in a pod and hung out together during their off time. At the store, Lisa helped Anne run the bridal and gowns department. With a great eye for the upscale fashions, she was helping us target better inventory and evaluating prices. She even started joining our workouts.

Much to my pleasure and displeasure, Whiskey, James, Bones and Tech usually stopped in at least once a week as well to watch and laugh at our expense. My hormones were driving me nuts, but my writing was at an all-time high with all the new material.

With all the money from my book sales and the store profits piling up, I closed on several surrounding pieces of real estate. I bought the property adjacent to the store and the long stretch of property behind that, and even the 50 acres of woodlands across the side street. I started construction on three houses along the side street. Two were good-sized ranch houses on one-acre lots.

The third house was a large two-story, situated closest to the store with six bedrooms, four full bathrooms and a couple of half baths. The master bedroom was more of a private suite on the first floor with a four-season atrium that would be both a sitting room and a writing space. The private suite also would have an entrance from the atrium into the house that Donovan, after I had him review the plans, was having fits about from a security perspective. The larger house sits on 10 acres, which consists mostly of the field behind the store. Construction of all three homes was going well, and I was hoping for occupancy by the end of the summer with large bonuses available if the crew finished early.

On the opposite side of the highway from the store, I bought the 150 acres of farmland. I was still working on the business plan for that property, but I was in no big rush. In the meantime, I was having fun turning down all the purchase offers that kept coming my way. The more customer traffic that The Changing Room brought into the area, the higher the property values climbed. And the store had been packed most of the time during the last month. We were once again having occupancy issues and my old friend the fire marshall was back. Neither of us seemed too excited about the reunion.

It was Saturday morning, and we hadn't left the store until after 10:00 the night before, restocking from the Friday rush. I started my Saturday at 6:00 a.m., dealing with the rest of my to-do list. I wasn't surprised to see everyone on executive salary in before 8:00. The store didn't even open on Saturdays until 10:00, but there was always too much to get done lately.

By 9:00 the rest of the staff had arrived. I saw Donovan approaching and waited for him to catch up as I did another visual sweep of the back room before heading to the sales floor.

"I'm a little concerned," he said.

"That's because you are a worrywart, my dear," I said as I stopped in the office and grabbed a name tag out of my bucket. Today's name tag read: Kween B. Kelsey, Owner. Katie had started coming up with goofy name tags for each of us, and I had to admit it was fun to trade them up weekly.

Just to bug him, I reached into Donovan's bucket and pulled one for him. Deputy Donovan, Official Spoilsport. I couldn't help but laugh as I handed it to him. He read it, rolled his eyes and threw it in the trash. I pulled it back out and set it on the desk. He continued to follow me out of the office.

"Kelsey, stop and listen for just a second. Have you looked outside lately?"

"I don't know. Why? Is it raining?" I sighed.

"No. There are about 200 customers already gearing up to ram the doors down. And more cars are lined up to pull into the parking lot."

"That's not good," I said.

"That was my thought when I looked at the security feed."

I heard him grumbling some complaint under his breath as I went up to the front window to look for myself. *Damn.* Donovan was right. It looked like a Black Friday war zone out there. If we weren't careful, someone could easily get hurt. I pulled out my cellphone and started dialing.

My brother Jeff answered on the first ring, "Hey, aren't you working?"

"Yeah. I have a problem, though. We open in less than an hour, and there is a mob out in the parking lot. Any chance you can come to help? And bring any available siblings?"

"I'm on it. See you as soon as I can get there." He hung up on me, and I smiled. My brother loved me.

"It's getting worse by the minute," Donovan said over my shoulder.

As much as I didn't want to look, I had no choice. The parking lot was now full, and cars were pulling onto the grass, starting a hillbilly parking lot in the side field. It was a madhouse.

"Katie!" I yelled.

She came running out of menswear when she heard the panic in my voice and immediately saw the crowds and cars.

"Hell's bells," she said.

"Close down bridal; appointments only will be honored today. Warn the rest of the staff. And, talk to Anne about Candi taking Sara for a few hours. I don't want to worry about Sara in this crowd."

She took off running to the back room. I turned my attention back to my phone to make yet another plea for help.

"Hello," answered James, half asleep.

"We are less than an hour from opening the store, and if we open the doors with the current crowd, there will be a stampede. Can I hire the club to come over and do crowd control?"

"Give us 15 minutes and stay away from the fucking doors until we get there," he ordered, and disconnected.

"Please tell me they are coming."

Donovan was nervous, which only spiked my own nerves.

"Yeah, he said to give them 15 minutes. Should I call the police too?"

"No. Devil's Players are more effective if they don't have to worry about the police arresting them. They can back the crowd up and keep them controlled." Donovan tried to assure me as I was biting my lower lip.

"Okay. I need to change my clothes," I said, hurrying off as Donovan threw his hands up in exasperation.

He just didn't understand women. There was no way I was going to face this crowd in some passive-feminine-business-casual slacks and blouse. In my experience, the clothes you wore made all the difference when it came to attitude. I wanted to make sure the customers thought long and hard before starting trouble on my playground.

Chapter Twenty-Five

Twenty minutes later, not only had I changed but so had Lisa, Anne, Katie and Alex. Anne even darkened our makeup, Alex's too. We walked out of the break room and met up with Donovan and the Players. I knew that we made an aggressive unit. Except for Alex, we all wore tight black pants, black leather heeled boots and skintight blouses. Our attitudes were right there with our outfits, which of course was the point. We were ready to open.

Not one of the men said a word, only stared at us as we turned and marched with clacking heels to the front doors.

Several of the Players were outside and had pushed the unruly crowd back. James came around the outside of the building and stood up on top of a planter.

"Listen up!" he ordered.

One of the bikers pierced the air with a loud whistle.

"All of you are going to form a nice, respectable, calm line, and when the doors open, you will enter as such. Anyone pushing, shoving, yelling or otherwise badly behaving will be dragged out on their ass and escorted off the premises. We don't care if you are male or female. The owner and her employees are our friends, and we will defend them and protect their store. Do you understand?"

The crowd, completely silent now, nodded their heads in unison. This is why James was the president of the Devil's Players. He really could scare the crap out of most people whenever he felt like it.

Whiskey gave me the nod through the glass window, encouraging me to unlock the doors.

We spaced ourselves out at the entrance, forcing the crowd from the outside and the inside to enter in a single-file line, nice and easy, through the doors. The customers stayed calm and settled into their shopping. When the bulk of the crowd was inside, we split up to our battle stations. I had everyone on staff in at least two-person teams.

I turned back to the window and watched a woman shove an elderly woman out of the way. Fortunately, I wasn't the only one to see it. Bones grabbed the shover by the arm and escorted her away from the building. James offered his elbow to the elderly woman and personally escorted her and her friends into the store. I heard him telling them that if they had any problems to let one of his men know and they would take care of it. The women beamed up at him and then shimmied off to shop their hearts out. *Aww.*

"What?" James said as he wrapped an arm around my shoulder and pulled me into him to give me a kiss on the cheek.

"My hero!" I said in my most sappy voice, leaning back to return the cheek kiss.

"Get to work, brat!" he chuckled, walking back toward the doors. "We are going to stop the customers from entering soon, and then we will monitor people exiting."

"Sounds good. Oh hey, my brother Jeff and maybe some of my other family members are on their way. If you see them, send them to the back door. Hattie will recognize them and let them inside."

"Will do."

By 2:00 the store was beyond scary. At one point, I saw Katie walking by without a shirt on, and minus her boots. She held her head high as she marched right down the main aisle with her tight black pants and purple bra, into the back room. Jeff and I just looked at each other and laughed before continuing to handle cash-only sales. Anne was behind me in another makeshift row also taking cash deals. We had four standard registers open for credit card and debit purchases, and Donovan and some of the Players were our bag boys. My other brothers and sisters-in-law were somewhere out on the floor, helping keep the stock moving out of the back room.

Tech was operating the security system and several times scolded and threatened customers over the PA system for trying to shoplift or bullying other shoppers. I was sweating and tired when Alex came running up to me.

"We're out," he said, panting, leaning over to brace himself with his hands on his knees.

"We are out of what?" I asked.

"Everything! We pulled all the stock that was clean from inventory. The grab-happy, psycho freaks took it all! We even checked the dressing rooms, and there's nothing left."

I finished the cash deal I was working and climbed on top of one of the counters to look around. I could see maybe three shirts and a pair of shoes, and the customers still on the sales floor were racing to see who got to them first. I saw a woman taking the clothes off one of the manikins and realized the rest of the manikins were already naked. Someone stepped up on top of the counter next to me and put their arm around my waist.

"Unfucking believable," Bones said as he looked around the store.

"Think you can spread the word that we're officially closing for the day?"

He simply turned around and yelled out the doors, "Shut it down. The store is closing."

The bikers started to break up the crowd that never made it inside the store. A few customers appeared irate. They had probably stood in line for hours. Bones jumped down and went outside. He led several of them around to the side of the building so that they could see through the windows that there was just nothing left.

I saw two women arguing over a blouse and got on the PA system. "Ladies, drop the shirt. Neither one of you gets it now. All customers, please proceed immediately to the checkout lanes. We are closing the store. Staff, please search all rooms and make sure everyone has cleared out and then proceed to the front."

The women stalled for only a moment before resuming their argument.

"Ladies, either drop the shirt or I will refuse to sell either one of you the other items you selected today!"

They both simultaneously dropped the shirt and Alex picked it up on his way to the back room.

The remaining staff made their way up to the front of the store, and together, we efficiently checked out the rest of the customers. Last in line were the three elderly women from this morning's parking lot incident. All three had the shine of excitement in their eyes as they checked out just a few items each. The one who had been shoved earlier came over to me and clasped my hand.

"That was the most fun I have had in years," she giggled. "And this nice young man," she said, gesturing to Bones, "was kind enough to protect us from the crowd most of the day, and even got us chairs to sit on so we could people-watch. We felt like royalty," she said with her friends standing behind her, bobbing their heads in agreement.

Bones seemed embarrassed, but took the ladies' bags and helped them out to their car. As we tried to muffle our snickers, he turned and grinned at me through the window.

"I wonder what that was all about," I laughed.

"I think it may have had something to do with you kissing James after he escorted the ladies in this morning," Lisa answered.

"What? That was a joke. And, it was a cheek kiss, not a real kiss."

"Well, I just heard it stirred up some friendly rivalry is all," she said as she pulled out some chairs.

Looking around, we were all sweaty and disheveled. Katie came out of the office with a case of beer and a package of bottled waters. Most of us collapsed on the closest chair, stool, or countertop to take a break as Donovan and some of the Players locked everything down.

The front door opened again, and I saw one of the Players had let in the fire marshall. He looked around the store and then gave me a stern look.

Ughh…not again!

"What do you want me to do that I didn't already do?" I asked him.

"I don't know," he said with a shake of his head, and walked back out the door.

I took a nice cool drink of my beer. *Ah*, better.

Donovan came charging into the room gripping two women firmly by their arms, escorting them briskly to the front doors.

"What's up?" I questioned.

"They were hiding in the back, sorting through the donation bin."

"But we would have paid for anything we found!" one of the women pleaded.

Bones opened the door and held it while Donovan pushed the women through it. Then Bones relocked the door behind them. The two women stood there pouting a moment before finally turning away. Donovan walked over to Lisa and stole her beer. Bones walked over to me and stole mine. That's okay. Lisa and I preferred liquor.

"Okay. Anne, we need big signs to go up on the doors and windows saying 'closed for remodeling.' Alex, I need the service vans moved up to block off the entrances for the rest of the day. Hattie and Lisa, can you close the blinds on all the windows? Katie, I need your help in the office for a minute."

Entering the office, I opened up the new Donovan-approved wall safe. We stuffed some cash into envelopes for the Club and my family members that had shown up to help.

"I put a couple of grand in the Club's envelope. Do you think the store would be okay if we offered it to them on a permanent basis for Saturdays?"

"The store can afford it. I will take it to James and see if they are interested while you dole out the envelopes for your family. By the way, the tall brother of yours is hot."

"I don't even want to know which one you are referring to, and regardless, they are all married," I laughed.

"Just saying…"

I handed out envelopes to my family. One of my brothers protested, but when his wife tried to take his share from him, he quickly tucked the envelope in his back pocket. Katie and James were still talking. James said something that I couldn't hear and Katie stiffened her shoulders when she replied. He looked at me, winked, turned back to Katie, nodded and put the envelope inside his cut.

I climbed on top of the counter and got everyone's attention while Anne cracked a beer and handed it up to me. It was cold and refreshing after all of the craziness. Clearing my throat, I addressed everyone:

"Listen up, bitches—," My crew cheered, and the Players whistled. "Today was intense, but it could have been a complete disaster. I want to thank my brothers and sisters-in-law for dropping their plans without notice, and driving an hour to get here to help. And, be sure to thank whomever you dumped all my nieces and nephews on too!"

"And to the Devil's Players who came to the rescue and prevented us from being trampled and torn limb to limb, thank you! We truly appreciate it!"

I held up my beer while everyone on staff loudly demonstrated their appreciation. I waited for it to get quiet again before continuing.

"Obviously, we need to make some major adjustments like reducing store hours, increasing inventory, increasing staffing - *again*, etcetera. We will close to the public for a couple of days and get it figured out. As for today, my ass is heading to South Haven for some much-needed R&R. Anyone who wishes to join is welcome, and drinks will be on me. See you at The Haven's Pub!"

More cheers went up from everyone. The sun was shining, and in Michigan, we just didn't get enough summer weather.

Anne took off running to the office, squealing in excitement, and we all curiously watched her. When she came back out, she was carrying several sundresses and jumping up and down like a teenager. "I snatched these off the line last week and forgot all about them! Let's go change!"

Katie pulled me down from my perch and pushed me hurriedly toward the back, grabbing Lisa along the way.

"You know, I could have sold those today!" Alex yelled at Anne.

"But then we wouldn't have anything to wear!" she yelled back.

Chapter Twenty-Six

Arriving in multiple vehicles, I wasn't surprised to see most of the Players had arrived at the bar before us. They had the back veranda already claimed for our group, and a manager was arguing with James when we entered.

"You can't just take over this whole section. We are always busy on Saturdays, and there are only a dozen of you," she said.

"And another dozen just pulled in. And in about 20 minutes, this section will be packed," I interrupted. "Hi. I am Kelsey. I also want everyone in this section on my tab for the day," I said as I moved away and commandeered myself a stool by the waterfront. Sara climbed onto the stool beside me and looked over my shoulder to watch the birds and boats.

"Well then, I guess that will be okay," the manager backpedaled. "But we don't allow kids in here on Saturdays. We have too many customers that drink past their limit, and it's not safe for a child to be running around."

"Let me put it to you this way: if this little girl leaves, we all leave. I'm not worried about your other customers getting near her. Sara is well-guarded."

Everyone crossed their arms over their chest, driving home my point. Nobody would dare to bother Sara.

"You may want to run your policy by the owner and ask if he wants to make an exception to the no-kids rule before we spend thousands of dollars somewhere else."

"Yes, that sounds appropriate. Let me call him." She pulled out her phone and stepped away while we all waited to see if we were staying or going. She turned back to the waitresses and gave them the nod. *Yeah. That's what I thought, honey.*

"I think you scared her, Aunt Kelsey," Sara giggled.

"When it comes to protecting you, little bug, they should all be scared," I said as I tickled her and moved her over to my lap.

"Where's Katie and Lisa?" asked Donovan, taking the chair diagonal from me, while Bones took the one next to him, directly facing me. That will be distracting, I thought to myself.

"They dropped us off and ran up to the Haven Inn to sign out some rooms. We can get more rooms up the road at the main hotel if needed. No reason for anyone to have to worry about driving tonight."

"Club is covered," James said, taking Sara's previous seat next to me. "Tech had to finish up some things, and then he is bringing the van out."

"Well, offer stands if needed." I waved a waitress over and asked her to bring several rounds of shots. I was way past my deadline to get rip-roaring drunk.

It wasn't long before Tech showed up and Sara jumped off my lap to give him a hug.

"How's my favorite computer geek?" he asked her.

"Good, but I've been waiting for you. Did you bring your laptop?"

"Never leave home without it."

"Aunt Kelsey bought me a laptop for my birthday, and she let me bring it with me. Do you want to see it?"

Tech had already seen it. When he told me she was a natural with computers, I handed him my Visa and asked him to order her whatever he thought was appropriate. Sara struggled to make friends and hung out with adults so much, I just couldn't deny her such a simple thing when I could easily afford it. She deserved to be spoiled.

"I heard. I was excited too. Now we can send messages to each other, and I can show you some more programming and gaming sites."

They set up at the table behind us, cornered off from the main room. I turned and watched them for a few minutes, but when they started talking giga-something and other bits and bytes, I decided I had better things to do, like drink.

We were lively for several hours. I enjoyed the sun and smell of the water. It was nice to relax and spend time together without all the stress of customers, budgets, and to-do lists.

My brothers and their wives left after only a few rounds. I was glad I had been able to spend some time with them, I loved them dearly, and I knew they loved me, but at the same time, it was hard to be around them for long without remembering how they took my mother's side when I was growing up. They didn't mean to betray me, but in the end, that's what it felt like. It would take years to fully forgive them for not helping when my cousin Charlie and I needed them the most. I shook my head, scattering the memories. That was a long time ago.

Katie was laughing loudly at something Goat had told her. It was good to see her relaxing too. She spent too much of her young life being too serious. Which reminded me, "Hey Katie? How exactly did you end up shirtless and bootless this afternoon?"

"What? What did I miss?" asked James.

Bones, Whiskey and Goat also turned in surprise, waiting to hear the story.

"Yeah. What the hell, girl? You were working in menswear last I knew and then you came strutting your stuff in a purple bra and bare feet. Those boots I gave you this morning were top of the line too. Don't expect me to find you another pair," Alex said.

"It wasn't my fault. Those women were vicious. They came flooding into menswear and just started grabbing stuff. I don't know if they were buying the clothes for someone in particular or just damn determined that they weren't leaving the store empty-handed. Then this woman with a big nasty oozy cold sore starts charging at me asking what size my boots are. I couldn't answer. I was too freaked out by her cold sore. She just kept getting closer and closer, as I walked backward away from her.

"I ended up bumping into one of the guest chairs and falling into the seat. Then she starts telling me how she saw the sign that all the clothes the sales staff wear are from the store, so she ought to be able to buy my boots. She proceeds to take off my boots as another woman comes over to help. I just let them. I just wanted her to get away from me." Katie paused to down a shot.

"When they had the boots, the other woman said she wanted my shirt. I didn't hesitate. I took the shirt off and threw it at them as I ran around them toward the exit into women's wear. I was by the registers before I realized I was walking half-dressed through the store."

"Oh dear. You poor thing. Cold sores can be very scary. I hope you don't have nightmares," Hattie patted her shoulder, laughing.

The rest of us had stared at each other, dumbfounded, before we broke out into laughter.

"It wasn't funny. I'm telling you, that cold sore was horrific!" she declared as she raised her glass to the waitress to indicate another round.

One of the waitresses set down another round before turning to me. "Ma'am, the manager is nervous about the tab getting too high. Can we get a credit card to hold to cover the bill?"

"That's not a problem," I said, digging in my shoulder bag and pulling my wallet out. "Katie, should I put this on the personal or business card?"

"Business would be better, but then we have to talk business to make it legit."

"Business," James insisted.

"I agree," Donovan added.

Handing over the black business card, I ordered a couple of dozen appetizer baskets to go around the room. I also ordered Tech and Sara more root beer floats, which gained me grins from them, a glare from Anne and an eye roll from James. Guess he couldn't truly appreciate a member of motorcycle club drinking a float in a bar.

"Okay. Why choose the business credit card? I thought this afternoon was about taking a break?" I asked.

"You're the most secretive woman any of us has ever met," Bones shrugged.

"You've bought the property across the highway, the property next to the store and more property behind that, where you're building three houses, plus all the wooded acreage. But you haven't told us a single thing about what you are doing with any of it," added Anne.

"Or how you paid for it all," Alex joined in. "You wouldn't have gotten a loan; that's just not your style. And, I know the store is bringing in a big chunk of money, but no matter how I figure it, it wouldn't be enough to buy all that and to start building."

They all just sat there waiting, staring at me. I thought about evading the questions, but I trusted them, so there was no point. Katie was grinning uncontrollably. She knew I was about to confess. She climbed on top of her barstool, with Goat bracing her unsteady legs and yelled to the bartender, "Tequila!"

Another round of whistles and cheers accompanied her declaration.

The waitresses brought out mini plastic cups and bottles and poured right at the table. When everyone had a drink in hand, I raised my shot to the group.

"To liquid courage," I said, and downed the shot.

"Okay. So here goes," I started. "I have other sources of income that pay extremely well. The land that I am building the houses on is for me, and any of my crew that wants to move there. Right now I am building the main house and two smaller ranch houses. I have enough property, though, that I can build a couple more along the road if needed."

"The houses are for us?" Katie asked, shocked.

"Well, yeah. I wanted everyone to have a nice place to live. I know Alex and Hattie like the duplex, but if either of them wanted to move over, I would welcome them. I want to see Anne and Sara closer. Lisa is a ball to live with, but we are cramped in a drafty old house. And, you are alone too much, my friend," I said, looking at Katie. "I want you to have the option of joining the pack too if you decide that's what you want. None of you have to move. I just want to make sure you have options."

They just stared at me. The silence was making me uncomfortable as I shifted in my chair.

"You don't have to live there. I don't want any of you thinking you're obligated or that my feelings would be hurt."

"No, Kel, I don't think any of us feel that way," Anne assured me. "Sometimes it's difficult for us to believe we got this lucky. Most of us have never known what it was like to be part of a family, a real caring, loving family, and then 'poof' out of thin air, you pulled us together and made us one. You watch our backs, give us jobs, hold us when we cry, and now you are opening up a massive, top-of-the-line house for us to live in if we want? It's more than I could have ever hoped for for my daughter and myself. And, if you mean it, and there's room enough, Sara and I would love to move in with you into the main house."

I was trying to stop the tears, but when I looked around at the others, I realized I wasn't the only one crying. Even the Players had looked away or down at the table to avoid the emotions that were flowing.

"My apartment sucks," Katie interjected. "I hate going home and being alone every night. I'm in too." Goat wrapped an arm around her, and she leaned back into him.

We all turned when Hattie cleared her throat. "I like living next door to Alex in our duplex, but I enjoy Sunday mornings at your house better. I like the fact that I can walk in and feel at home. I'm in too if there is room for me."

"Hattie, there is plenty of room. Since you're the early riser of the group, I thought the room above the kitchen with the back stairwell would be the perfect room for you. The others can fight over the remaining four bedrooms."

"No offense, love, I'm honored, but there is no way I can live in a house full of women," Alex said seriously. The other men nodded, laughing and agreeing with him. Chops thumped the table a few times with a jovial 'here, here.'

"I didn't figure you would. That is exactly why the third house is a simple two-bedroom with a three-season room off the back. You can make yourself a cozy man cave, or woman cave, whatever works for you," I grinned.

"Girl, you are the bomb!" He did a happy dance that only Alex could get away with in public.

We all turned to Lisa. She turned to Donovan, then back to me. "I don't know. I like living with you. I just ..."

"You are finally ready to be a little more independent. You found someone you're crazy about, and he's crazy about you. You both need more privacy if you're going to move forward," I said for her.

She nodded, seeming embarrassed as Donovan wrapped an arm around her and kissed her on the forehead. "How did you know?" she asked.

"Please. We live together. Besides, people don't fool me easily. And, I wasn't the only one to figure it out. We just didn't bother saying anything," I grinned. "I figure the two of you would be the most interested in the middle house. It's a three-bedroom with an oversized, fully loaded kitchen so you can cook to your heart's content - as long as you feed me on occasion."

"Why three bedrooms?" Donovan asked.

"Not only is our current house drafty, but there is no soundproofing either. I can hear, *everything*."

Donovan grinned as everyone laughed and Lisa ducked her head in Donovan's neck, embarrassed but laughing too.

"All right, enough of this sappy shit," Whiskey said. "What's up with the rest of the properties?"

"Well, I am not set in stone on any of it yet, so plans could still change. As of right now I am thinking the corner lot will be for local farmers and concession vendors with a picnic area. The customers can both eat there during the nicer weather and buy fresh fruits and vegetables before they return home. Sounds corny, and there is no profit in it for me, but for some reason I just like the idea. I don't know what to do with it during the winter. Maybe just pile it with snow. On both sides of the store, I'm working on the designs for new additions for menswear and bridal and gowns. Both departments will have separate customer entrances, but connect to the main store through the back rooms. Construction will start at the end of August. I am also closing down the kids' clothing line, except for keeping our friends' and families' kids clothed. It's too competitive of a market, and we could better utilize the space.

"With all these changes, we can expand the inventory in the main store for the women's clothes. I think the current bridal section will become all jeans, and the current menswear section will become an accessories area: shoes, scarves, belts, jewelry and handbags. The parking lot, in general, will triple in size.

"The woodlands that I bought are just to keep other people away, though I think I might build a cabin out there just for the hell of it. Across the highway, I am working on designs for a country-style motel with a small courtyard. The motel would be on the back, west corner of the property. A bar with an attached diner would be in the front center portion of the property. The bar is just something I have always wanted to try and think would be fun, something rugged but not dingy, casual but not lazy. The diner would be open from midnight, for the after-bar crowd, until three in the afternoon. No dinner hours, only breakfast and lunch menus. I have space for some other type of business, but haven't decided what that will be yet." I was lost in thought as I downloaded all the information. I think that covered most of the construction. "If we switch the store hours to Wednesday, Thursday and Saturday, we will have a better handle on inventory and staffing. It will also give the motel guests the option of either staying during the week or weekend. The store also provides a customer base for the bar and diner, along with the locals who are tired of going all the way into town."

I rattled all this off without looking up at anyone. I didn't realize how quiet it was until I quit talking. I heard Sara giggle, and I turned her way.

"Was I the only one that knew all that?" she laughed.

"How did you know?" Anne asked.

"I asked. Aunt Kelsey is always working with her sketchbook. She has drawings of everything and always has them in her bag along with her writing pads. That's why she carries a shoulder bag instead of a purse," Sara said, grinning ear to ear.

James reached into my shoulder bag and pulled out a few of my notebooks and my sketchpad. I took the notebooks and stuffed them back into the bag but let him keep the sketchbook. Everyone gathered around James as he flipped through the pages.

"Hot damn, you're serious!" was Alex's reply.

"Well, it's not all going to happen at once. I don't have time to think it all out, let alone manage the construction of all the buildings and hire the needed staff. It will most likely take years and years to get everything done."

"Exactly how much money do you make?" asked Bones with both eyebrows squinted in serious concentration.

Taking a deep breath, I answered honestly, "Millions."

Once again, everyone was staring at me. *This was why I didn't tell anyone.* My friends would treat me differently now. I held my empty shot glass up to the waitress, and she rushed over to fill everyone's plastic cups.

"Kelsey, what exactly do you do in your room every night for hours, and sometimes through the night into the morning?" Donovan asked.

"I write books," I answered, downing my shot.

"And, you're good enough to make *millions*?" Goat asked.

"No," I chuckled. "I don't know. It started out when I was still in high school and I needed a way to pay the bills. It's not easy to find a job that can pay for groceries and an apartment when you can't even legally drive yet. Later, my writing paid for college and other things that I needed, but I started investing the rest of the money. That money made me more money, and it just kept going. Until now, I've never spent any of it on myself. But lately the book sales have been skyrocketing so I have a lot more available," I shrugged.

"So, you write to make money?" Bones asked.

"That's how it started, but it has become just a part of my life that I keep doing because it relaxes me and I enjoy it. Don't you ever just have these stories that keep repeating in your head and you feel the need to put them down on paper?"

They all stared at me blankly and said "No" in unison.

"Okay, so let's pretend I never said that then," I laughed.

"This is exciting!" Hattie exclaimed. "We have a famous author in the family! What kind of books do you write, dear? I want to read them."

"She writes porn," Katie blurted.

Bones spit his beer across the table, barely missing me. *Oh, holy hell.*

"Katie! It's not porn. It's- It's called erotic romance," I quickly tried to recover.

"Bullshit!" she laughed. "Honey, I have read your books, some of them multiple times. You put porn to a page like no other. And, it sells. Kelsey barely pays attention to the sales, but if she didn't write under a pen name, she would be trampled by her fans, much worse than the crowd at the store today."

"What name do you write under?" Anne asked.

"Kaylie Hunter," I admitted without pause. What the hell, in for a penny, in for a pound.

Three of the Players dropped their beers to the floor while Whiskey and Bones both stood abruptly and stepped back from the table in shock.

I was so startled that I flinched. I heard Tech behind me break out laughing. Sara was suddenly climbing the leg of my stool, and I pulled her onto my lap. The Players didn't say a word, just continued to stare at me.

"Aunt Kelsey. What's wrong? They're scaring me." They were scaring me too, but I didn't want her to know that.

"It's okay, little bug," I said, wrapping my arms around her. "Let's go for a walk and check out the ducks."

I grabbed my bag and carried her away from everyone. I stopped to let one of the waitresses know that I would be back but that Katie or Alex were approved signers on the card, so it wasn't an issue. She seemed a little uneasy about our silent group that continued to stare at me as I walked out with Sara.

Chapter Twenty-Seven

I put some quarters in the feed dispenser and sat on a bench while Sara played at the water's edge, feeding the ducks. As soon as we were out of the bar, she relaxed. I felt my phone buzz and checked the screen. It was a text from Katie: *I'm sorry. I don't know what's going on.*

Katie had no reason to feel bad. If the Devil's Players didn't want anything to do with me because of something this trivial, it was their loss, not mine.

I sensed someone approaching and checked over my shoulder. It was Haley, one of the club girls who also happened to be Candi's best friend. Several of the girls had made the trip out today to keep the bikers company and enjoy the weather.

"Mind if I sit?" she asked.

"Not at all, help yourself. I figured you guys would be heading out soon, though."

"No. We'll be here for a while yet. It will take a couple of hours for all the boys to eat crow," she grinned.

"Why? The club doesn't have to like my books or me. I just hope that my friends can accept it."

"Oh, you don't have to worry about that. Your crew was setting the MC straight when I walked out. After you and Sara had left, James said, '*I didn't see that one coming,*' and Katie turned around and punched him so hard he landed on his ass. She followed it up nicely with a *'Did you see that one coming?'* It was classic," Haley laughed.

I could picture it so easily in my head, along with Katie's smart mouth remark, that I had to laugh. I would be worried for her safety, but I knew James would never hurt her, even if he could outfight her, which was doubtful.

"Your crew is tight. They have your back. The club didn't mean to hurt you either. They will explain it themselves, I'm sure," Haley said.

"As I said, it doesn't matter," I said.

"Look, Aunt Kelsey! A turtle!" Sara said, holding a little painted turtle up in the air for me to see.

"Oh. He is cute. He's just a baby, though. You should put him back so he grows big and strong."

Sara happily complied and encouraged him on his way with little shoves until he plopped back into the water.

All of a sudden, a chill chased through my body. I felt someone watching us. I carefully scanned around without being apparent, but couldn't find the source.

"Aunt Kelsey?" Sara whispered, still crouched down, looking into the water.

"I know, little bug. I feel it too, but I don't know the source. Do you?"

"Two men on the bridge," Sara said just as quietly.

"Then come up here all casual like, and hang out with me for a bit. Fish my phone out of my bag and pretend you are like any other little seven-year-old playing a game. Be careful, though, my gun is in there. Text Donovan."

Sara played along perfectly, giggling and skipping up to me, giving me a hug and then sitting in the grass at my feet as she pulled my bag over and retrieved my phone. I turned to Haley with a big smile on my face. She was trying to keep expressionless, but she was reading our reactions and tensing up.

"You are wearing sunglasses. Can you get a look at them?"

"Already did. Two men, they look like twins with matching clothes, white shirts, dark glasses, olive complexion, black hair, medium height, black pants. Both men are armed, carrying on their lower backs."

"And their demeanor?"

"Watching, waiting, still looking for something or someone. They look too clean to be a club problem."

"Crap. Sara, tell Donovan to get ready to disappear with Lisa. Let him know to wait for me to create a distraction and then to take my SUV. Go bags are already in the back."

"Sent," Sara said. "He wants to know about us."

"Tell him we're safe. I will get us back to the bar after he gets Lisa out of the area."

"Orders received," she whispered back moments later.

"Haley, I am sorry, but it's time for us to make a huge loud scene. And, hopefully, while we are doing that, Sara can get a picture with my phone of those guys."

"Let's do it," Haley said as she stood up and pointed a finger in my face looking like she was chewing me out for something. I stood up and attempted to get in her face as well, but with her being so much taller, it required me going up on my tippy-toes and leaning my head back.

"So," she snarled, "What are we fighting about?"

Acting of any kind was not my forte, and I started to laugh. Haley grabbed me by the hair and pulled my head down. I screeched loudly.

"I'm sorry!" she whispered, "Please don't hit me but you suck at acting. I don't want to fight you. The Players are constantly coming home with bruises from your workouts and say you're vicious."

I grabbed her by the hair, returning the favor, and we staggered around cat fighting, screaming cuss words back and forth. "I won't hit you. I promise. Just keep me from laughing, because I feel like a jackass," I giggled in a whisper.

"No problem," she said before giving me a hard shove - right into the water. *Shit.*

"Ummm. Aunt Kelsey? I got the picture, and Uncle Donovan texted that they were clear," Sara said with saucer eyes, looking at Haley and then looking at me.

I was sitting on my butt in the murky water with the waves lapping at my chest and my sundress floating around me. Luckily, my hair was at least up in a clip, so it stayed dry.

"Good. Let's move inside before I start laughing again. Haley, sashay your perfect little ass back into the bar. Sara and I will only be a minute behind you."

Haley pointed and shook her finger at me again to complete the ruse and then stomped back to the bar. Several of the bar patrons, including our group, stood there watching. Katie was approaching with a concerned expression and one of our beach bags that I knew would contain a change of clothes. I dragged myself up and out of the water, and onto the dry grass. I had to hold the top of the sundress up to keep myself covered.

"Well, that was interesting," Katie said as she handed me a towel.

"Hope you enjoyed the show." I grabbed the bag and pulled out a tank top. I put it on over the sundress, and then with the towel loosely held around my waist, I pulled the strings on the dress to let it fall to the ground.

"I did. But more importantly, who was the show for?" Katie asked.

"We will have to put that conversation on hold for the moment," I said as I struggled to pull on jean shorts over my wet thighs and keep the towel in place at the same time. Finally, the shorts gave, but I think I chaffed some skin off in the process. I finished drying off the best I could.

"Let's get Sara inside," I said and followed Katie and Sara into the bar.

When we entered, I noticed James had cornered Haley and was chewing her out. I stepped up to Tech and Goat.

"Goat, please let James know that I said to knock it off. Haley was doing me a favor. I will explain later." Goat didn't wait for more information. He went straight over and stepped protectively in front of Haley. Knowing Goat would make sure the conflict was resolved, for now, I turned my attention to Tech.

"Tech, I don't want the club involved in my mess, but I don't have time to reach out to Donovan's partners," I said in a low tone.

Tech picked up on the fact that someone was watching and acted accordingly.

"Sara has a picture of two men on my phone. I think they came from New Jersey, and they are looking for the same person that we erased several weeks ago. I need to know who, how many, where, when and how. If you can provide me with any of that knowledge, I would gladly pay you a sizable sum of money. Katie can help get you started, and Sara may be useful as well."

Tech reached down, swinging Sara up into his arms and looped an arm around Katie. "Well, Sara, I think you and Aunt Katie need to meet with me at my private table over here." Sara giggled as Tech led them back to the laptops.

Large hands settled on my hips and pulled me back against a tall, strong body. Bones leaned in and whispered in my ear, "I'm sorry."

"For what?" I asked, completely confused.

"We weren't judging you. We weren't appalled by you." With everything that had happened in the last few minutes, I had forgotten about their reaction to my books.

"Whiskey tells everyone about your books and several members have read them," he continued. "To find out that the woman who has distracted me for months, is the same person that writes words that can make me cum without anyone touching me-" One of his hands dipped under my tank top, gliding smoothly across my stomach, before moving back to my hip. "It was just a lot to absorb," he whispered.

I could feel the heat of his breath on my exposed neck. I felt warm, everywhere. I was having trouble concentrating, and my breathing was heavier as I leaned slightly back into his body, enjoying the feel of his warm hands on my water-chilled skin.

Whiskey, Goat and James walked up, ruining the moment. James' lower lip was swollen and cracked.

"So. You are Kaylie Hunter, aye?" Whiskey asked with arms crossed in front of him.

"What of it?" I asked, a bit snarky.

The hands, which remained on my hips, flexed and soothed me.

"I just want to thank you. I jack off to your books at least twice a week," Whiskey admitted.

"I did NOT need that image in my head, Whiskey!" I laughed.

We settled back into our original table, except this time I sat at the end closer to the door. I motioned Anne to sit on the other side of me. Everyone except Anne, Alex and Bones were oblivious that anything was out of the ordinary. Bones stood behind me but didn't say anything. Alex took a stroll over to Tech's table and started whispering with them.

"So, what does Bishop think about your writing?" James asked.

"Unless one of you texted him in the last few minutes, he doesn't know. Why? Why would it matter what Bishop thought?"

"I thought you two were dating?"

"Hell, no. Why would you think that?"

All the players stopped talking and looked up in surprise.

"Because Bishop has been telling us you two have been dating for months," James answered in all seriousness.

"What? That makes no sense," I said in disbelief.

"It makes sense to me," Anne said. "He's arrogant and possessive. He knew if he told the club you two were dating, they wouldn't pursue the matter. It would buy him some time. But, all of you are idiots to have believed him. I mean, she dropped him on his ass a month ago in the store. He is the only person ever to be banned from The Changing Room."

I noticed Haley approaching. She made a wide half-circle in front of me, and I realized what she was doing. Directly over her shoulder, the two men from the bridge sat at a table along the wall. Her position allowed me to get a visual of both of them for myself.

"You done being pissed at me?" she asked, loud enough for others to hear.

"Yeah, short fuse, sorry."

She held out her hand to shake, but I got off the bar stool and gave her a hug. She seemed uneasy by the gesture until I whispered in her ear, "Do you know if anyone here is a really good pickpocket?" I released her and returned to my stool.

"Hey, Bridget! Meet my new friend, Kelsey!" Haley hollered to one of the other tables.

A little sprite of a thing with bouncy, spiked black hair came over. She was in her early twenties and looked a little nervous to be meeting me. The nervousness might have had something to do with the fact that Haley and I were both publicly cat fighting a few minutes ago and now claiming fond friendship. I don't know about Haley, but those types of mood swings weren't normal for me.

"Hi! I love your store. I've been in several times and get such great deals. I heard you say that you write the Kaylie Hunter books too. I'm a huge fan, though not quite as much as Whiskey. He overdoes it a bit," she rattled. I liked her right away, nervous and all.

"Hi. It's nice to meet you." I shook her hand. Over Bridget's shoulder, I saw Bishop walk into the bar.

"Can you set this up on the fly?" I asked Haley. She nodded affirmatively.

Before I could chicken out, I charged across the veranda, heading directly for Bishop. I ran into him with enough force that he conveniently crashed into the table with the two men. Both men jumped back in opposite directions as their beers crashed to the floor. I didn't stop. I charged at Bishop again as he tried to turn out the door and he practically landed on top of one of the men. I then jumped on top of Bishop, and while trying carefully not to inflict any real damage, I started acting like a crazy woman.

Several people from our group attempted to separate us, bumping everyone around even more. I made eye contact with Bishop, and once again struggled not to laugh. His eyes were dancing wildly, and he was sweating and breathing hard, as real fear overtook him.

He deserved it for saying we were dating. He couldn't handle a girl like me.

Strong arms wrapped around my waist and pulled me off of Bishop. I continued to swing my appendages like I was bat-shit crazy.

After carrying me back to our table, Bones moved in front of me, shoving my head into his chest while yelling at me to calm down. He then leaned in to whisper in my ear, "You are a damn nutcase," he laughed. "I don't know what is going on, but Bridget got the wallet. Now quit laughing because the manager is coming over to kick us out."

"Ma'am, I'm sorry, but we have strict rules on violence. You will need to close your tab and leave."

"Fine," I said, looking stone-faced up at her. I knew my eyes were wet with tears, but little did she know it was from laughing so hard. "It was worth it. That prick told everyone that we had been dating. He deserves what he got and a lot more."

One of the waitresses brought over the tab, and I signed, leaving a generous tip. We gathered up all our belongings and agreed we would regroup at the Haven Inn before deciding what to do next. Surprisingly, Hattie accepted an offer from Whiskey to ride on the back of his bike. Anne and I kept Sara tight between us, as we followed Alex to his SUV and Tech and Bones covered our backs. After settling Anne and Sara in the backseat, I turned to open the front passenger door, but Bones stopped me.

"Go straight to the Inn. Take your time fiddling around with bags in the truck when you get there. Wait for us to walk you inside." I nodded as he stepped back to allow me to get in the truck.

"Can you have both Haley and Bridget come to the Inn too?" I said before closing my door.

Bones dipped his head in acknowledgment as he scanned the lot and walked away.

Chapter Twenty-Eight

It took a good half-hour for everyone to gather. Some of the club members stayed around the outside perimeter or in discreet locations throughout the Inn. The club members I considered friends were in my top-floor suite, though.

"Anyone want to tell me why a black sedan with tinted windows followed the SUV back to the Inn and is currently sitting in the lot watching the building?" Goat asked loudly, coming in with his arm wrapped around Bridget.

He handed a piece of paper to Tech. I could see what appeared to be a license plate number. Bridget pulled a wallet out of the waistband of her shorts and passed it to me. I quickly glanced at the driver's license before passing it to Tech. New Jersey.

"Before we all go down that never-ending serious path of shit always hitting the fan, I have two questions," Haley said.

"Go for it," I said, while pacing back and forth in front of the suite's balcony.

"First, how in the hell did you not bust up laughing when you went after Bishop like Jennifer Leigh in Single White Female?"

"I did start to laugh! That's why Bones hid my face in his chest when we got back to the table!"

"But you were crying?" James said, trying to catch up.

"Only because I was laughing so hard. I couldn't stop. I mean, the look on Bishop's face was priceless."

"Lucky for us, Sara gave me the heads-up that you were about to do something crazy, and we recorded it. We can watch it in slow-mo later," Tech grinned.

"How did you know something was going to happen?" James asked Sara.

"Because, Aunt Kelsey hugged Haley. She's not a big fan of hugging, only if someone is upset or sometimes if she drinks too much. I knew she was getting a message to Haley. Then when Haley called Bridget over, I knew for sure. We were recording by the time Aunt Kelsey saw Bishop walk in the bar."

"Kid, how do you know all this stuff? You're only seven years old!" James asked.

"Unlike some people, I pay attention!" she snapped sarcastically.

Hmm. Sara was annoyed with James, and she doesn't tend to get annoyed with people. It was time to change the subject.

"Okay. Well then, you said two questions. Hurry up, what's the second one?" I asked Haley.

She turned to Alex, who was leaned back on one of the two sofas with his feet stretched out on the coffee table. "Are you gay or not?" she asked him directly.

Alex leaned forward, grabbing the waistband of her jean shorts. He pulled her onto his lap tightly, straddling her body to his and wrapped his arms around her as he kissed her. He even lowered his hands to her ass and pulled her tighter, groin to groin, as we all sat there listening to her moan in pleasure. By the time he released her, she was panting.

"I guess not then," she said breathlessly.

"Now that that mystery is solved," Bones rolled his eyes, "Who were those men and what did they want?" He looked directly at Tech.

"Sorry, man. I am working as a private consultant on this one. It's not club business." Tech nodded his head toward me.

"Kelsey, tell us what is going on," Bones demanded.

I raised my eyebrow, crossed my arms and stared him down. I was never very good at taking orders. In fact, everyone pretty much knew I despised it.

Hattie giggled as she got up and pulled bottled waters out of the kitchenette's refrigerator. Bones took a moment and sat down next to Alex. "Please," he added.

"Well since you asked so nicely, they're the mob," I said.

"The mob?" Bones said.

"Yeah. You know, the mafia, the godfather, men in fancy suits holding cigars, the mob. At least, I think they are. I haven't had a chance to confirm it with Tech."

Everyone turned to Tech, who nodded.

"What does the mafia want with a resale shop owner?" Bones asked.

"Nothing at all, but Lisa is a different story. She could start a war between the families, and if the wrong family got their hands on her, they would kill her."

Hattie handed me a bottle of water, but my hands were shaking too badly to open it. She put her hands over mine and looked me in the eye.

"We won't let that happen. We won't let them get her." She took the bottle back and opened it, before returning it back to me once more. "Now, think positive. I know you can fix this. Meanwhile, I am going to make myself useful and get some groceries."

Hattie grabbed her purse and one of the sets of keys from the stand. I looked at Bones. He pulled out his phone, calling some of the other Players. I knew Hattie wouldn't make it far without a leather-clad security unit following her.

"Where's Lisa? And Donovan?" James asked.

"Gone," I said.

"When did they leave?" James asked.

"When you were watching the staged cat fight I had with Kelsey," Haley quipped.

It must be 'Pissed at James Day' and I didn't get the memo. It seemed everyone was a little short-nerved with him.

"That was staged? Why the hell didn't you just tell me?" James asked.

"First, you didn't ask, you just assumed. Second, it didn't involve you or the club. It was a matter of helping out a new friend. It wasn't your business," Haley said.

"The hell it wasn't. You are here today by club invite only. Watch your place, Haley, or you'll be out on your ass," James barked back.

Haley was fuming but bowed her head. Anne and Katie had clenched fists and were waiting to see what I would do or say.

"Has he always been a jackass, and I just didn't notice? Or is this a special day for him?" I asked.

Haley cracked a smile at that but didn't look up. She was humiliated.

"Look, Kelsey, I'm sorry, it's just," James started.

"Don't apologize to *me*. I wasn't the one you just treated like a mindless whore." I walked over to Haley, lifting her chin to face me. She had tears rolling down her cheeks. "Are you ready to walk away?"

"Yes," she admitted.

"Then as of this afternoon, I have an open bedroom at my house. I also have a business that never seems staffed adequately. Are you in?"

She threw her arms around my shoulders in a hug. "Hell, yes. I'm in."

"Kel, you can't just steal club pussy away from us," Whiskey complained.

I was too far away to stop Anne. She threw a solid right hook, cracking hard into Whiskey's nose.

"If you didn't treat your girls like brainless whores, maybe they wouldn't be so desperate to leave. Show some respect for the women who make sure your clothes are clean, your food is hot, and your bed is warm," Anne said as she stormed out of the suite.

I didn't like her out alone with everything that was happening around us. Goat nodded to my silent request, following her. Whiskey turned to me but knew better than to say anything and just sighed. Bridget lightly shoved him to the couch, before retrieving some ice and a towel from the kitchen.

"Haley, I'm sorry," James said, not looking up.

"Yeah, me too," Whiskey said, bowing his head as well.

"I know. You both have been good to me for years. I just can't keep living my life this way. I want something more for myself than just being a club whore." She sat down on the other side of Bones. Bones leaned over and kissed her temple, as she leaned into him, accepting the quiet comfort.

"Aunt Kelsey. I got something," Sara said, eyes glued to her laptop.

Tech leaned over and started reading her screen. "Crap" was his only response.

"What is it?" I asked, coming around to see the screen. The website appeared to be a log of flight plans with the FAA. Sara pointed to one.

"This one is a private jet with four total passengers that came in early this morning. This one," scrolling down the page, pointing to another flight, "appears to be a second private jet that is leaving tomorrow morning and should be here by noon."

Leaning over close to Sara's ear, I whispered, "Sara, if this means you illegally hacked into the FAA's flight plans, you and I need to have a serious talk."

"She did, but I taught her how to cover her tracks. They can't trace her," Tech defended her.

"Are you kidding me, Tech?" I fumed quietly. "She's seven years old, and you are helping her commit a felony! Her mother is going to kill me!"

Katie, being the only one close enough to hear our conversation, chuckled. "Let's make sure she doesn't find out. Sara, get out of that site. From now on, you are banned from hacking any federal or state government sites." Katie attempted to sound serious, but she couldn't keep from smirking.

Sara nodded with a grin. I waited, watching her exit the site.

"*Ugh.* So how many are coming tomorrow?"

"It wasn't listed yet. But, I accessed the hotel's server and found rooms booked at the same time. Three adjacent rooms were listed under Phillip's name," Sara answered.

"Do we know where the first group is staying?" Katie asked.

"As a matter of fact, it appears they are one floor down. It would work out well if they simply ran into each other," Sara smirked.

I nodded, agreeing, but still needed more information.

"Tech, can you get into the hotel's security feed and get some stills of the four that already checked in?"

"Sure. You need to see the other two guys?"

"She needs to see if this guy is with them," Sara said as she clicked a couple of keys and pulled up a picture of Tommy Russo. And Sara was right. I needed to know if only his goons were here or if he came to collect Lisa himself.

My phone vibrated. It was a text from Donovan: "Confirmed threat?"

I replied: "Confirmed. Go dark."

Donovan and I had a few weeks to come up with a plan if anyone came after Lisa. I knew when he read the text that he would destroy their phones. I wouldn't expect for either of us to reach out with updates for at least a week. Donovan would keep her safe, forever if necessary. My goal was to end this nightmare for her, though. I wanted her to be able to live her life out in the open again.

"Pull it together, Kelsey. We need you," Katie said, giving me a much-needed shoulder nudge.

Anne and Goat returned carrying grocery bags. Kicking Alex's feet aside, Anne set the bags on the coffee table.

"I bought booze, booze and more booze from the liquor store. I also have a feeling that Kelsey quit drinking for the day, so I bought decent coffee as well. And now I am going to get drunk," Anne announced.

I walked back over to the sitting area and took a seat on the couch next to James.

"We need the story if we are going to be able to help," Bones said.

"I don't want anyone else in this room involved with this situation. But, I do think it's a good idea if you know who the bad guys are, so no one is dragged in accidentally. I don't want anyone getting hurt because of decisions that I made to help Lisa."

Chapter Twenty-Nine

"Lisa's real name is Annalyssia Bianchi. Her father is a New Jersey crime boss, Antonio Bianchi. Her older brother, Phillip, also sits at the table along with other influential families that fall under Antonio's control. Basically, Lisa is your average everyday mafia princess," I chuckled. "She was raised that her place would be beside the man of her father's choosing. She described her childhood as a happy one, loved and filled with laughter, despite the crime and chaos of the mafia life.

"On her twentieth birthday, her father told her he wished for her to stay as a guest with the Russo family. He wanted her to become better acquainted with Aristeo Russo, the eldest son of Francesco Russo, who was the patriarch of one of the most powerful families under Antonio's control. Her father did this as a courtesy to her. It was her duty to marry whomever he chose for her, but he loved her enough that he wanted to make sure it was a good match.

"Her belongings and one of her longtime guards accompanied her to the Russo estate where she spent time becoming familiar with Aristeo, and to some extent, his sister, Amelia. She never told anyone, but she disliked Tommy, Aristeo's younger brother, and didn't care much for his father Francesco either. She avoided them when possible and remained quiet and respectful when it wasn't.

"One night, Aristeo was out of town on business and Amelia and Lisa were having dinner when Tommy and Francesco showed up drunk. They tried to excuse themselves, but Francesco said he needed to talk to Lisa about something. After Amelia had left, both Tommy and his father tried to make physical advances. Lisa was able to flee and went to her room. Her guard knew she was upset, but she wouldn't tell him why. She wanted to wait and talk to Aristeo in the morning.

"Her guard retired for the evening, and Tommy came into her room in the middle of the night and covered her screams until the syringe filled with a sedative knocked her out. When she awoke the next morning, she found herself locked in an unfamiliar bedroom, naked, covered with bruises."

I had to pause to take a deliberate breath before I could continue.

"Tommy took some pictures of her while she was still under sedation and sent them to his brother. He spread rumors that she had snuck out of the family home for a liaison with him. Her reputation was ruined. Her family turned their backs on her without ever speaking to her."

"Bastards," Goat growled.

"She spent the next three years being the personal whipping girl to Tommy and his father. I won't betray her confidence by detailing any of the specifics other than to say that it was bad, really bad."

I wiped the tears that slipped past my guard. I had seen the marks on Lisa's body. I knew the dark violence that she had suffered.

"One day she was able to surprise the guard when he dropped off her lunch and after knocking him unconscious, she fled. She went directly to the bank, emptied her personal trust account, and left New Jersey. A week later she walked into The Changing Room."

I was trying to keep my breathing calm, but flashes of the bruises and scars on Lisa's body consumed me. I started shaking, and fresh tears rolled down my cheek. James put his arms around me and pulled me over to lean against him. I inhaled deeply before I started again.

"So today, when we spotted the men watching us, I had Donovan get Lisa out of town. Tech and Sara have confirmed that a private jet did come in today from New Jersey. I think this is Tommy and his men. A second jet contains her brother Phillip and his men, scheduled to arrive tomorrow morning. If I can convince Phillip that Tommy is the enemy, we have a chance that the families will resolve this situation amongst themselves. Otherwise, I have made an enemy of both families, and they will kill me and anyone else that stands in their way. That's why everyone else needs to stay away from this. We can't beat them. I can only try to persuade Phillip to protect Lisa."

There was silence throughout the room. Even Katie and Anne, who suspected Lisa had been abused, were shocked to hear the story. Most of the Players were struggling to harness their anger. They all had come to know Lisa as the gentle and refined woman that she was.

"I confirmed it," Tech said without looking up to meet anyone's eyes. "Tommy is part of group A. He arrived with three henchmen."

"Where did that bottle of tequila go?" Anne asked, getting up to pull the bottles out of the bags. She was in pain. I could hear it in her voice. Anne and Lisa had survived similar types of hells and had both partially healed by supporting each other. I snagged the bag of coffee and took it to the small kitchenette to brew a pot.

As I waited for the coffee, Hattie returned with two of the Players and set down the grocery bags. The Players started putting the food away as Hattie came over and rested a hand on my shoulder.

"You will figure it out. You will find a way to solve the problem. It's what you do best," Hattie comforted me with her words.

"I just can't see it this time. I have known for a month about everything, and the more time I spend thinking about solutions, the more my mind clouds with doubt. And, if I don't find a way, people that I care about could get hurt."

"You can't see it because you keep trying to figure out what you would say or do," Sara said walking into the kitchen. Tech, James and Bones stood behind her as she handed me one of my notebooks. "But, you need to think about what you want him to read. Tell the story, Aunt Kelsey. He won't be able to stop reading until he reaches the end."

"And, if I don't get it right?"

"You will," Bones answered. "But if something backfires, we are all here. Regardless of you not wanting the club involved, Donovan's old lady is in danger. I owe him a debt from overseas. James does too. We won't abandon him."

Hattie handed me a fresh cup of coffee. "Off you go now. Write a masterpiece that will save the world," she cackled, nudging me out of the kitchen.

Chapter Thirty

I stayed up all night writing, re-writing and re-writing again. By the time dawn broke, I thought the letter was pretty good, but I was too exhausted to know for sure. I had to break confidences of Lisa's to bring home the brutality she endured, so I couldn't let just anyone read it. If Lisa were here, I believe she would approve of only two individuals knowing the gruesome details: Anne and Katie.

I found Anne passed out, snoring loudly, in the Queen Anne chair, which I thought appropriate. Katie, however, was waiting for me at the kitchenette table. Hattie was making eggs and toast.

"Good morning, sunshine," Hattie greeted.

"Is it done?" Katie asked, straight to the point.

"I don't know. I need a fresh set of eyes on it, and I need it typed. You and Anne are the only ones that I can have read it. Anne appears to be unavailable. Can you read it? Let me know what you think needs to be changed?"

"That's why I'm up at the butt crack of dawn."

She took the notebook and started for the bedroom. She faltered at the doorway and asked over her shoulder, "Is it going to make me cry?"

"Unfortunately, I hope so. It has to get through to Phillip. He has to understand."

She nodded. Katie didn't like to cry.

"I'm going to take your laptop to your room to read and type it. Then I might take a quick shower. So give me a bit, okay?"

She wanted to make sure no one interrupted her if she did start bawling.

"Where is everyone?" I asked Hattie.

"All over the place, I don't know for sure. Anne was loaded. She threw all the room keys on the coffee table, telling us to figure it out for ourselves. I know the club rotated sleeping shifts last night to keep eyes on everyone. I grabbed one of the three bedrooms in the suite by going to bed early and made Sara join me. Katie must have missed the last one because I woke up to her in bed with us this morning. And, let me tell you, she is not a nice person when she wakes up in the morning."

"I remember. She stayed with me for a week once. I don't expect her to stay in the main house for more than a few months. That's why I am having an apartment made out of the upper floor of the garage. It will give her some space to be by herself but still keep her close enough to come and go as she pleases," I smirked at my deviousness. Hattie laughed. We knew our Katie well.

Hattie set a plate of eggs and toast and a small glass of milk in front of me.

"What about you?" I asked.

"I ate with Katie earlier. I only started cooking again when I heard you rummaging around in your room. Eat up. You filled up yesterday on booze for several hours followed by a pot of coffee. You need to get something in your stomach before too much more damage is done."

I didn't argue. I had the coffee jitters, and Katie was going to have a hard time reading my handwriting in some places. Hattie turned her head and listened to something I couldn't hear and then added more eggs to her pan. Minutes later Sara came in and crawled up onto my lap only half-awake. The third suite bedroom door opened, and Tech entered with the same zombie-like appearance. Hattie set glasses of orange juice out for both of them, and they were like twins reaching and drinking at the same time.

"So, I was up late last night working on an idea that Sara had," Tech said.

I raised my eyebrow, waiting. Sara lifted her head and focused on Tech, also waiting.

Hattie set fresh plates of eggs and toast on the table, and Sara reluctantly climbed off my lap to the other chair to eat. They both seemed distracted by the food for a few minutes, scooping up the eggs and taking a bite of their toast. Their actions mirrored each other, perfectly synchronized, but neither one of them noticed the other.

"That's just weird," Hattie mumbled and set a bowl of cut cantaloupe on the table that I served to both of them before adding some to my plate.

"Anyway," Tech finally remembered he had been about to explain something to me. "Sara told me that she overheard that Lisa's injuries were bad enough that she needed a doctor once. The clinic described was just over the New Jersey border into Pennsylvania. She also remembered Lisa saying a nurse named Tracy kept pushing her to call the police, and took pictures of Lisa's injuries in case she changed her mind."

I nodded. Lisa had told me all of this one night on the back patio. Sara must have been listening while playing in the yard.

"So before Sara went to bed *early, like a little girl—*," Tech rolled his eyes at Sara, and she giggled, "we searched for clinics in that area. We narrowed it down to seven possibilities. From there I had to fly solo, so it took longer, but I found the nurse. She called me about 3:00 a.m. She has the pictures of Lisa and her injuries at the clinic. She agreed to email them to me first thing this morning. She also knows not to repeat this to anyone. She sounded completely legit and eager to help. I think she will come through for us in time to slide some of the photos into the envelope with your letter."

Hattie and I just stared at Sara and Tech as they focused their attention back to eating. They seemed completely unaware that they probably just landed us the closing argument we needed to win Phillip and his family over and keep the rest of us alive in the process.

Katie came out of the bedroom looking freshly showered, but her eyes were still swollen and puffy. She handed me an envelope with white sheets of paper folded inside. She nodded at me, and then her eyes started flooding again as she turned and ran back to the bedroom and closed the door.

Bones came in as Katie was leaving. As he sat, Hattie placed coffee, eggs and toast in front of him. "Good morning, Hattie. Thank you," he smiled. He turned to me, "Is Katie okay?"

"Sure. Allergies are just getting to her this morning," I said as I drank my coffee.

"Did you get the letter done?" he asked as he dug into his eggs.

"Yes. We are hoping later this morning we will have some pictures to add to it, thanks to our little brainiacs here."

Tech and Sara both smiled.

"Is the letter good enough to do what it needs to do?" Bones asked.

"Yes," Katie answered, joining the room again. "I have been called a cold-hearted bitch most of my life, but I can't stop sobbing after reading that letter. If Lisa's brother cares about her at all, it will bring him to his knees." She started bawling again. Bones got up and held her while she cried.

Goat came into the kitchen, and I cleared my dishes so he could eat as Hattie set another round of food down. I washed my plate and then washed

Tech's and Sara's as they ventured off to their laptops.

"Does anyone know if they are still watching the inn?" I asked Goat.

"They went back to Kalamazoo about 2:00 a.m. They haven't moved since. We have men watching the hotel, and Tech got us access to the security feeds. We should have plenty of notice if they leave."

"Thanks. I think I will go for a walk on the beach. Do you want to come along, Katie? The fresh air might help."

Everyone who was awake, minus Hattie, decided to tag along. Hattie, the mother hen, wanted to stay behind to make sure everyone ate breakfast.

Goat and Sara ran back and forth along the water's edge, seeing which one of them was quick enough to avoid the next wave. Goat was the first to lose. Tech threw his arm over Katie's shoulder, and she leaned into him as they strolled ahead.

"You okay?" Bones asked me.

"I will be when I know for sure my family is safe. All of them." Thoughts of Nicholas drifted into my mind, but I quickly put up my mental wall and shut them out.

"It will work. It's a good plan."

"I made a promise to Doc when Lisa first arrived. I plan on keeping that promise if I have the opportunity, and if I am sure there won't be any blowback."

He was quiet as usual and looked out past the water to the rising sun. "Can you live with that decision for the rest of your life?" he asked softly.

He knew. He knew I planned to kill Tommy if I could get away with it.

"Yes." Images of Lisa's wounds flashed through my mind.

"If it comes down to that, let me take care of it. It won't be the first time."

"No worries there," I snorted. "He won't be the first man I've killed. And he won't be the last. Besides, you don't know what I know. You didn't see the things I saw. No, he's mine unless I can arrange it somehow so Lisa can do it herself. Then it's up to her."

"I don't have to know the things he did, or see the images that you see. It's written all over your face. I just want to take away any chance that you will regret it later."

"I won't have any regrets," I assured him.

He reached out and entwined our fingers. The gesture felt warm, supportive and comforting. It wasn't real though. It couldn't be real when almost everything he knew about me was a lie.

I pulled away. "I can't," I whispered to Bones as I walked away to the water's edge.

I felt Bones watching me, but he didn't follow. I was grateful for the privacy as I looked out upon Lake Michigan. Days like today, the lake appeared as massive as the ocean with no land in sight and the waves rumbling at your feet. Nicholas loved the ocean. He would have loved Lake Michigan too, though we never left Florida during all the years we were together.

The smells were different. The sand was coarser. But the peaceful, calming feeling when you leaned back and felt the cool breeze blow off the water was the same.

Standing by the water's edge, I felt closer to Nicholas. It was as if he was calling me. Calling me to save him. Calling me to find him. Calling me to tell me to hurry.

Tears streamed down my cheeks, but I closed my eyes and let myself feel it. I needed to feel him near, even if it was for just a few moments.

A small hand clasped mine, breaking my moment. I looked down to see Sara standing next to me, looking out across the water.

"Are you sad, Aunt Kelsey?" Sara asked.

"Yes, little bug," I answered, wiping the tears away with one hand and gripping hers tighter with the other. "I'm okay now, though," I smiled. "Let's head back to the inn."

Chapter Thirty-One

When we arrived back at the inn, it was still early enough that I went to my room to take a nap. I awoke a few hours later hearing Sara yelling and flew out of bed, my fingers already wrapped around my gun.

"Quit being a jackass!" Sara screamed as I ran into the sitting room.

"Watch your mouth, kid!" James yelled back at her.

"You're not my father. You can't tell me what to do! And, if you were my father, I would have called you an asshole, *you jackass*!" she screamed again.

I couldn't believe what I was seeing. Sara was standing on top of the coffee table in James' face. She was furious, face beet red, snarled lip, glaring eyes and clenched fists. I looked around, and everyone else in the room was looking just as shocked, except for Hattie, who was in the corner giggling at the scene and taking a picture with her phone.

"You are too young to swear! And, you need to learn to butt out of adult conversations!" James continued to yell.

"You're just acting like an ass because Aunt Kelsey doesn't want you! You keep trying to be her boyfriend or something, but she has already decided it will be friends or nothing. So you're pissed, and taking it out on everyone else! *Grow up*!" A seven-year-old, standing toe-to-toe with a grown man, let alone the president of a motorcycle club, telling him to grow up, was too much for most of the spectators. Chuckles broke out around the room, everyone trying to muffle them.

James stormed out of the suite.

I tucked my gun into the back of my jeans and went to Sara.

"Give me one good reason," I spoke calmly to her, "why you shouldn't be biting a bar of soap right now for your language, young lady."

"Because he was mean to Hattie," she mumbled her reply.

I turned to Hattie.

"He was behaving poorly, but I wasn't worried about it," Hattie shrugged.

I went in search of James and found him in the downstairs lobby. He was leaned back on a couch with his eyes closed. I sat down beside him and waited for him to finish calming down.

"Please tell me that I did not just get into a screaming match with a seven-year-old."

"Don't leave out the part about you losing the screaming match. That was the funny part," I said.

He released a chuckle in agreement.

"She is an amazing kid. I don't understand her, but she is amazing. She just doesn't fit the profile of other seven-year-old kids, and it confuses the hell out of me."

"That's the problem. You keep treating her like a child. In her short life, she has known more about pain, suffering, loss and fear than any child should ever know. Between her history and her intellect, she can't relate to other kids. We keep trying, but she's never going to be a kid that is content to sit on the floor and play Candy Land. We would be forcing her to be someone she just isn't. And, she deserves the respect of an adult when she can usually behave better than most adults."

"Is she right about you and me? Is it friends or nothing?"

"Yes."

"And Bones?"

"I don't have the desire or the time for a relationship. Most days I'm so busy juggling my friends, my business, my writing and the other projects I have going that I don't have time for anything else," I answered honestly.

"But you are attracted to him and not to me. I see it, and it drives me crazy. I have never had anyone turn me down other than to avoid the MC life. You're not concerned about the club life. Hell, you barely notice the cut. I guess it's just thrown me. And, Sara's right. I got pissed and started taking it out on others."

"What did you say to Hattie?"

"I was an ass about breakfast being cold."

I took a slow, deep breath, trying to stay peaceful. "You need to know that Hattie is off limits. She's the softer, kinder side of all of us and she both wants and needs us to protect her from the harshness of life. You need to make this right, or everyone in my family will turn their backs on you, whether Hattie is upset with you or not."

He nodded but didn't say anything.

I got up and walked away. Hopefully, he would figure this out, but he needed to do it on his own.

We checked out of the inn and piled into separate vehicles, traveling down Highway 43 in convoy fashion. James, Whiskey and Bones led the way on their bikes. The rest of the club followed behind Alex's SUV and the club van. The closer we traveled toward home, the more my nerves screamed in panic. I couldn't do it. I couldn't allow everyone else to be in danger.

I turned on my blinker, indicating I was pulling into the gas station ahead. Tech did the same behind me, and luckily, Whiskey noticed in time to signal Bones and James. Everyone followed my lead as I pulled over to the far side of the lot. I asked Hattie, Anne, Alex and Sara to wait in the SUV as I walked back to the club van.

"What's up?" Tech asked, and Katie leaned toward the driver's window from the passenger seat.

"Katie, I need you not to fight me on this and drive the SUV. Take everyone to the clubhouse.

They'll be safer there. I cannot allow anyone else hurt by this mess."

"What about you? Who protects you if we are all in lockdown?" Katie asked.

"I will," Bones said from behind me, wrapping his arm around my waist. "Goat and I will go with Kelsey. Everyone else can stay at the clubhouse." He turned to James, and James nodded his agreement.

"Promise me, Bones. Promise me you've got her back in this," Katie demanded.

"You have my word."

Katie got out of the van and stomped up to the SUV. Before she opened the door, she looked back at me. "Don't do anything stupid or I will kick your ass," she yelled.

I just grinned. I turned to Tech. We were going to print some of the pictures from my house, but I wanted him at the club too. "Can you forward me the photos? I will go through them and print what I need."

"What if something else comes up? I might be of more help if I am with you guys."

"You are more valuable to me using your superpowers to keep my family safe. That is the priority. I need to know you are with them, protecting them. Please, Tech. What if something happened to Sara or Hattie? What if Katie got hurt trying to protect me? You know them. You can watch out for them. Make sure they don't do anything reckless."

He stared at his hands, white knuckles tightly clutching the steering wheel. He finally released a sigh and firmly nodded.

I turned to Bones.

"Don't even think you can ditch us too," he glared down at me, ready to argue.

"I was thinking more along the lines that I need a ride home."

He snorted, raised his arms around my shoulders and led me to his bike. I got on after him and when he started the bike, the deep baritone vibrations of the bike hummed through me. I moved my shoulder bag, so the weight was at my back. Bones locked both his hands under my knees and pulled my legs forward, so my thighs tightly surrounded his ass. *Oh, my.*

I wasn't just tingling anymore, I was hot and wet and trying to think of anything else when he reached a hand back again and squeezed my upper thigh before turning the bike and accelerating out of the lot.

Chapter Thirty-Two

It was the longest 20-minute ride of my life, and when Bones parked the bike, I wasn't sure if I could move. I was on the verge of an orgasm and afraid that I was going to moan in ecstasy any moment.

"You need some help back there?" Bones chuckled, looking back at me.

"Nope. I'm good." I slowly pushed myself off from him and dragged my leg over the bike to stand. My legs were a little wobbly and Bones reached an arm around my waist as he swung off the bike.

"I'll go clear the house," Goat smirked, walking past us up to the back door.

"Wait, Donovan installed an alarm."

"I know. I got it," Goat answered without stopping.

I took a few steps, but my legs were still vibrating. Bones leaned in, reaching his hands down to massage the back of my thighs.

"Don't," I moaned.

"Give me one good reason."

"I need to focus."

"Not good enough."

He pushed me against the side of the house, gripping my thighs tighter.

"I want to make you cum," he whispered into my neck as he tasted my skin. "I want to feel you in my arms as you go over the edge."

He lifted me and wrapped my legs around his waist as he gripped my ass hard and pulled us groin to groin.

"I want to feel my cock against your pussy as it spasms."

He started rocking against me, and I knew that I wouldn't be able to stop. His hands clenched and unclenched on my ass, pulling me closer as my clit rubbed against our combined jeans. I was close, right on the edge. I was panting and felt dizzy. He leaned down and sucked an already-erect nipple, shirt and all, into his mouth. He rubbed harder against me while he slid one of his hands over my jeans down my backside to firmly tease my entrance. I imagined his cock entering me, and my insides gripped and twisted.

"Yes," I whispered clenching his body, as white bursts ricocheted through me.

"Yes. That's it, baby." He moaned, continuing to rock against me as my whole body shivered and shook under his control.

It took a few minutes to steady my breathing, and I finally pushed him away enough to slide down the side of the house and stand on my own. I turned toward the back door and realized that Goat was standing there.

"Umm. House is clear," Goat said, looking down at his boots, smiling.

I didn't say anything. Compared to the fact that I let it happen at all, Goat watching was a minor blip on the radar. Entering the house, I grabbed an orange juice from the fridge before heading to my desk and starting up my laptop. Tech's email was at the top of my inbox, and I double-clicked on the file. There appeared to be twenty pictures in all so it wouldn't take too long to pick two or three to print.

My photo viewer screen opened and there in front of me was a picture of Lisa; both eyes were swollen, her upper lip split, a gash on her temple, blood coating her hair and the side of her face, and rope burns embedded into her neck. I barely had time to reach for the trash can before I lost my breakfast.

"Shit," I heard Goat say as he ran over and closed the laptop.

Bones reached down, picked me up and carried me into the bathroom. He filled a cup with water for me to rinse my mouth while he balanced my weight with his other arm.

"Sorry. I just hadn't prepared myself. I'm okay now. I need to go through the pictures."

"No."

"Bones, I have to do it. She's my friend."

"And, that's why it can't be you." He stroked my hair away from my face. "Goat's already working on it. He will pick a couple and print them out. You need a hot shower and to relax for a little while. When the pictures are ready, Goat and Whiskey will run them up to the hotel with the letter to Lisa's brother."

"But I don't want anyone else getting involved. I don't want the club hurt by this."

"They won't wear their cuts. They are just the messengers. Now take a shower before I decide that you need help and strip you down and wash you myself," he teased as he kissed my forehead.

I was getting internal whiplash trying to figure out what was going on between Bones and me, and more importantly, what I wanted from Bones. He was right that I needed to relax, though, so when he walked out and closed the door, I started up the water.

Forty-five minutes later, I emerged feeling more in control. My hair and make-up were done, and I was wearing a navy pantsuit that Lisa pulled out of inventory for me last week. It was a sharp suit and with my navy and white heels, I felt ready for my face-off with Phillip Bianchi.

I went to the kitchen and stole a cup of fresh coffee from the pot. Bones was already at the table, so I joined him.

"You look great."

"Thanks." I wasn't sure what else to say to him, so I decided not to say anything.

Goat came in and set the manila envelope on the counter before joining us at the table. I started to talk, but emotions clogged my throat. Breathing deeply, I pushed the emotions back and tried again.

"Did you find what we needed?" I asked Goat.

Goat nodded. "I picked the first picture that you saw and another one of her body with sheets that cover her more intimate areas. The second picture shows the cuts."

I was familiar with the cuts he was referring to. They looked horrid enough melted into red and white faded scars across her body. I was glad that I hadn't seen them covered with fresh blood. I shook my head to clear the images. "Thank you, Goat."

"I'm in for anything that has to happen here, just as long as when it's all over, that asshole is no longer breathing."

I looked up at him and saw he was fighting to bank his emotions too. The pictures were probably much worse than what I thought. I nodded, agreeing with him. "His days are numbered."

Whiskey arrived, and they left to deliver the envelope. We included a note of Tommy's location and the goons that had accompanied him. With any luck, the families would be too busy ripping each other apart to come after us. Unfortunately, that required a lot of time wasted waiting to see what happened next.

Chapter Thirty-Three

Two hours later, we still hadn't heard anything.

"Kelsey, you need to stop pacing. And, you need to stop drinking so much coffee," Bones said, taking my cup away from me. Goat handed me a bottle of water from the fridge.

"What would you normally be doing if you were home and not waiting to see if a war broke out?" Whiskey asked.

"I don't know, researching or working on my next book. But there is no way I can concentrate right now."

"What about the business plans?" Bones asked. "Why don't you get those out and go through them with us? Whiskey and Goat both have construction experience and can give you some free feedback."

I definitely couldn't keep pacing for the next several hours. I was driving myself nuts. "Follow me and we'll look at the larger prints."

They followed me into my bedroom to the fold-down drafting table. I lowered the table and pulled back the cover sheet.

Whiskey whistled, leaning over my shoulder. "Did you do all these?" He flipped through several sheets and then pulled some rolled plans from the bin and looked at them.

"Yes. I prefer to draw things up for myself. They are not architect rated, but when I have a plan in place, I have a guy I hire who transfers my plans into the final building-project plans with the electrical, plumbing and HVAC layovers. This one," I said, pulling another roll from the bin, "is the mock-up for the main house that's under construction. I have the other two houses too, but this one was a lot more fun."

I stepped back so they could go over the plans. They went through each room, commenting on various likes and occasional dislikes. None of their dislikes concerned me, though. When they got to the second floor, Whiskey started to flip back and forth between the sheets and I knew what he saw. He turned to me with a questioning look.

"It's a safe room. And there is a drop ladder that will get them down to the first floor into another safe room and a hidden exit to the outside if needed," I explained. I pointed the entry points out. "Only the architect, the foreman and one other man on the crew know about it and are building it. It's not in the county inspection plans either so I would appreciate it if this is kept quiet."

"You told them they had a choice of where they wanted to live and which bedrooms," Bones said. "But you designed this house for each one of them individually. Anne's room has a view of the road and driveway. You even have security coaxial running to her room so she can watch the exterior camera feed.

Sara's room has a built-in desk with several high-speed internet ports. The panic room is between their rooms and above your room so you can also get to them from downstairs. Katie's room is more basic, but with lots of smaller windows and a huge closet. Hattie's has a sitting area alcove that looks over the field and is next to the small stairway going down to the kitchen. They don't have a choice of rooms; you have already decided," Bones summed up.

"They still have a choice, but I know them well. They will pick the rooms based on their likes and comfort. I would never force any of them or control them. But that doesn't mean I don't want them to be happy," I said, running my hand over the plan to smooth it back out.

"But why would a panic room and emergency escape make Anne and Sara happy?" Whiskey asked.

"It just would," I answered without answering, and rolled the plan back up. "How about we move on to the motel plans, and you guys can tell me what you think. If we get through that, I need a lot of help on the bar still." I put away the main house plans and pulled out the motel designs. They stood around me as we went over the overall building layout and then the room designs. They offered some good feedback, and most of it was easy to change immediately.

"I still think the rooms need to have small kitchenettes," Goat grumbled.

"And, I agree that if I am staying a week at a hotel or motel, I want a kitchenette as well. But, I plan on charging a little more and attracting only the one-, maybe two-night guests. I figure we will turn over the rooms three times a week. If you only stay one or two nights, having a kitchenette is not a big deal. The guests can swing into the diner for a real cup of coffee. Then, of course, they smell the fresh cinnamon rolls, *and voila!* – they are hooked into breakfast. As a bonus, I save on insurance premiums by not having the kitchenettes too."

"You are a little devious, you know that, right?" Whiskey looked at me, fully amused.

I grinned.

"Fine. You sold me. No kitchenettes. But now I need to refill my coffee and look around for something sweet to eat like cinnamon rolls." Goat lumbered out of the room, rubbing his belly. I set aside the motel drawings and pulled out the overall layout.

"So here is the overall property layout and this would be the main drive that would go back to the motel, or you can turn to the right and go to the diner or bar."

"What about these buildings over here?" Bones pointed out the east side of the plans.

"I don't have all that worked out. Right now they are just miscellaneous thoughts that I doodled onto the plan," I lied.

Bones smirked at me, knowing that I was lying.

Focusing back on the diner and bar, I started asking questions about the entrance locations and parking.

"That's it. I need a break," Whiskey admitted an hour later. "How much time do you spend on this stuff?"

"That depends. Between the store, my books, my other business investments and some research projects I work on, I don't get a lot of time to focus on these, so when I do, I usually stick to it until I fall over from exhaustion."

"Well, my brain can't handle all this thinking. I'm going to Lisa's room to see if there is a ballgame or something on TV."

"I will see what I can whip up for us to eat," I said.

"I'll help," Bones got up to follow.

"You cook?"

"Yup. Heard you are a big fan of Donovan's cooking," Bones grinned.

"I am a huge fan of his cooking. His pasta dishes are fabulous."

"Good. Since I was the one that taught him how to cook, that's points in my favor," he smirked as I stopped to gawk.

He kept walking into the kitchen and started looking through the cupboards.

"Okay then, chef, you tell me what we are cooking. And, if Donovan told you that I liked his cooking, he probably also told you that I have no business hanging out in a kitchen unless it's for morning coffee."

"He did. But I reminded him that once upon a time he had no business being in the kitchen either."

"Good," I laughed. "Then I will tell you that I can cook quite a few dishes. I make a killer pot roast, a hearty but not-going-to-kill-you chili, and breakfast foods are a snap for me."

"And why do you keep this a secret?" He pulled some noodles and cans from the cabinet before raiding the refrigerator.

"I just don't have the time to cook," I shrugged. "Everyone just assumed that I ate frozen dinners because I couldn't cook. They feel sorry for me and provide me with homemade meals, placed right under my nose. I wasn't about to correct them."

"You're kidding," he laughed. "There really is no end to your deviousness, is there?"

"I prefer to call it smart."

Bones retrieved fresh vegetables out of the fridge and set them on the table.

"Did you teach Donovan how to cook broccoli?"

"Probably, why?"

"Because he overcooks it and then tries to cover it up with butter and spices."

"Then I taught him because I do the same thing. Are you going to teach me how to cook broccoli?"

"If you teach me to make that marinara sauce, I will teach you the trick to broccoli."

"Deal."

An hour later, we put the food on the table and called the guys in for dinner. Donovan's secret marinara sauce turned out to be two different brands of sauce mixed together and then spiced up a bit with fresh garlic. I kept my word though and showed Bones how to cook broccoli to perfection. When Whiskey and Goat sat down, they immediately started to shove the broccoli aside.

"Hey, eat that. It's good for you," I scolded.

"I don't like broccoli," Goat grimaced.

"This is imported broccoli. It's amazing," I said, taking a big piece and eating it. Bones took a big bite as well and smiled at me in approval. Both Goat and Whiskey looked unsure but finally followed suit.

"Hey, this is pretty good," Whiskey complimented.

"Yeah, it's not all mushy. Where is it imported from?" Goat asked.

"I don't remember. I will check later and let you know," I said vaguely. Most likely, it was imported from the local farmers' market to my kitchen.

Chapter Thirty-Four

We were just clearing dinner when a black sedan pulled into the driveway. I went to the window and watched as Phillip exited from the back seat. He walked up to the front porch alone; his henchmen stayed beside the car.

"He's walking up alone. Let me greet him with the same respect."

I didn't wait for their reply, but went to the front door and stepped out onto the porch, closing the door behind me.

"Mr. Bianchi, I was expecting you," I said with confidence. Where it was coming from, I wasn't sure.

"Ms. Harrison, it's an honor to meet you." He held his hand out, which I accepted.

His eyes flickered to the window, and I figured the boys were openly monitoring the situation.

"I would invite you inside, but I must admit, I am not clear as to what you or your family's intentions are at this time."

"It may be best if we talk out here. I don't think my men and your men would be able to stay calm in a room together."

I nodded in agreement, gesturing over to the porch swing.

"Is my sister safe?" he asked as he sat down next to me.

"Yes. She's not here. I sent her away as soon as I spotted Tommy's bulldogs. They were distracted and didn't see her slip out. She will stay in hiding until she receives word that Tommy is no longer a threat."

"Thank you. My family and I mean you no harm. I received the letter and pictures. I can't describe what that information did to me. I am in your debt."

He took a moment to look away before he continued.

"I didn't know. We never understood how Annalyssia could betray her family, but Tommy had pictures. He was very convincing. I'm ashamed now for not demanding to talk to her. I could have protected her."

"Why did you come to Michigan?"

"We heard rumors that Annalyssia ran away. I wanted to know why. Despite shunning her, I needed to know she was safe. When I found out Tommy flew to Michigan, I booked a flight to follow him and see what he was doing."

"Now that you know the truth, what happens next?"

"My father and I will be handling this matter personally. Tommy fled the hotel before I could get my hands on him. We are searching, but so far, nothing has turned up. We have two of his men, and they confirmed that Tommy intends to kill Annalyssia. My father set up a meeting with Francesco and Aristeo as well. I am flying back tonight to see that through."

"Annalyssia goes by Lisa now. You should know that it is her opinion that Aristeo knew nothing of his family's abhorrent behavior."

"I will pass the information on to my father, and Aristeo will have the opportunity to plead his innocence. However, Aristeo was ultimately responsible for Annalyssia's protection. He will have to answer to that."

He leaned forward and braced his elbows on his knees, looking down at the porch.

"What of his sister, Amelia?" he asked so quietly I would have missed it if I hadn't been studying him.

I sat silent for a long moment, taking my hundredth purposeful slow breath of the day. "Lisa believes Amelia has dark secrets of her own. Amelia never helped her father or Tommy, but Lisa believes Amelia always knew the truth and never stepped forward. I would see how much damage Amelia endured by them before you judge her too harshly."

"Wise words. I only hope that I can control my rage when I am face to face again with that family."

"And if Amelia has been barely surviving that kind of rage turned against her by her own father and brother? Does she not earn a pardon?"

"We shall have to see."

There was a long pause in the conversation before I leaned back in the swing and looked up at the clouds. There was one more thing I hoped to gain from this meeting.

"I need your promise that when this is all over, you and your father will not force Lisa back home. She has built a good life for herself here and after everything she has been through, she deserves to choose which life she wants."

"I cannot make that promise. It's a promise only a father can make. I will speak to him and let you know where he stands."

"Please also let us know of any word on Tommy. She will never be safe until he is gone for good."

"I will. And, I won't stop looking for him," Phillip vowed.

As he walked away, I could see how Lisa saw him as a simple man, and not the right hand of a crime family. His affection for her was apparent every time he turned his eyes away to keep them from clouding up. He loved her.

Chapter Thirty-Five

Three long days later, I still had not heard from Phillip. We were all tensely awaiting any news, but tried to stay busy with work while keeping an eye out for Tommy.

Tech was able to confirm that a private jet with six passengers traveled back to New Jersey late Sunday. The Players kept close, rotating shifts at the store and at my house. They used Donovan's room as a rotating guest room for whomever was on night duty assignment. Katie and Haley both moved in with me as well and traded between the couch and Lisa's bed. Whiskey had taken it upon himself to move in temporarily with Anne and Sara. While Sara was enjoying the extra company, Anne seemed ready to stab his eyes out most of the time.

Arriving at the store early, I saw that the painters had finished the second coat in the main salesroom. The walls were now pale yellow, with accents of orange and brown with white lattice overlaid and ivy intertwined. The new look set off the size of the space. I would have to thank Lisa for suggesting it.

Katie updated the website and our email fan club. We were officially opening again next week with new hours and open only Wednesday, Thursday and Saturday. We could be ready by this Saturday, but none of us felt overly excited about it with Lisa gone and Tommy's whereabouts unknown.

Alex made some big finds that helped us restock faster than expected and the back room was already bulging at the seams waiting for the salesroom to be ready to move the stock forward. Anne also found some new gowns that she was eager to sell.

Our biggest obstacle was finding more employees. Haley was trained on registers, and I thought she would be a good fit until she decided what else she wanted out of life. But we still needed two or three more solid new employees.

"What about new hires?" I asked Katie.

"I know, I know. I keep going through all the applications, but they all seem the same. And, every time I hire someone, you hate them, and they end up getting fired."

"They don't get fired because I hate them, Katie. They get fired because they suck." I sighed while taking a seat on the office couch.

"That too," she grinned, leaning back in her desk chair. "I'm not as good at reading people as you. I mean, look around. You picked up Alex from a street alley. You found Hattie at the grocery store and me in a crowded airport. Anne and Lisa might have come into the store, but not for an interview. You have Spidey senses or something that just start tingling and you just know. I don't have Spidey senses."

"Okay, so maybe you are looking at this all wrong. When I am not good at something, or frankly, just don't want to do it, I hire someone who is good. Maybe you need to stop the interviewing and go out and find the people yourself. And, maybe, you need to take someone who is good at reading people with you."

"So you will go with me?"

"No. It won't do you any good if I go," I laughed. "I will just bulldoze through the process, hiring whomever I want, and you don't learn anything. No, I have someone else in mind to help. But it will probably cost you, at least, a hot fudge sundae."

"Sara! Brilliant! No one would suspect a seven-year-old of screening for job applicants. I love it. I'm going to find Anne and see if it's okay if I steal her."

"Later." I walked back up front to check on the contractors.

About an hour later, Alex announced on the PA system that I had a personal call in my office. I thought this was a little strange since I could answer any phone line at any phone in the store but took the hint and went to my office to pick up the line that was blinking.

"Kelsey."

"Ms. Harrison, it's Phillip."

"Please, call me Kelsey. I have been waiting to hear from you. Do you have an update?"

"I do, but I must be a little discrete. Modern technology can be tricky sometimes."

"I understand." And, I did. They probably had their phones tapped, being the mafia and all. I wondered if mine would be too after this conversation.

"First, I want to let you know that Mr. and Mrs. Francesco Russo passed away last night. Their deaths were the result of a violent home robbery that involved the death of several of their staff members as well. It was truly an unfortunate event. Their son, Aristeo, and daughter, Amelia, wanted to be sure I passed on this news to you."

"Thank you for calling and letting me know." For Lisa's sake, I was happy to hear that Aristeo and Amelia were pardoned from the executions. "I will be sure to send flowers or something. What about the youngest son, Tommy? Was he hurt during the break-in as well?"

"No. It's strange really. No one has seen Tommy. His brother has been frantic, trying to track him down. Of course, we offered to help. The only lead we could find though was a private flight that landed in Italy last night at 9:00 Eastern time. We are assuming he is there with close relatives, but have not found anyone that can confirm that."

"Well, that is distressing. I will be sure to call you if I hear from him. As for the initial purpose of your call, I can have several suits sent to you this week that might meet your needs. Should I send them to your home address?"

"Yes, that would be perfect. I trust your taste. How is everyone? How is the business going?"

"Well, we are a little short-handed right now. One of my star employees is on an extended vacation, but I hope she will be back soon. I just talked to her this morning and assured her that we would be fine without her for a little longer."

"Yes. I understand. My father is hoping to make a trip that direction with me in the future. He just wants to meet everyone. He doesn't want to interfere. He likes the thought of such independent women running a business together as long as everyone is safe."

"Well then, when he visits, I will be sure to show him all the security measures we take. I think he would be pleased."

"I'm sure he will. Take care, Kelsey."

"Bye, Phillip. Thank you for calling." I hung up and released a huge breath.

Within minutes, Tech came rushing into my office with his laptop. "You are not going to believe this," he said, slightly out of breath, dumping his laptop and other equipment on the desk.

"What? That Francesco, his wife and several henchmen were killed in their home last night?"

"How do you do that? It just came out on the news!" Tech looked completely disappointed that I already knew.

"Phillip called," I laughed. "Last lead on Tommy was a private jet to Italy last night at nine, our time. They're still looking but haven't been able to get confirmation of his location."

"I'll backtrack the flight and see if I can pick up anything. It might tell us if he is using any aliases or how he managed to get out of Kalamazoo without us knowing." He started to gather all of his stuff again.

"Stay. There is no point in you leaving, just to track me down again. Have a seat and make yourself comfortable. Help yourself to the snacks and drinks in the mini-fridge."

Tech seemed pleased by the offer and made himself cozy in my desk chair, swiveling around in circles.

Making my way back to the front, I ran into Bones and Whiskey. I hadn't seen Bones in a couple of days, and I was a little surprised he was here. It was Whiskey, though, who shocked me.

"Wow. What the hell happened to you?" I asked stunned.

Whiskey's shaggy hair and been trimmed up to just below his neckline and his facial hair had been shaved to a light scruffy layer. He was, as usual, sporting his MC cut and clothes he had purchased from the store, but the chains and heavy belt with a skull buckle were shockingly missing. He still looked manly and dangerous, but a little less Mad Max scary.

Bones grinned while the look on Whiskey's face was that of a bear woke in the middle of hibernation.

"Fricken Anne," he grumbled. "Said she didn't have issues with the MC, but if I was going to stay at her place, I was going to look," he motioned air quotes and mimicked Anne's voice, "*presentable*." He continued to sneer and added, "Either I complied, or she was locking me out and calling the police."

I knew Anne would never call the police. She wouldn't want them running her name through the system and looking too closely. I smiled as I continued to check out the new and improved Whiskey. "She did right by you, my friend. You look smoking hot."

Whiskey looked embarrassed, but I saw a slight grin and turned to Bones. "So, what's up?" I asked passing him to look at the new checkout stations from a different angle.

"I heard Tech came this way in a hurry. We wanted to see if he had an update," Bones said.

"Yes, a partial one. We are still missing the most important player. Tech is in my office researching the new information to see if it helps to figure things out," I answered while partially distracted by the register lanes. "What is wrong with these counters? I can't figure it out, but it's not right."

"You need to turn the counters in the other direction, away from the incoming customers. It will keep the waiting-to-check-out line to the west and the heavy stream of people entering to the east. And, if you move them so your tellers are back to back, you can utilize one bagger for each set of cashiers."

"Perfect," I agreed. "Jack," gaining the contractor's attention, "Sorry, but we need to change this again."

"Will this be the last time?" he asked, a little huffy.

Whiskey chuckled and took that as his cue to walk away.

"No. I am sure it won't. This is an evolving business, and things don't stay stationary for long," I snapped back. "Which brings me to yet another change, I now want the checkout counters to have lock-in casters installed. So next time I want them moved, I can do it myself, and we will both be happy."

"Fine, but it will take us awhile to order the casters, and we will need at least four per counter."

"No. You need at least six per counter, probably eight, but only half of them need to be a lock-in style. They sell them just down the road. Be sure to check the weight ratio," I said as I walked away.

Bones came up beside me and wrapped an arm around my waist. "He has no clue that he's fired by the end of the day, does he?"

"I just hope my casters are installed by then, or I will have to get out my drill and finish the job myself," I grumbled.

"I would help," he grinned.

"I bet. I have to head to menswear. Tech is in my office. Make yourself at home if you decide to hang out a while."

"Hey, Kelsey!" one of the prospects, Tyler, called out.

Assigned to the front door, it was Tyler's job to keep an eye on those coming and going during the construction. Standing next to Tyler was a man dressed in a stiffly pressed suit. He flashed a badge my way, and I motioned to let him enter.

"Problem?" Bones asked.

"No. I know him," I lied.

Bones took the hint and left to find Tech.

The man in the suit followed me into menswear and then into the back hallway, which as usual was empty.

"So, what brings the FBI to my doorstep?" I asked, slightly annoyed.

"I'm Agent Kierson. I wanted to thank you for the assistance you and Katie provided in the child abduction case. In return, I was able to get my hands on the file she requested. It wasn't easy. I have never had to kiss so many asses and threaten so many cops to get a copy of a murder file. I even received a call from a cop down there, chewing me out for twenty minutes. She knew the file was for you and said I should be ashamed of myself. She's a holy terror."

"That would be Charlie. She's my cousin. And I know how scary she is when she is working against you."

He handed me a flash drive, and I stared at it in my open palm. I had waited years for this information. It would either confirm my suspicions or dissolve what little hope I had left. My chest tightened in panic.

"Let me know if you find anything. I would be glad to help. In the meantime, if you run across any new patterns in the missing-person files, be sure to call me."

"Why the personal delivery? You could have mailed the flash drive," I asked, still staring at the flash drive.

"Curiosity. When you had Katie call in the tip, I looked you up. The FBI has an extensive recruiting file on you. You turned us down twice. That doesn't happen often."

"Three times, truthfully. Agent Benson was persistent, but I had bigger priorities in my life at the time."

"Am I to take that as you are interested now?"

"No. I still have bigger priorities. Thank you for the file, Agent Kierson."

We parted ways when we re-entered menswear.

The walls in menswear were freshly painted this morning, so I was careful to step around supplies and tarps to get to the locked cabinet in the center of the room. A few weeks ago, we acquired some high-quality suits that Lisa commented Phillip would like. I doubted he would ever wear them, being from a used clothing store, but I still intended to send them. If his phones were tapped, it was wise to ship the suits as discussed.

I placed the flash drive on the inside shelf and relocked the cabinet after removing the suits. As much as I wanted to race to my laptop and review the case file, I needed to be alone when I looked at it. Lisa and I were the only ones with the combination to this cabinet so it would be secure until then.

I found Alex jamming to his stereo in the stockroom where he was packing up the new donations for one of the homeless shelters. Luckily, he saw me, so he turned down the volume, preventing me from having to yell over the thumping base.

"Hey, Queen B, what's up?"

"I need these suits packaged for shipment. I will be back in a minute with the address. Can you make sure they go out for delivery today?"

"Sure thing," he said. "These are the ones that Lisa liked so much. She is going to be upset to see them gone. Where are they being shipped to?"

"New Jersey."

Alex laughed. "You are turning soft! I'll do up the packaging real nice, just like Lisa would want."

"Thanks, Alex."

"No problem, Queen Softy."

"I can still beat the tar out of you, you know."

"Only in America would someone rather be called Queen B than described as soft-hearted." He shook his head, grinning.

He had a point. Being a bitch was just easier.

I walked back onto the sales floor and stopped short. A very large clown entered the store wearing what appeared to be biker boots and holding 'I'm Sorry' balloons. Tech, Bones and Whiskey stepped out of the office already laughing, and I knew this was James' way of making things up to Hattie.

I walked over to the PA phone and called for all employees to make their way to the sales floor. As soon as everyone arrived, James set down a little stereo and started to dance around Hattie. She was already laughing. Then he started to sing while we all clapped along.

"I'm told I am a jackass," he sang, "and a jackass I must be. For upsetting my pure Hattie, is not what I meant for anyone to see. I know I am a jackass because smart Sara said it was so. I'm just so sorry that I did it, that I sunk so very, very low. So please accept my apology, and I promise I won't sing to you no more!"

Hattie wasn't the only one laughing so hard that tears rolled down her cheek. She wrapped her arms around James and gave him a hug. Sara ran to James, giving him his second hug and telling him he did a good job. James smiled and looked at me. I gave him a nod that we both understood.

He was forgiven. Now he just had to survive the fallout with his club. It appeared that Whiskey and Bones weren't going to let it go any time soon.

Chapter Thirty-Six

It was 2:00 a.m. when I quietly crept into the living room and woke Katie. Sneaking out secretly would have been better, but I didn't want anyone to worry if I wasn't back before morning.

"What's wrong?" Katie asked.

"I didn't have a chance to tell you earlier that Agent Kierson dropped off the Florida file. I am heading to the office to go through it."

"I'll go with you," she said, starting to get up.

"No. I need to be alone to go through it the first time."

She nodded, understanding. "Call me if you need me. I'll keep my fingers crossed that the information will help you find Max."

I hadn't been completely honest with Katie as to why I wanted the file. It was doubtful that the information would help to find Max. What I wanted to know, needed to know, is if Nicholas' death had been real or staged. Charlie argued that the DNA results came back as Nicholas' and that I was in denial. But neither of us could get our hands on the sealed case file to know for sure, and even she had her doubts after I listed all the logical reasons for believing that Nola faked her and Nicholas' deaths.

After exiting and relocking the back door, I was startled to find the Devil's Players' prospects, Tyler and Sam, both standing on guard duty on the back porch.

"What the hell?" I gasped.

"It's a little early, isn't it?" Tyler asked with raised eyebrow.

"I couldn't sleep, so I figured I would get some work done," I lied.

"I'll go with you," Tyler said, stepping on his cigarette.

I knew better than to argue. As prospects, they had no choice but to follow orders, and I was part of their assignment. It also worked in my favor to have Tyler back my SUV out of the driveway, so I didn't hit the light post again.

At the store, I told Tyler that I needed some privacy to focus on my work, so he moved the TV from my office out to the main room and set up a sitting area for himself. He said he was content just to be indoors away from the mosquitoes and watch TV. I retrieved the flash drive from the cabinet in menswear and plugged it into my office laptop. The computer hummed as the files quickly downloaded.

Twenty minutes later, I buried my face in my trembling hands and cried. I was right. The bodies and evidence were staged. Nicholas might still be alive. At least, he was as of two years ago. If I had stayed in Miami, they would have killed him for sure.

My chest constricted, as the thought of finally allowing myself to hope filled me with a twisting fear that I would fail him again. Fear that I may already be too late to save him.

I was bawling so hard that I didn't hear Tech enter the office. He pulled me up from my chair and held me while I cried. I clutched my fists into his cut and buried my face into his shoulder as my body shuddered, and I felt the full weight of my burdens.

It was a long while before I managed to calm myself enough to pull away. I realized when I did that Tech was staring at the monitor, reading the ME's report over my shoulder.

"You shouldn't read that," I said.

"What is this?" he asked, taking my chair and using the mouse to flip through the pictures and witness statements.

"It's a murder case from Florida."

Katie entered the office, carrying a thermos and three cups. She closed the door behind her. I grabbed a handful of tissue and wiped my face.

"Sorry. I know you wanted to be alone, but I was worried about you. I called Tech to give me a ride over here so Sam could stay with Haley."

I nodded, letting her know that I wasn't upset with her.

"Seriously, Kelsey, what is this?" Tech asked again.

"I was a cop. After that murder, I walked away. I left the force and left Miami."

"Holy shit," Tech said, looking up from the computer. "You were a cop?"

"Seems like a lifetime ago," I nodded. "I was recruited to work undercover assignments by the vice unit when I was still a rookie, so I wasn't in uniform much. I was actually on the fast track for a detective slot and fulfilled most of my class requirements." I sat in a guest chair.

"Do you miss it?"

"Sometimes, but I could never be that same cop again. A good cop has to be objective. And that case—" I nodded toward the computer, "—that case is personal. I haven't read everything yet, but I read enough to confirm some suspicions."

I rubbed my forehead to try to alleviate a stress headache that was building. My emotions were raw and I wasn't sure what to do next. But one thing was certain: I couldn't allow myself to buckle under the pressure. I needed to fight back. I needed to save Nicholas if he was still alive. I stood, turning back to Katie and Tech.

"This has to stay quiet. I've told Katie parts of the story, but there are pretty big chunks missing. People's lives depend on keeping this information quiet."

"It's not club business, so it's not a problem. Walk me through this, though. I'll help with anything you need."

"What don't I know?" Katie asked.

"I don't know how to even explain it all," I sighed.

"Start at the beginning. If I'm going to be able to help, I need to know the whole story," Tech said.

I thought about the information on the flash drive and how it exposed many of my enemies. I was going to need help following all the new leads and bringing everyone to justice. And, the fact was that I did trust Tech. He was smart, quick on computer research and loyal. I also believed he would keep the club out of it since it didn't have anything to do with them. It was time to recruit help, and Tech would be a good ally to have. And, it was time to tell Katie the whole truth.

"Years ago, I was working an undercover job in a seedy section of the city. We had already busted the main players in a drug ring, but I needed to keep my cover for another week or two to make sure everything was settled. I went back to the crappy one-room apartment. The apartment door across the hall was open. I could hear a young child squalling. He was so loud, I didn't think twice. I entered and found a crib with a neglected toddler, barely over a year old. Big alligator tears streamed down his face. He was hungry and needed to be changed, but other than that, no permanent damage was done. His mother, Nola Mason, was nowhere around. I cleaned him up and fed him. I moved him and his belongings over to my place and called an attorney.

"Nola came home two days later, and I handed her adoption papers and asked her if she was willing to give up custody. She didn't hesitate to sign. She even laughed and joked at her good fortune. She gave my attorney the information on the baby's father so we could get his signature too. That night, she threw a party to celebrate."

"Shit, that's cold. She didn't care at all?" Tech asked.

"No. I don't think she was capable of caring. During the adoption process, I looked further into her past, and some of the things I found were disturbing. I kept track of her, even after the adoption of Nicholas was final. She was mixing company with some very bad people involved in prostitution and possibly sex trafficking. By then, Nicholas and I had moved to my real apartment and I quit working undercover."

"Nicholas?" Tech asked, looking back at the computer. "The boy in the file whose DNA was confirmed? He was your son?"

"It's not him. I can prove it now too," I said.

"Nicholas is alive? Nola's alive?" Katie asked, looking at me in shock.

"Yes, I think so. You see, Nola was crazy, and I mean that literally. She kept tabs on me too. She was pissed when she found out I was a vice cop and even angrier when she found out that I had enough investment money to provide Nicholas with a nice life. But by the time she realized I wasn't some poor woman, living in a roach-infested apartment, it was too late. I had all the legal rights."

"She must have been furious," Katie said.

"She was, but it had more to do with the fact that I had all the power. I was a well-respected cop, untouchable. I had influence over the street because I worked the streets. I had informants everywhere, and many of the leads I was getting were pointing in her direction. I heard her name pop up in investigations too many times, and suspected she was into some pretty heavy shit. The guy she was sleeping with at the time, Maxwell Lautner, was almost as scary as she was. They made a pretty creepy couple, even in the criminal world.

"I never expected her to come after Nicholas though. Her hatred was always directed at me, not him. She was indifferent about him. But, four years after I had adopted him, I came home from work to find him missing and his babysitter murdered – and," I shook my head, trying to admit the words out loud. "– I lost it."

Fresh tears streamed down my cheeks with the weight of the admission.

"I went on a rampage search for Nicholas, for Nola. Every cop in the city was working the case. We had BOLO's and news alerts with both their pictures. I didn't think it out. I should have kept a low profile and worked my contacts."

I wiped the tears off my face, trying to collect myself, but new tears continued to surface. My body trembled, and I leaned forward, my arms braced on the top of Katie's desk to hold me upright.

"Almost a week later, I heard over the police scanner that some bodies were found in the old warehouse district. The warehouse district was Max's stomping ground, so I went to check it out. Eight bodies were set on fire and left on display, seven women and one child. Two of the bodies were identified to be Nola and Nicholas. I wasn't sure how they were identified, though."

I pushed away from the desk and paced the small stretch of floor.

"I wasn't allowed to see the file. I was put on mandatory leave and told to bury my son. Bury my son? My sweet five-year-old son? No," I shook my head, still fighting the orders. "I couldn't do it. I couldn't accept that it was him. I wouldn't believe anyone that tried to convince me either."

I was fighting the memories, arguing with the past.

"What happened next?" Tech whispered.

"The next day, I went back to the crime scene. One of the crime techs who I had worked with in the past, motioned for me to move over to the other side of the van. I worked my way through the crowd and slipped through to where he was waiting for me. He told me that my boss, Trevor, wanted me to see a letter that was left behind. It was addressed to me. It said: Leave Miami."

"And you still didn't know if the body was Nicholas' or not?" Katie asked.

I shook my head no. "I didn't know what to do. I went to a bar that Charlie and I frequented when we first moved to Miami."

"Who's Charlie?" Tech asked.

"My cousin. We've been closer than sisters since we were both little kids. We moved to Miami together when she graduated high school. After college, we joined the police academy together. She's the closest person other than Nicholas in my life," I answered. My pacing had increased into a frenzy, and I forced myself to stop and lean against a wall. "She somehow knew where to find me that night. We stayed up all night. Her trying to convince me that my son was dead, and me explaining all the reasons that it didn't fit. By morning, I had finally convinced her. We staged a big fight so it would appear we were enemies, and I left Miami. She stayed behind to work the case and bury the child everyone believed was my son."

"But how could Nola have gotten away with it?" Katie asked.

"Oh, she had help. I suspected that she had someone in the medical examiner's office. And Trevor had that crime tech show me that note. Trevor was publicly against me being involved in the case from the start. He wouldn't have let me see that note unless he was worried that I wouldn't get the message. He tipped his hand, but I still had no proof."

Tech flipped back to the crime scene photos and the autopsy report.

"It's possible. But, that's a lot of work to fake a couple of deaths. What makes you so sure?"

"Nola is a textbook version of a psychopath with no boundaries. She knew that I wouldn't stop looking for Nicholas as long as I thought there was a chance he was alive. She did a good job setting the scene. Other than Charlie, not one single cop I had worked with believed me. And, not one of them would let either of us see this file."

"Fuck, Kelsey," Tech reached out and grabbed my hand, offering his support as he stared at the floor. "I don't even know what to say."

"Say you will help Katie and me. Say you will keep my secret and help me track down Nola and find my son. I can't find him, Tech. Katie and I are constantly trying to dig up dirt on Max. He's the key to finding Nola. And, Nola is the key to finding Nicholas." I dragged my hand through my hair in frustration.

"I'm in. You have my word that no one will know about this from me. I'll go through the case and see what else I can track down."

"Why didn't you tell me that you suspected Nicholas was still alive? Why did you tell me that you and Charlie no longer got along and that she was keeping the case file away from you?" Katie asked.

"I couldn't Katie. Even now, I am putting their lives in further danger by admitting it. If anyone finds out that Charlie is helping me, they'll kill her. They won't hesitate. And, as for Nicholas, I wasn't sure you would believe me without proof. No one else involved in the case believed me. I couldn't have another person in my life trying to convince me to let it go. Trying to convince me that my mind was playing tricks on me to avoid the grief."

"I believe you," Katie said, while folding her arms around me.

My body trembled as I returned the embrace. I felt tears start to flow again, and pulled back to regroup my emotions. I had work to get done. I needed to find my son.

"Now," she said, turning away from me to offer me some space, "tell us what we can do to help."

I opened the credenza behind Tech and pulled out a small decorative treasure chest. Picking up my keys, I unlocked the chest and set it on the desk.

Tech flipped the lid open. It was filled with flash drives.

"You will want to make copies of all of these, and the one in the computer. I need the originals to keep researching on my end."

"I'll copy them tonight and get started. It will take me awhile to catch up on all of this, though. And, Kelsey," he said, "we'll find him."

I nodded but didn't say anything else as I sat in my desk chair and started reading through the ME's report again. Tech and Katie settled in at her desk and began copying the other flash drives.

Chapter Thirty-Seven

Two more days passed. I was restless, pacing back and forth in the front of the store.

Most of the store was back in order. As expected, I installed the casters on the register counters myself after I fired the snarky contractor. I didn't bother calling Bones, but the prospects, Tyler and Sam, helped me flip the counters over and set them back up.

All the rooms except bridal and gowns were stocked and ready. Sara earned herself a huge hot fudge sundae by helping Katie find three new employees in two hours. Katie was convinced that I wasn't going to hate them. I decided to reserve my opinion until they started next week.

Not able to clear my head, I called Tech as I continued to pace.

"No," he answered. "Again, I can't find anything on Tommy. I even had the little genius look, and she couldn't see anything that I missed. I have no idea where he went. He's underground somewhere."

"That's not good. I talked to Lisa this morning, and she wants to come back."

"She can't. It's not safe," he said.

"I know, but I don't know how much longer I can stall her. She's homesick and worried about everyone here. Hell, I fully admit I miss her princess designer ass strutting around the store educating us all on the Parisian fashions. And, I have the store to keep my mind busy, so she must really be going crazy. I don't like this at all. My fear is that Tommy could be hiding close by, waiting for her to return."

"Tell me something else to try?"

"I don't know. Sorry, I'm snapping at the messenger. You've done a great job helping us out. I told Katie to cut you a consulting check too. You should have it later today."

"Thanks. I would have done all this for free, but I could use the money for a new tire on my bike."

If he was thinking a tire-size paycheck, he was in for a shock. The payment was more along the lines of a downpayment on a house. I had called Donovan's partner, asking what the going rates were for similar computer jobs. He even wanted to know if Tech was interested in sub-contracting out some jobs for them. Of course, I didn't know. I recommended that they wait until Donovan returned to talk to Tech. I also didn't say that Tech was busy sifting through the flash drives looking for Nicholas, Nola and Max.

"I need to go. Keep in touch if you find anything." I disconnected and continued pacing.

Tommy had a plan, and I just needed to figure out what it was if I was going to stop him.

"Hey, boss lady," Anne approached. "The contractors that are working on Alex's house called. They wanted to let you know that it looks like someone slept there last night. Nothing was missing or broken, but they want you to make the decision of whether to call the police or not. I already asked Alex and it wasn't him."

The hairs on my arms stood up, and I grabbed the PA system handset.

"All employees to the front of the store. All employees to the front of the store, immediately."

Anne took off running to find Sara, but Sara was already running toward her from the back room. Hattie and Alex hurried through the doors as well. The contractors that were working on small projects also moved out to the front, probably due to the frantic tone of my voice. Haley flew out of bridal. Two part-timers entered from menswear. I was searching and cataloging everyone's faces as they arrived. Taking roll call in my head, as my pulse beat faster and faster. No one else came rushing out.

"Where's Katie? Where the hell is Katie?"

"Relax, Kelsey. It's okay. She had a headache and went home to lie down for a while. I'm sure it was just all the paint fumes getting to her. Everything is fine," Alex assured me, placing a hand on my shoulder.

I stepped away from him and started pacing again. Despite his words, my gut was telling me something was wrong.

A memory flashed through my mind of everyone telling me that I was losing it. They all thought I was crazy.

Was it paranoia driving me now? Or the honed instincts I learned being undercover on the streets?

I needed to know everyone was safe. I needed to see it for myself. I needed to pull myself together and focus.

"I am going to check on Katie. Anne, please call Bones and James and ask if they can check out the break-in at Alex's house. Stay here until I get back. Don't let anyone you don't recognize in the building, and that means, as of right now, lock it down. The contractors can either stay inside or quit for the day, but I want the doors locked and the alarm activated."

I grabbed my shoulder bag out of the office before walking out the back door of the building. Luckily, I didn't get pulled over on my way home, because they probably would have pulled my license at the speeds I was traveling. I knew I wasn't acting rational, but I didn't care. When I pulled into the driveway, I saw Katie's car, but no other vehicles. I was feeling a little better until I got to the back door and saw it was partially open. I knew instantly: Tommy had Katie.

I dropped my bag on the porch and pulled my gun from its holster at the base of my back. Without breathing, I slowly entered through the back door. I checked the alarm panel and saw the wires ripped out. There was no way for me to use it to signal for help. Backtracking to the porch to retrieve my phone was the right move, but I chose to move forward instead. I had to get to Katie.

Clearing the laundry room, I proceeded into the kitchen. It was an open space, so it was easy to confirm it was empty. The bathroom was off to the left, so I moved slowly along the wall, peering around the doorway to see that it was also clear. I turned to approach the entrance to the dining room.

Pain ricocheted up my arm as I was struck with one of my baseball bats. I watched in horror as my gun dropped to the floor. I felt another gun press tightly to the back of my skull.

Shit. I forgot to check the basement door, off the laundry room. He must have been waiting there for me to pass by him.

"No sudden moves or your friends will have one hell of a mess to clean up," he laughed.

I didn't see the humor. A shiver of real fear snaked down my back.

"Where's Katie?" I asked, faking confidence that I no longer felt.

"She's in the living room waiting patiently for us. Let's say hello." He nudged my head with the gun, and I slowly approached the dining room that opened into the living room.

I was halfway through the dining room before I saw Katie. Tied to the weight bench along the far wall, she cried and choked on the gag that was tied around her head. She had a bruise forming on her tear-soaked cheek. Her shirt was torn open, but her bra was still secure, along with her jeans. He hadn't raped her yet. When she saw me, her panic increased, and she started trying to scream through her gag.

"Katie, calm down. It's going to be o-" I felt something slam into the side of my head. I slid to my knees and fell forward on my hands, feeling the blood on the side of my face before watching it drip on the carpet beneath me.

The last thing I heard before everything went black was Tommy whispering in my ear, "It's never going to be okay again, for either one of you."

Chapter Thirty-Eight

When I woke, I was tied to my bed. My hands were bound together, with another rope looped through to secure them above my head to the headboard. My head was pounding. Trying to turn my body to the side, a rush of nausea swept through me and my vision blurred. I closed my eyes and took deep breaths to calm my rising panic.

I heard Katie whimper from the other room. I had no idea what the monster was doing to her.

"Hey, dickhead!" I yelled.

Pain lanced through my head from yelling, but I took another breath and continued.

"Would you mind cutting me loose now?"

My stomach rolled at the thought of provoking him. If I could keep him focused on me, though, he wouldn't hurt Katie. I just needed to survive long enough for the others to realize something was wrong. They would call either the police or the club. Maybe they already had. I wasn't sure how long I had been out, but I guessed not more than 15 minutes since the blood on the side of my face wasn't dry yet.

"Ah, sleeping beauty is awake." Tommy entered, holding a long knife in one hand and his gun in the other. "Truthfully, Katie is the beauty between the two of you. She has those long shapely legs and long luscious hair. In fact, she reminds me a lot of my Annalyssia."

He moved onto the bed next to me, setting his gun on the nightstand. "But don't be jealous, they don't have tits like you do," he laughed. "Yes. These are an amazing set of tits. I'm sure a whore like you already knows that, though."

He roughly grabbed one of my breasts and started kneading it painfully.

"I have watched you with those dirty bikers, coming and going, putting their filthy hands on you. Lucky for you, as much as you tease them, you go to bed alone."

He leaned forward, slowly inhaling along the side of my neck, whispering in my ear as he continued to fondle my breast. "And, such perfect skin, so smooth and soft. You and I are going to have a lot of fun. Well, at least I promise I will."

Releasing my breast, his hand traveled down my shirt to cup my sex in a gripping hold. I tried to move away, but it was futile. And, the more I moved, the deeper the ropes cut into my wrists.

"You are one sick *son of a bitch*!" I spit at him.

He punched me in the face.

It happened so quickly, I didn't have time to turn away. My cheek and eye shared the impact. My face instantly throbbed in excruciating hot, searing pain.

"No swearing!" he screamed. "Women should never swear!"

He landed another fist to my abs, knocking the wind out of me. He climbed on top of me, setting the knife down beside him and gripped one hand tightly around my throat as he shrieked at me and hit me with the other.

I took the beating and the choking, all the while gritting my teeth. I tried to remain as quiet as possible. Chances were good that he was going to kill me. I didn't want Katie's last memories of me to be echoes of screams of pain. I also didn't want to give the psycho the satisfaction.

I focused my eyes on the nightstand beside the bed. Hidden behind it was the picture of Nicholas and me on that beach. I held the image in my head, forcing the here and now out as much as possible. I could smell the sand and salt. I could hear Nicholas' laughter mixing with the sound of the lapping waves. But my body continued to throb in pain and by the time he quit hitting me, the image of Nicholas vanished and tears rolled down my cheeks. Tommy released my throat, and I gasped for a solid breath of air.

"I'm sorry I had to hurt you. You have to learn the rules, though." He stroked my cheek, wiping the tears away. It would have been a gentle gesture if he wasn't such a monster.

He stood up, ready to leave the room. I could hear Katie crying, trying to yell through her gag.

"That all you got, asshole?" I weakly challenged. My voice was hoarse and sounded foreign to my own ears.

"Well, you are a stubborn one, aren't you? No wonder Annalyssia hid out here. She used to be stubborn too until she was properly trained, of course."

He picked up the baseball bat that I kept in the corner of the bedroom. Without hesitation, he raised it over his head and bashed it down on my leg.

I grunted, groaned and ground my teeth as the pain sliced up through my body. I uncontrollably twitched and jerked against the ropes, digging them deeper into my skin.

I stared at my leg in horror, as I gasped to breathe through my panic-constricted lungs. Even through the tears that blurred my vision, I could see it was broken, lying at an odd angle.

I barely turned my head in time to vomit on the pillow next to me. Gasping for air, the vomit, tears and blood threatened to cut off my oxygen from my already-bruised throat. My mind drifted back to Nicholas, and if I was going to die, I was glad that I had given Tech the files. He would help Katie find Nicholas. They would never stop searching for him.

Hysteria had finally set in. Images flashed in my mind of the club, Lisa's family, and my new family getting their hands on this man, tearing him to pieces limb by limb. He was a dead man. And, it would be a brutal death for him.

I pulled my head up as far as my restraints would allow. "You made a mistake," I said. "Whether I live or die, you'll get what's coming to you. Just like *dear old Daddy*. They're going to kill you, *slowly*," I laughed at him.

By his reaction, I knew he had heard of his father's death. He glared at me with such hatred that I was certain the next swing of the bat would be my last. Instead, he turned and threw the bat across the room. His face was a blistering red, and I could see his pulse rapidly pumping in his neck as he began to pace back and forth.

"I think you would have liked dear old Dad. He especially had a fondness for knives."

He picked up the long serrated blade. He stalked toward me with the knife, glaring, hatred radiating off him in waves.

"Yes. I think it would be good to teach you a few lessons using one of dear old Daddy's favorite techniques."

He dragged the blade under the edge of the buttons on my shirt, sending them flying one by one. After the shirt, he slid the knife under the center of my bra and swiftly cut the thin piece of fabric. My breasts pushed out of their confines.

He placed the knife against my skin and slowly dragged the sharp edge over my breast, slicing into my skin. I gritted my teeth and tried to focus on something else. The blade dipped lower, as he slashed across my upper abs. I was having trouble breathing through the pain, and my eyes continued to blur through the tears. The knife dragged farther down, scraping under the button of my jeans, sending it flying. *God no.*

"I see the fear now," he taunted, his eyes never leaving my face.

He inhaled loudly. "And I can smell it too," he grinned.

I wasn't sure how much more I could take. I still clenched my teeth. I clenched them so tightly I was sure they would snap under the pressure. My muscles contracted and shook as every nerve in my body screamed.

Without another word, he turned and walked back to the living room.

I could hear Katie's cries but tried to block them out.

I needed to think. I needed to protect us if we were going to live through this.

My knives, I thought.

I kept a switchblade hidden inside each of my boots. My only chance of fighting him was cutting myself loose. The blade inside of the boot with the broken leg was useless, but I could use the other one.

I grabbed ahold of the headboard, and through the pain, I rolled my lower body upward. My broken leg didn't move, but I was able to twist enough to get my other leg up by my hands. Holding the position by clenching my muscles, I released my grip on the headboard and pulled my knife from the hidden sleeve inside my boot. I hit the switch, and the blade clicked out into place.

Dropping my weight back to the bed, I quickly started sawing at the rope that held me to the headboard. If I could only cut myself loose, I could access several guns that I kept hidden around the room.

My hands were sweaty and shook with fear. Twice I almost lost a grip on the knife as Katie's cries became louder. I felt the rope start to give, and in my rush for freedom, I pulled my weight against the ropes to break their last threads. The headboard creaked loudly as the rope gave, and my body was thrown off the side of the bed as the tension was removed.

I scrambled to my hands, pulling my good leg under me and tried to rise as Tommy came rushing into the room, tackling me flat to the ground.

With his body weight on top of me and my front pressed to the carpet, I was at his mercy. In his rage, he lost his control and rolled me swiftly. That was his first mistake.

With both hands still bound together, I plunged my switchblade into his chest. With the use of my good leg, I slid back and realized that I still held the blade in my hands. I raised my arms and plunged the blade into his chest again. It planted itself deep under a rib.

He shrieked in pain, pulling away from me, and I rolled out of his reach.

Once again on my stomach, I pulled my good leg underneath me and used it to push upward and forward from the floor, landing only a foot away from my dresser. I grasped the carpet with my sweaty, shaking fingers and pulled myself forward the remaining distance.

Reaching underneath, I tried to feel the holster attached to the underside of the dresser, where I had a revolver hidden. Tommy screamed out in pain across the room. I turned to extend my reach under the dresser and saw recognition register across his face that I was trying to reach something. He fumbled, trying to reach for his gun on the nightstand, as he used the bed to pull himself up off the floor.

He screamed again in a mixture of pain and rage, my switchblade still embedded in his chest. My hand gripped the handle of my revolver. As he stood, gun in hand, turning back to me, I pulled my gun out of the holster, leaned back and took aim.

"This is for Lisa," I said as I pulled the trigger.

The bullet hit him in the face.

I watched blood and brain splatter the wall behind him as his body crumpled in slow motion into a pile on the floor.

I could hear Katie screaming through her gag, but I couldn't move. I was too tired, too weak, and part of me knew that I still might die.

My body slumped to the side, no longer able to support me. I wanted to reassure Katie that I was okay, but I couldn't find the strength to form the words.

Right as darkness closed in around me I heard heavy boots running toward me. "It's going to be okay, babe. Hang in there. Call an ambulance!"

Then I slid into the blackness.

Chapter Thirty-Nine

"Bones, keep your shit together," I heard James demand, followed by a loud thud against a nearby wall.

I moved slightly, and every bone, nerve and muscle cinched up as spasms of pain rippled through my body. Moving slower, I forced myself to turn toward the sound. I opened my eyes, or at least one; the other one didn't seem to be working. James and Whiskey held a heavily panting Bones against the wall. He appeared furious, glaring past the foot of my bed.

Turning my head, I saw two cops I didn't recognize. Doc was blocking their path.

"Kelsey is my patient," Doc sputtered, "and you will not be allowed to question her until I determine she can handle it. She has two broken bones, several fractures, a concussion and well over 100 stitches. Now is not the time to get a damn statement," Doc steamed. *Go Doc.*

The cops must have taken him seriously enough because they left the room without another word. Whiskey and James stepped away from Bones, catching my attention. Bones was no longer looking that way, though. He was watching me closely. He slowly stepped toward me with his hands up, as if to let me know that he wouldn't hurt me. Of course he wouldn't, it was Bones.

I attempted to smile and nod at him the best I could through the bruising and swelling. The relief in his eyes was as apparent as the large breath of air he released. He continued walking over to the bed.

"Hey beautiful," he whispered as he leaned over and gently kissed my forehead.

"I lived," I murmured in a scratchy voice.

"We are all so proud of you. You're safe now. You need to sleep more."

"Katie?" tears pooling in my one good eye, blocking what vision I had left, as I started to panic.

"Shh. Shh. Shhh. She's fine," he whispered, soothing me again, petting my hair from my face. "She only has one bruise on her cheek. You protected her from the rest. You protected her, babe."

Katie was okay. Katie wasn't hurt. I managed to keep the monster away from her. These were the thoughts roaming through my head as I stopped fighting the drugs that pulled me back under in a deep sleep.

One week after the attack

It had been a week from hell, and I'd had enough of being at the hospital. I honestly couldn't understand how anyone could ever get well in such a place. The hours of people coming in and out, waking me up for various reasons, was ridiculous. Nurse shift changes, resident checks, doctor rotations, x-rays, meals, visiting hours, … it never ended. Once I was off the morphine, I didn't sleep for more than an hour at a time.

Except for my broken leg that was loaded down with a heavy cast, the rest of my injuries were starting to heal. I could even see out of my left eye again, though the skin surrounding it was a rainbow of colors.

Tech snuck the detectives assigned to my case in yesterday. I gave them my statement while everyone that was in overprotective mode was away. They explained that there was enough evidence at the house to support that Tommy's death was in self-defense. They only needed my statement to close the case.

Hattie had arrived this morning with a home-cooked breakfast that I managed to devour just before Doc arrived in my room.

"You're looking better," Doc said.

"Yes, she is," Hattie agreed. "Does this mean she gets to leave today? I know she is anxious to get out of here."

"Well, we were hoping to release her this morning, but we hear fluid in her lungs. Dr. Tasket and I agree that she should stay here another day or two until it clears up."

"You have got to be kidding me!" Katie screeched from the doorway. "Of course she has fluid in her lungs." She finished entering the room with Tech and Whiskey following behind her. "Look at all these flowers. She has allergies. Get them out of here!" she barked.

Doc, Whiskey and Tech started bailing the flowers out of the room as if my life depended on it. Katie ransacked the bedside table and pulled out my shoulder bag. She retrieved my pill bottles and handed me an antihistamine and an expectorant tablet. Hattie handed me a glass of water. I gladly swallowed both as Katie adjusted my bed.

Doc examined the pill bottles and shook his head. "You should have said something, Kelsey."

"Everyone shouldn't have kept me away," Katie ranted. "This would never have happened if you would have let me visit sooner. Kelsey's too polite to turn away the deliveries, even if she can't breathe. Didn't anybody ever notice the flowers at the store are silk?" she grumbled, shaking her head.

"Does this mean I get to leave today?" I interrupted her tirade.

"I will come back in an hour. If your lungs sound better, we will start the discharge process. I will also alert the nurses to turn away any further deliveries for you." Doc tried to sound stern, but couldn't hold back his smirk as he turned and left the room.

I smiled at Katie. "You totally saved me. I couldn't have survived another day in this place."

"I owe you much more than that, my friend, much more." She turned away and started cleaning up the room. I knew it would take time before either one of us would put this behind us.

Two hours later, I had signed the release papers, and I was getting dressed when Bones entered. Luckily, I already had a tank top on, covering the stitches on my chest. I wasn't ready for anyone else to see the horrific damage. Bones helped me finish dressing in sweatpants, one shoe and a second tank top. I was going to have to layer my shirts for a while until I could wear a bra again.

"I don't know if I can sleep in that house," I admitted quietly, my hands shaking.

"You don't have to," he answered. Placing his hands over mine, he leaned forward and gently kissed my forehead.

After helping me slide gingerly off the bed, he pivoted me into a wheelchair and propped my broken leg up on the stand. As he pushed the chair into the hall, he handed my bag and crutches off to Tyler. I was a little surprised that none of my overprotective friends came to escort me home.

When we exited the building, I inhaled the fresh air and coughed when I inhaled nearby cigarette smoke. The smell didn't bother me, having been a smoker for many years; it was just a surprise to my lungs.

The man who was smoking nearby realized the smoke had come my way. "Sorry. I should be standing farther away from the building," he said sincerely, as he tried to waft the smoke away.

"Probably, but I will forgive you if you let me take a hit off your cigarette," I smiled back.

"Miss, you can have it. Looks like you need it more than I do," he said, handing it over.

I took a deep drag and held it in, appreciating the flavor and calming effect.

"That's enough," Bones ordered, taking the cigarette from me and handing it back to the stranger.

"Thanks," I said, winking at the man before Bones pushed me to the entrance curb.

Tech was behind the wheel of my SUV as it pulled alongside the curb. Katie jumped out of the passenger seat and helped me into the back. She still couldn't make eye contact with me. I didn't know how to ease her pain. She closed my door and settled herself back in the front as Tech pulled away from the curb.

I was startled by the surround-sound of Harleys. Looking out the front, I saw James, Bones and Whiskey leading the way in front of the SUV. Turning around, I saw what must have been forty bikes, following us in rows of two.

"I don't understand," I said, bewildered.

"Yes, you do," Tech said.

Thinking about it, he was right. I did understand. Because when one of your own is scared, you surround them. You protect them.

Tech passed the turnoff for my road and kept heading west. I figured we were going to the store for some reason, and I was okay with that. When I saw the bikes pass the store and turn left onto the side road, I was confused. The new houses wouldn't be complete for another month at least. When I had last walked through the main house, they were still putting up drywall.

I was further surprised to pull into the driveway and see all of my friends standing in the front yard waiting for us. Behind them, contractors stood occupying the rest of the yard.

I opened my door and removed my seatbelt. I wasn't ready to jump out on my own. Bones was at my side quickly and carefully lifted me out. I balanced on my good leg while I aligned the crutches. He walked beside me with a hand on my back, ready to grab me if I wobbled too much.

"Why are we here?" I asked, looking around at everyone.

"Because it's your home," Bones answered.

"But we are a month away from completion."

"All three contracting companies, your crew and the MC joined forces to finish the main house so you could come here when you were released. We even had strangers showing up to help at all hours of the day and night when word got out what we were doing. Katie even threatened the inspectors and made them stay for same-day re-inspections. Which, by the way," he leaned in and spoke quietly so only I would hear, "She kind of scares me."

● ● ●
330

"That's my girl," I smiled.

"I can't believe you all did this," I said to everyone. "I can't tell you what it means to me. The thought of going to the old house—," I said, stumbling over my words. I couldn't finish that sentence and just shook my head and abandoned the thought. "Thank you."

The front door opened into the dining room. A large formal mahogany table with high-back chairs sat in the center of the room. A staircase to the right led to the second floor. To the left was a wall that hid the galley-style kitchen with a small table and another small staircase by the garage door that also led to the upstairs. Behind the staircase was the door to the basement where I had planned not only a full-size home gym but several locked storage rooms that would be available for my investigative work.

In front of the dining room was a large living room with French doors that led out onto a balcony. A hallway split off to the right between the living room and the dining room. The first room on the right was a spare bedroom that I hoped someday would be Nicholas'. On the left was the entrance to a large family room filled with casual, oversized furniture. The last door, though, was my private suite.

I opened the door to see the oversized bedroom with dual side-by-side walk-in closets. Beyond the bedroom was a private atrium that already held a good number of beautiful green flourishing plants. I took a moment to sit on one of the beige couches, staring about the peaceful room. It was everything that I had hoped it would be. It was a home that I hoped someday would keep Nicholas happy and safe.

Everyone was hell-bent on keeping me entertained and comfortable, but after a while, I couldn't tolerate sitting anymore. Using my crutches, I managed to make my way to the back balcony where James and Whiskey were.

They both smiled when I stepped out. James offered to pull a chair out on the deck for me.

"No thanks. I just want a fricken cigarette." I tilted my head at Whiskey and gave him my best pouty face.

"Fine, but if Bones asks, you didn't get it from me." He discreetly snuck one out of his pocket, looking around nervously, and handed it to me.

Good grief. Guess if I decided I wanted a joint, I would need to find someone else to ask. I took the cigarette and the lighter and lit up.

12 days after the attack

The stitches came out this morning. It took a long time and was uncomfortable, as an intern and the plastic surgeon carefully removed them. With my left breast still swollen, it would be at least another week before I could attempt to wear a bra. I was larger breasted for my body size, and it was obvious when I didn't wear one. But, as sore as I still was, I didn't care.

I had stopped taking the painkillers after I left the hospital. Without them, I was having trouble sleeping through the night and often woke soaked in sweat from nightmares. The lack of sleep was making me jittery, and I startled easily. I had two panic attacks, and either luckily or unluckily, both were in front of Sara; lucky, because Sara knew from personal experience how to bring me down from them and unluckily because I could see in her eyes that they scared her. I am supposed to be the one reassuring her, not the other way around.

15 days after the attack

I was getting worse. Everyone's worried facial expressions had become impossible to tolerate. I couldn't sleep long enough between the nightmares to function. I started working alone at night and then leaving late morning to sleep while everyone was away from the house. The new schedule at least kept me from waking everyone in the middle of the night because of my nightmares.

I was never actually alone, though. Someone from the club was always close, no matter where I was. It was usually one of the prospects, Sam or Tyler. Both were polite and friendly and didn't interfere. They had the impossible job of making sure I felt safe, even though I was no longer in danger. But, what I desperately needed was to feel in control again. I needed the nightmares to stop.

18 days after the attack

It was on that 18th day that I arrived home late in the morning to find a box lying on my bed, wrapped in shiny baby blue paper with a big white bow. Initially, the thought of someone being in my room made me uneasy, but I slowly forced myself to approach the box and look at the card lying on top. "*For Kelsey,*" it said on the outside of the card. I pulled the card off and opened it. Inside it read: "*Maybe this will help. Love, Bones*"

I pulled the white ribbon away and slipped the lid off the box. Inside were several notebooks and a shiny new silver pen. I didn't need any further instructions. I understood his intent. I carried the box of supplies into the atrium and began to write.

36 days after the attack

I got up this morning and, without anyone reminding me, showered and put on clean clothes. When I entered the kitchen, Hattie seemed surprised but greeted me as if nothing was unusual.

"Good morning, sunshine."

"Good morning, Hattie," I said, placing a kiss on her cheek and retrieving my cup of coffee. "Is everyone already at work?"

"Yes. Everyone except Sara and I went in around 7:00 this morning."

Glancing at the clock, I noted it was approaching 8:00.

"What day is it?" I asked, surprised that I had no idea.

"Monday," she answered as she put some eggs in a pan and started to scramble them. She paused, looking toward the garage door before she smiled and added some more eggs to the pan. I knew her super-human hearing picked up something I had missed and wasn't surprised when Bones walked in a minute later and greeted her with a kiss on the cheek as she handed him a coffee.

I just smirked and shook my head. Hattie had us all wrapped around her finger.

"So why is everyone at work so early on a Monday? It's a restock and laundry day," I asked, sipping my coffee, sitting at the small kitchen table.

"Oh, I don't know, dear. It's a mystery," she said, giving Bones a strange look.

Bones sighed and shook his head. "I hear you sent an email to Tech last night asking him to do some proofreading for you," Bones questioned me while he focused his attention on his coffee.

"I finished my writing project last night and wanted his opinion on it."

"He stayed up all night and wouldn't let anyone else see it. This morning he flew out of the clubhouse at the crack of dawn with his laptop."

"Hmm. I will call him later and make sure it didn't upset him too much. That wasn't my intent. Maybe I shouldn't have shared it with anyone."

I was staring at the table when Hattie set plates of eggs and toast in front of both of us. I grinned at finding fresh fruit cuts on the plate as well.

"You're better. I can see you finally slept last night, and got dressed this morning without argument too. Just don't take the weight of everyone else's problems on your shoulders until you know you're up for it, dear. We missed you." She kissed the top of my head, and I grinned up at her.

I was vaguely aware that Hattie had been in and out of my room the last couple of weeks. She was the only one that had entered my suite. She never really disturbed me, just reminded me when I had gone too long without bathing or eating. I slept when I couldn't keep my eyes open any longer and wrote when I was awake.

"Maybe a little weight," Bones countered. He looked upset about something.

Hattie tried to make eye contact with him, seeming a little irritated, but he turned guiltily away.

"Okay. What is Hattie is trying to shield from me?" I asked as I added a pile of jam to my toast.

"Katie. Katie is super scary. You need to fix her," Bones said.

He still wouldn't look up, and Hattie took his plate away from him. He didn't seem surprised by the punishment as he leaned back in his chair.

"Hattie, you can't punish Bones. I knew Katie was having issues before I disappeared into my girl cave. I should have talked to her. I just didn't know what to say."

Hattie paused by the trash, turned and set Bones' plate back in front of him. She didn't say anything as she stomped up the back stairway.

"So, how bad is it?" I picked the conversation back up.

"I wouldn't be surprised if they don't pack her stuff up and force her out if it goes on another day. The only one that is not furious with her is Lisa. And, Lisa's the one that is taking the brunt of Katie's fury. Donovan even locked everyone out of the basement gym because he's afraid they will try and kill each other."

Bones pushed the eggs around on his plate before tossing his fork down and leaning back in his chair again. "Hattie's right to be upset with me. I'm expecting too much too soon from you. I was just hoping that since you sent the writing to Tech, you would be up to stepping in and bringing in enough calm to settle Katie down a bit."

When I broke out laughing, Bones looked at me a little nervously.

"Calm? Settle her down? Is that what you all have been trying to do? Manage Katie?" I continued, laughing. "Well, no wonder it's all going to hell. Katie on a normal day runs on edgy, spirited and downright bitchy, but never calm."

He smirked but didn't say anything.

"Give me a minute to grab my stuff while you finish your breakfast. You can drive me to the store, and I will sort this mess out. I'm ready to get my life back."

And I was. I felt in control again.

Chapter Forty

Bones parked my SUV near the loading dock. I was moving around pretty well these days with only one crutch, but stairs were still tricky. Bones picked me up, holding me out in front of him and carried me to the top. I laughed, and he leaned forward and kissed my temple as I entered the passcode to the side door.

I barely took a step in before I could hear the yelling.

"Yeah," Bones sighed. "That's what I was afraid of."

"Well, I am glad to know it's Monday, and the store is closed."

"I get that. Last Saturday was not pretty."

I didn't want to know what happened last Saturday and proceeded to the sales floor. When I opened the door that separated the two rooms, the yelling bounced off the walls and windows, and I was finally able to make out the words and voices.

I saw Katie and Lisa squared off in the middle of the sales floor as I continued moving their way. They both were playing tug of war with a dress as Lisa stepped closer to Katie. Donovan stood rigid on one side. Whiskey and James stood nervously on the other side. If this turned physical, they knew it could get bloody.

"You are a selfish, self-centered, spoiled brat, and I am not going to put up with any more of your bullshit!" Lisa shrieked. Her expression was a twist of rage and pain. Tears rolled down her cheeks unchecked. What broke my heart though was how vulnerable she appeared.

I continued hobbling toward them unnoticed.

Katie had her back to me, as she lurched toward Lisa, finger pointing aggressively, "And you are nothing but a sniveling piece of shit that lets her friends get beaten and sliced up while you sneak off to safety!" Katie screamed back.

I saw the crushed look on Lisa's face and snapped.

I am not sure if my brain even processed everything that was said by the time I had thrown my crutch, dragged Katie by the throat to the nearest wall, and pinned her there. I was shaking. She stayed frozen in place, reading the fury on my face.

"Tell me," I said slowly, trying to calm my breathing, "Katie, tell me that I did not just hear you blaming our friend for me being beaten."

She didn't move. She seemed both shocked and slightly afraid and didn't answer.

"If I ever hear you speak like that again to anyone I care about, I will come after you." Shaking her by the neck, I emphasized my words. "Do you understand?"

Still wordless, she nodded, as a single tear slid down her face. It was enough for me to slowly release her. I turned and looked around. Donovan held Lisa as she cried into his shoulder. Alex walked over and handed me my crutch back. Anne stood leaning into Whiskey, looking ashen.

"Anne, honest Anne, do you feel that Lisa was responsible?" I asked.

"No. Not at all. It sucked beyond words how it all went down, but you knew the stakes. You chose to send Lisa away. We all chose to play it out. We all could have run. We decided to stand behind you while you tried to end this for her, to protect her, like you protect all of us."

Whiskey handed her a handkerchief, and she wiped her face before continuing.

"Like how you chose to go home to make sure Katie was safe. That wasn't on Lisa. That wasn't on Katie either. You made that choice, and it should have been fine. We all thought everything was fine. But it just wasn't." More tears streamed down her cheek, and she leaned closer into Whiskey as he wrapped an arm around her.

"Bones?" I asked.

"I wish that things would have been different, but that's never going to change what happened."

"Alex?"

Alex had his head bowed and wiped his face with the back of his hand before looking up. "The only person to blame is already burning in hell."

He patted Lisa on the shoulder before he went over and tried to comfort Katie.

"Lisa, you need to know that the decision to send you away was never in question. I don't repeat that over and over in my head. It was the safest move for everyone. If he could have gotten to you, he would have put a bullet in Katie and me, before kidnapping you. I have no doubt about that. You know how obsessed he was with you. You cannot put this on yourself."

She nodded, but I knew it would take a long while for her to absorb all I was saying. Donovan held her tighter as she cried.

I stepped back over to Katie.

Alex still held an arm around her, but she wasn't responding to him.

"Katie," I said stepping in front of her. "Katie, look at me."

She lifted her head and a few more tears streamed down her face.

"I love you, my friend. I'm sorry that I didn't get there sooner. I am sorry that he hurt you. I am sorry that you were trapped there listening to the things you heard. But, if you want to be angry, you take it out on me. Because this –," waving my arm around the room of distraught people, "this is not ever going to happen again."

She nodded as more tears fell and she curled into Alex's arms.

The club van pulled up to the front doors and Bones walked over and let Tech and Goat inside.

● ● ●
342

Tech carried in a box and set it down in front of me. He had dark circles under his eyes, and I was instantly worried.

"What's wrong?"

"For the first time in too many weeks, nothing is wrong," he assured me with a hug and a kiss on my cheek. He opened the box and pulled out stacks of banded rings of paper. "I honestly don't know if this is something you should ever publish, but after I was up all night reading it, I decided it was something you needed to share with your friends and family. We were helpless while you battled through this."

He looked away, choking up.

"But you found a way to heal, by writing this. I read it and could feel you healing, page by page. Everyone else is still stuck, though, some more than others." He looked to Katie and Lisa. "They need to read this too. They need to know what you knew. See through your eyes how it all happened and how you felt about it."

He handed me one of the banded rings of paper, and I recognized it for what it was. It was my story. It was the story of my attack that I spent the last two weeks pouring my tears and screams into, and coming out the other side feeling as if I could finally breathe again. Tech was right. They needed to heal, and maybe this would help them to understand that I never once blamed anyone else.

I picked up another booklet and took one to Lisa and one to Katie. They were still crying, but I knew it was a sign for the better. They needed to stop holding it all in. They needed to let it go, to put it in the past where it belonged.

"Tech's right," I said, turning to look at everyone. "I can't talk it out in a way that would help, but if you read this, you will understand. I love you all and want everyone to be able to move forward with me. I *need* you all to move forward with me."

I nodded at Tech to pass out the rest of the booklets. I hobbled toward the front door and exited into the morning sun. Bones followed me out.

"You're not going to read it?" I asked.

"I already did." He leaned over, kissing me on the forehead, smiling. "It was the hardest thing I have ever read in my life. It helped, though. I know it will help them too."

"I thought you said Tech wouldn't let anyone else read it?"

"I'm not everyone else. Can you see Tech, or anybody for that matter, telling me no?" he smirked.

I laughed at that. "I can't see anyone in the club telling you no. Probably all of my family would tell you to buzz off, but not anyone in the club."

"And why is it that they aren't scared of me? Everyone's scared of me. But they shrug me off like I am no big deal. Hell, Hattie was going to throw my breakfast in the trash this morning."

"Why should they be scared of you? Because of your little temper tantrums? Please. They all know you would never hurt them."

"I do *not* have temper tantrums," he laughed, pulling my head into his shoulder.

We stood there peacefully until I finally pushed away. I reached into his shirt pocket, stealing a cigarette and lighting up.

"You are going to get stuck being a smoker again if you keep it up," he scolded.

"I was always a smoker, always will be a smoker. I just refrain from it for long stretches of time."

"Why did you quit in the first place?" he asked as he steered me over to a nearby bench in the sun.

I shrugged, not answering, exhaling a steady stream of smoke. The truth was that I quit when I adopted Nicholas, but I couldn't tell Bones that. I wasn't ready to give anyone else access to that part of my life.

The nice thing about Bones was that he always knew when to drop a conversation. Leaning back, enjoying the breeze, I stared off into the clouds. I wasn't going to talk anymore today about the past. I would take today just to re-adjust myself back into the world and tomorrow I would start looking for Nicholas again.

"Thanks for the pen and paper," I said.

"You're welcome," he answered, wrapping his arm around me.

Thank you for reading Kelsey's Burden: Layered Lies. I hope you enjoyed reading it as much as I enjoyed writing it. Not ready for the story to end yet? Get ready for Book Two: Past Haunts in the Kelsey's Burden series!

Past Haunts

The story continues with whacky customers, dark pasts revealed, and sexy suggestions from the Devil's Players in the second book of this series.

Will Bones and Kelsey finally connect?
Or, will secrets from both their pasts destroy their chances?
Is there love on the horizon for our sassy Katie?
Or is she just having a bit of fun?

When trouble once again crosses Kelsey's path, decisions must be made whether to face the evil straight on or run for the hills. And, who will be left standing in the end?

Be sure to stay in touch to receive book release information. Updates will be provided through my Facebook page: Author Kaylie Hunter; or, you may follow my author page on Amazon.

From the Author –

Thank you for purchasing Kelsey's Burden: Layered Lies. I must admit I have a strange addiction with the characters in this series. Often, I wake in the middle of the night, realizing that I am dreaming of their antics. I hope I have succeeded in describing them the way I see them acting out the scenes in my head.

I have always enjoyed writing, but the last few years I have dedicated my time to working on my craft—researching formats, writing styles, grammatical rules and publishing options. I was overwhelmed with the amount of free advice available. As the characters became more and more realistic, I became more and more obsessed with getting this book right. I stopped counting how many rewrites I did after forty. Any time I found another piece of the writing puzzle, I would start at the beginning and make improvements.

Please be sure to follow the series as Kelsey's world continues to explode.

I look forward to hearing from you!
Best Wishes,
Kaylie Hunter

Kelsey's Burden Series:

Layered Lies

Past Haunts

Friends and Foes

Blood and Tears

Love and Rage

Made in the USA
Columbia, SC
24 April 2021